Stephen Matthew Nolan

Space Library

Revenge of the Vampire Zombie Bunnies

iUniverse, Inc.
Bloomington

iUniverse books may be ordered through booksellers or by contacting:
iUniverse
1663 Liberty Drive
Bloomington, IN 47403
www.iuniverse.com
1-800-Authors (1-800-288-4677)

ISBN: 978-1-4502-8029-7 (sc)
ISBN: 978-1-4502-8030-3 (ebook)

Printed in the United States of America

iUniverse rev. date: 12/29/2010

Table of Contents

Preface

It is Halloween and I have just written the last words of this book. Halloween is a time for magical and fantastical events to occur and this manuscript is certainly that. The book that you have in your hands comprises a small piece of me, your humble author. Please handle with care. No, I have not been to outer space but as a librarian I have worked with and served many people who seem to have come from there. I have been on the Staten Island ferry, been to the hockey hall of fame and most of the other places visited by the main character in this book. He is an aspect of me and now that this book is a reality I guess in some way he now actually does exist. I'd like to meet him someday and compare notes, he is a fascinating fellow.

If you are familiar with my previous work you no doubt are wondering what the hell is the author of two successful histories writing about vampire zombie bunnies? Well, I could explain it all to you but I'd rather you discover it for yourself. I don't want to spoil any of the surprises that await you as you go on this little adventure I have written. I hope you like it.

As for you librarians out there I salute you! It is not always the most glamorous of jobs we have but the vast majority of us working in special, pubic and academic libraries do a great job. If the citizens of Earth were ever to go into outer space they would definitely have to have one of us onboard the ship that takes them there.

So without any more chatter from me I will leave you to it. Here is the magnum opus that everyone will be talking about forever and a day. Enjoy my friends, enjoy the adventure and thank you.

Stephen Nolan
October 31, 2010

Acknowledgements

The road to the end of this particular paper trail would have been much harsher without the support of my friends and family. They are the rocks that make up my foundation. Included in this multitude are: Neal (Hot Buttered) Crossan, Jason Conway, Ed Headerson, Steve Barron, Sean and Chat Phelan, Don Webber, Mike Kean, Derm (DK) Kelly, Leona Raymond, Big Frank Snook, Terry (TMZ) Murphy, Paul Barrett, Ram, Shola, Karu, Heather Kelly, Patrick O'Toole, Lisa Delaney, John Edwards, Paul Smith, Stephanie Hannaford, Hal Jordan, Peter Collins, Carolyn Parsons, and oh so many more.

I also wish to give thanks to those special humans, the librarians to whom I will forever hold in my memory and who will always hold a place in my heart. The incomparable two Heathers Cooke and Roberts, the lovely Janet Eke, the mad Duane Spracklin, the kind Laura Burkhart, Randy (The R-Man) Rice, and the poet Patrick Warner.

My invaluable library technicians: Marjorie Barnes, Brenda Peach and Lee Ann (LA) Rogers. Thank you for putting up with me for all these years. I want to thank my dear friends Violet Pardy and Crystal Snow for the wonderful illustrations that are in this book. The work you both provided when I asked for certain scenes to be created is both compelling and unique. Thank you so much for your efforts. I would also like to give my deepest appreciation to Katherine Daley for starting me on my way, Rebecca (RJD) Dawe for just being brilliant, Joe Mullins, Gary Tucker, Wanda Butt, Sherri Quirke, Derek Young, Matt Brazil, Paulette Butt, Sharon LeShane, Lisa Perrault and Denise Dooley for just being you.

My deepest thanks go to my family: my three brothers Dermot, Martin and Michael and my mother Elizabeth who have supported me no matter how mad the scheme was. Finally my thoughts go out to my dearly departed father Stephen and my grand mother Aileen Healey who are dearly missed. This book is for all the above mentioned and the many more people who have touched my heart. Thank you all.

Chapter One

The Space Library

It was a slow day at the space library. Chubba, a 6 foot, 6 inch tall, hairless, muscular Gormorian library assistant wandered through the tall, narrow shelves of books twirling his head entirely around his thick, extended neck as he was wont to do when he was immersed in the shelving experience. Gormorians are telepaths. Unable to speak they communicated by emitting their thoughts and emotions to others through telepathic chanting; today he hummed contentment. Chubba enjoyed working in the library as the cold silence reminded him of his home world. Up and down, in and out, backwards and forwards the dedicated library worker slowly filed through the stacks fixing the small inequities on the shelves that were part and parcel of his library workday.

The space library where he worked occupied a small desolate asteroid in a remote potion of the known universe. Thanks to this fact most books that newly arrived in the acquisitions department were already hundreds of years old and as a result the library had the reputation of having the galaxy's greatest rare book collection. Stasis fields preserved the massive collection and protected the materials from deterioration and it was this important fact that eternally ensured a job for a native Gormorian in the library for, as everyone knows, no energy shield can impede a native of Gormoria.

Chubba continued to wind his way through the long shelves of books. He rarely looked at the titles as he wasn't himself an avid reader. He liked going to pubs and drinking with his friends during his weekends off. It was this trait that got him kicked out of the prestigious Olympic Library of Thessalonica 5 and demoted to this lowly branch of the space library. Still, he rarely thought on the demotion as he enjoyed the relative light workload of his new position. Here in this branch he could come and go as he pleased as long as his work hour totals were complete and his workmates were overall a harmless bunch. Chubba knew a good thing when he came across it.

The space library's staff was comprised of a silver, humanoid android named C.A.L.R.U, which stood for Completely Automated Library Reference Unit, the other staff called him Cal for short. The robot stayed permanently on duty at the reference desk where it answered inquires from around the known universe. The android's only quirk was that it refused to answer any question with regards to how much ice one should put in their drinks. Without fail the three times in which this particular question was asked the reference machine froze solid and had to be rebooted. Yet as this was the only fault of an otherwise perfect computer it was kept in place as is. The aforementioned Gormorian Chubba retrieved books for patrons and ensured the integrity of the stacks.

The only female member of the team was Zoe, a five foot six inch tall female Cypherian who catalogued all the "new" materials that arrived in the library. Cypherians looked almost exactly like humans save for a bluish tint to their skin, the fact that most of them were at least 6 foot tall and that the female of the species all had fairly large bosoms. No one was quite sure why they had such large breasts but there were many theories why this was the case. Zoe was often ridiculed on her home planet for being tiny in a world filled with giants and so, fed up with the constant references to being short, she transferred out of the cataloguing station on her home world and ended up at the space library where she worked with and put up with her co-workers.

Finally, there was the male human that ran the library, a librarian named Steve. Steve was from the planet Earth, a small, fairly insignificant world that had no inter-planetary flight capability. That a human had ended up running a library millions of light years from his home planet was due to a local newspaper ad in St. John's, Newfoundland, Canada. The association that runs the collection of libraries of the universe, the Inter-Galactic Library Board, made a slight error by placing their ad on Earth rather than a planet whose name is quite similar.

By the time the error was realized the interviewers seemed quite happy with their respondent and as the job recruitment small ad budget was already completely exhausted they decided to throw caution to the wind and hire the Earther. When told the job was to be off-planet Steve seemed blasé to the fact as his affection for the globe was dubious at best. Thus, humanity's real first contact with a species from another planet was in fact just the end result of a typographical error.

The quartet ran their library efficiently, but on this particular day the human was in one of his peculiar moods.

While going about his normal routine he came across a message that set his librarian blood boiling. "That bastard!" Steve blasted as he stormed out of his small, tidy office. All eyes looked at the medium-sized librarian who held a small crumpled piece of paper in his hand. "Gregos told me to get lost!"

Gregos, or more widely known to the populace of the galaxy as Gregos the Tyrant, was the undisputed ruler of a vast, tyrannical empire. Long was the list of cruelties that Gregos had inflicted upon the many planetary systems under his dark rule. His name was feared and reviled throughout the galaxy and no one, not even Baldric the Brave who was renowned for his great heroism and it goes without saying his amazing bravery, had the necessary power or courage to oppose the dark ruler.

This information was totally irrelevant to the fuming librarian whose only concern was the now crumpled paper in his clenched fist. "This, this, this, this thief! This disgusting swine absolutely refuses to bring back a book that I've recalled a dozen times over! Overdue after overdue notice I've sent him but now he, or rather his smarmy assistant, has written me telling me that I'll never see my book again. Well, I'm gonna get that blasted book back if it's the last thing I do." The fuming librarian could hardly contain his anger over the deliberate disrespect towards his precious library and its overdue book policy.

"Well, if you even try to get that book back then there's no question that it will be the last thing you do because Gregos will have you eviscerated," the dark haired Zoe calmly commented from behind a tilting stack of books that hid her pretty, slightly blue face.

"Never mind that," countered the angry librarian. "No one steals from my library and gets away with it. Gregos is just another library abuser to me. He has got to learn that taking books out of a library is a privilege, not a right."

Moving quickly to the reference desk Steve set the library robot, C.A.L.R.U., to automatic, then walked off towards the hanger bay at the far back of the library where the space library's book mobile spacecraft sat. Zoe sprang up from her comfortable seat, rushed past the determined librarian and with arms outstretched blocked the way to the hanger doors. "Are you insane? You want to go after the sickest, most deadliest guy in the universe just to get some old book that has been out of print for five hundred years?"

"Hey," Steve shouted back, "***The Definitive Guide to Cooking Jummies*** may be old and, well, probably irrelevant considering that Jummies are currently almost extinct, but that doesn't make the offense to this library any less onerous. It was a reference book for goodness sake!"

"And who put the Jummies on the critical list in the first place?" Zoe retorted. "Gregos!" she yelled, quickly answering her own question. Steve just stared unblinking at the frazzled cataloguer and Zoe instantly knew that there was no stopping this book-obsessed librarian from entering the hanger bay. Zoe thought about the situation for a moment then silently stepped aside. She all of a sudden remembered that the Earther had absolutely no idea how to operate the spacecraft and so there was no danger of him actually taking off. With a wave of her hand and a sarcastic bow she stepped aside and let the angry man pass.

Steve walked through the hanger doors, slowed as he looked up at the spacecraft in front of him, stopped, turned back and returned to the library. Without any hint of irony he looked at Zoe and said, "Oh, by the way, you're coming too." What followed was a titanic shouting match where the Cypherian said in no uncertain terms that she was not going on a suicide run just to appease the crazed obsession of a demented Earth creature. For his part the demented Earth creature countered with the fact that Zoe's contract included an 'and other related duties' clause. As far as he was concerned getting library property back from homicidal tyrants qualified as an other related duty. Chubba, taking it all in from the back of a book truck, merely looked on half-interestedly at the scene and wondered when the sweet quiet would return.

Finally, with both verbal combatants hoarse from shouting and therefore in plain violation of the library "Shush" policy, Zoe relented on two grounds, one was the fact that if she didn't fly the ship she would have a surly boss moping about the library and second was the hope that the replacement for the soon-to-be-deceased would come from a more reasonable species. Making an about-face and smiling a tad menacingly she strode past her boss, through the hanger bay doors and straight into the library spacecraft. She went straight for the captain's controls and sat waiting for the librarian to join her.

Inwardly marking a smart tick in the metaphorical win column, the head of the space library stepped into the cluster class book mobile to discover that sitting next to Zoe in the co-pilot chair was Chubba. Steve, obviously chagrined, looked disapprovingly at the tall Gormorian. "Who's going to mind the store?" he asked. Chubba indicated in a telepathic tone that he had programmed Cal to enter the stacks' stasis fields safely. "I didn't know you could do that," Steve said. Chubba merely shrugged his immense shoulders and turned to face the large forward screen.

Knowing there was no hope of changing the big fellow's mind Steve gave the order to lift off. The engines revved, the hanger bay roof opened, the nose of the ship pointed to space and with a push of a button the space mobile was up and away. The staff of the space library headed off towards the most hostile planet in the universe, the center of terror, Maladred. The small planet where the terrible Gregos ruled his evil, galactic empire but more importantly where he owed the space library branch # 6941 a very overdue book and that was the greatest offense of all.

Space travel for Steve was still a new experience. As a native of Earth only astronauts and the extremely rich got to fly into space and he was neither. Certainly a 31-year-old librarian had no chance to leave Earth's gravity let alone travel where no man had gone before. As he watched the stars zip past his window Steve took some pleasure in the thought that no one else on his world had ever experienced what he was experiencing at that particular moment.

Space travel, for those that actually have experienced it firsthand and considered it mere travel, is boring. The basic gist of it is that you get into a spacecraft, blast off then wait until you arrive at your destination which, depending upon where you are going, could take months. During the time you are on your ship there are no wonderful sights to view out the windows, if indeed your spacecraft is fortunate enough to have windows in the first place. There are no monoliths, no space battles, no giant whales or anything else of that nature that the average space traveler could witness from the comfort of their window. The only view is a haze of stars, which as anyone who has flown in a space craft for more than ten minutes can tell you, will become extremely boring very, very quickly.

To combat this problem of boredom, space craft designers installed a plethora of amusements to divert passengers on their journeys. Casinos, entertainers, movie theatres, sport facilities and many other thrills both tame and wild were neatly packed on all the best star-cruisers to help decrease passenger boredom and to increase profits. Thus for those who could afford it luxury space travel was a hell of a ride, many indeed forgot the reason why they took their trip in the first place and rather than getting off at their stop merely stayed on board for the return voyage.

The space mobile had absolutely none of these pleasures packed into its innards. The ship came with a pack of playing cards, three of which were missing, a board game so boring that no one on the ship wanted to play and a tiny selection of books and journals that no one wanted to read. So instead of fighting monsters and rescuing princesses in virtual reality simulations that the ship did not have the crew went about their ordinary library work, liaising with Cal on a remote link.

Fortunately for the crew, the trip to the planet Maladred was a short one in space travel terms, only a four week round trip. This ETA assumed that all went swimmingly. Unfortunately, the second-hand spacecraft in which they were currently traveling had a long history of mishaps. To put the situation in plain terms the space craft that was the space library book mobile was not an entirely reliable machine. Strange and mysterious things sometimes happened to the ship, such as unexplained loud noises or erroneous readings on the pilot's display. Steve once thought he saw the ghostlike forms of Alfred Hitchcock and Marilyn Monroe appear in the engine room of the ship.

It was because of the ship's history as a troublemaker that Zoe ignored the fuel gage reading, believing that surely the low fuel warning was a mistake. The vessel had been refueled only the week before and it had not been in use since. So it came as a complete surprise to Zoe when an alarm rang out and a calm female voice came from the ship's computer telling everyone who was interested that the fuel level was at a dangerously critical level. "Damn it!" Zoe cried out, "You just don't get the light years out of this piece of junk like you used to." Zoe shouted obscenities at the ship for a good ten minutes. During this time the quiet Chubba debated whether or not to mention that he had borrowed the ship to go to a weekend long kegger on Veridian III. He decided to keep that little piece of information to himself.

At last the fiery Zoe quieted down enough to listen to reason. It was decided that there was nothing else to do but to find the nearest planet that had a fueling station and land. Luckily, they were near a planet called Quan which was known for three things: a very relaxed, peaceful populace, excellent alcoholic beverages and a cheap supply of fuel for space travelers. Quan also welcomed alien business and was a member in good standing of the Inter-Planetary Business Association. In short, if you had to land on an alien planet and needed fuel and a quick tasty drink then Quan was a pretty good choice.

Like most planets in this particular sector of space Quan was subjugated by the might of the overlord Gregos and like most citizens of the empire the populace of Quan didn't relish the oppressiveness of their ruler but they felt that there was nothing to be done. No one dared oppose the mighty Gregos. So life went on normally for the people of the planet as it had for many centuries; they were displeased but ultimately resigned to their fate.

After receiving clearance from Quan's planetary docking control the space mobile sat down in a city space dock reserved for visiting spacecraft. It was to be a quick break for the library crew; one quick landing, one trip to the depot to arrange refueling then up and away back in the black. The space library had formed a new policy for emergency money situations after the newly appointed Earth librarian pointed out that it would be cheaper to simply pay for some items rather than go through the hassle of filling out time consuming purchase orders. So now thanks to Steve's forward budgetary thinking and so the library credit card had more than enough to pay for the refueling.

The crew of the library ship disembarked and took the opportunity to stretch their legs. The search for fuel would be a short one. Steve had already decided that since he knew nothing about spaceships or their fuel requirements he would leave the details to his able shipmates. He would instead head to the nearest local pub for a taste of the planet's famous local ale. The librarian had a taste for beer and hoped that the planet's offerings would live up to its reputation.

The human jiggled his pants pockets and was pleased to hear the satisfying sound of coin hitting coin. Currency in the civilized galaxy is, for the most part, standardized.

The credit is the main piece of money, which meant that no one had to carry fifty different types of coins about on a trip across space. Trotting down the narrow streets and sharp corners of the spaceport Steve came upon the unmistakable sounds of a local pub in action.

The Kitten's Caress was the equivalent of an upper class wine bar in downtown London, England. Here people were served with small, dainty glasses of the trendy beverage of the day. The wealthy citizens of Quan were drawn to such places as they could sample the latest creations of their planet's master brewers as well as gossip about local concerns. Steve, just wanting a quick drink and tired of wandering the streets, entered a place that on Earth would have qualified him as a snob just by walking in the door.

The librarian surveyed the establishment, walked to the elegant bar and motioned for a server to attend him. The waitress was tall, about six foot three and weighed about 120 pounds with red skin and a tail, but beyond this she looked like a chorus girl on Broadway. Steve thought for a moment as he surveyed her about the lack of uniqueness of form in the intelligent species of the galaxy. It seems that the science fiction writers had gotten it all wrong. Some legs, a couple of appendages, a few eyes and opposable thumbs got the job done every time. Variations such as horns, skin color, hair or retractable tongues may be a condition of environment but overall everyone looked reasonably humanoid. Sometimes it wasn't esthetically pleasing to his human eyes, but the basic design worked.

Ordering the local brew was an easy chore. Before beginning the job with the space library a translator was implanted into the inner canal of his ear making him more or less capable of understanding any language within reasonable limits. The fact that he could also occasionally pick up sixty-year-old radio transmissions from Earth he was assured was due to a manufacturer's error and as soon as a replacement could be found his faulty translator would be replaced. So every now and again Steve would hear a news item about the Korean War or a play by play of a bygone New York Yankees/Brooklyn Dodgers game but this was easily ignored.

In fact it was somewhat reassuring. Other people heard strange voices in their heads and assumed they were insane but Steve knew that he was all right. Indeed had he known that the Euridian Company that owned the patent on the tiny translators had for centuries tested their little devices on the people of Earth he might have suspected that the large, odd man who mumbled to himself on the steps of McMurdo's Lane in downtown St. John's was in fact a product tester for the company's latest line of merchandise. To this day the Euridian Company's media representative states that no sentient beings were harmed in the production of their products.

Soon the waitress that took his order returned with a small glass for which the librarian had to pay the equivalent of three hours of his hard earned pay. "This better be worth it," he thought as he handed over sixty credits for the drink and two for the lady just because he liked the erotic curve of her tight tail. He took a brief glance at his glass before closing his eyes and downing a cautious sip. His eyes popped open and he couldn't help but say out loud, "Man, this stuff is excellent!"

A patron sitting two seats next to the pleased consumer looked up and replied, "Oh, you think so do you? I thought that yesterday's sample was of a much finer quality."

"Well, I wasn't here yesterday so I can't compare," Steve said turning back towards the view of the tail of the bartender.

"My name is Bogatta. I am the district controller for this area," the small man told the librarian. Reluctantly turning back to his unwelcome drinking companion Steve noticed that the citizens of Quan were, from the samples he had seen, on the whole of a small stature. Perhaps, he mused, that was why their beverage glasses were so tiny.

The two began to talk and during the course of the conversation Bogatta became excited over the librarian's mission to Maladred. It had never occurred to him that anyone would ever try to defy Gregos' will. This was nothing to the shock, however, that Bogatta received when he heard that the humanoid he was speaking to had come from a planet where no one had even heard of Gregos, let alone was under his rule. Surely the off-worlder was delusional to think that there were worlds outside the control of the great tyrant. Yet there was something about the way the Earther spoke in so matter of fact a tone that led the area controller to think that perhaps there was a portion of truth to his story.

"Well, I gotta go," Steve said and rose to leave. Bogatta stood up, nervously looked around then whispered in the Earth man's ear a sincere "Good luck." The librarian nodded then walked out the door. Bogatta watched the man leave and quickly turned to the fellow seated next to him. After a moment of chatter, both men became excited.

It took a little while but finally Steve found the space mobile's parking spot. Once there Chubba, who seemed a little tipsy, and Zoe, who had just finished paying for their fuel with the library's credit card, greeted him and told him they were ready to leave Quan. With nothing more to keep them the three boarded the ship. Within moments they were back in space, none of them realizing in the slightest that they had already changed the course of the universe forever.

Within two more days of tiresome space travel the library crew was pleasantly surprised to learn that they could accomplish a great deal of work from the confines of their ship. Two reasons for this efficiency were that there were no outside distractions such as patrons, for the crew to be bothered with and second, the staff of the space library hardly spoke to each other outside of the discussion of their duties. This was not to say that they disliked each other it was just that they preferred to work alone unhindered by the unnecessary disturbance of small talk. This made for an efficient team that especially made their head librarian happy.

On the beginning of the tenth day of the trip Zoe sensed that something was wrong. On her long range scope she noticed that there was an unusual amount of traffic going to and from the planet of Maladred. She hoped that this would not bog down the space mobile in unnecessary congestion. Zoe wanted to quickly get to the planet, witness her boss die an imaginative and gruesome death, then head back in time to see the beginning of the Tiluran planet eclipse, one of the most beautiful events in the universe and something that she had always wanted to see. This year she had finally scored tickets to the big event and she knew that if she didn't get to go this year then she'd probably never have the chance again. With all this in her mind she thoughtfully increased the ship's speed.

Unfortunately, more speed was not to be a solution to Zoe's problem. As the ship neared Maladred, she noticed a wall of ships surrounding the planet. The planet was under an emergency blockade and no space craft were allowed on or off the planet. This was a mixed blessing for Zoe as she was happy that she would now be back in time to see her celestial show but she was half-heartedly disappointed at the same time that she would not see her boss's comeuppance.

Stopping the space mobile, Zoe rose from her pilot's seat to inform the library crew that their mission had to end on the boundary of Maladred space. Little did she realize the extent of her boss's stubbornness. "What the hell do you mean we've got to keep going? There's a blockade of the planet! Don't you know what a blockade is?" Zoe was very upset and her large bosom heaved rapidly, punctuating every excited word.

Steve, slightly dazed at the spectacle, paused for a moment before explaining that he had not traveled all the way to the border of another planet to be turned aside when he was so close to getting his book back. Surely this blockade, he argued, was for large ships carrying contraband or weapons, not a small ship carrying library workers trying to retrieve an overdue book.

After much debate a compromise was reached between the irate pilot and the determined librarian. Rather than merely turning back directly they would see if they could legally pass the blockade, if not, then they would leave a note. With this stratagem agreed to they headed to the back of the long line of space ships being examined by the security patrols. To Zoe and Chubba's great surprise the blockade commander let the space mobile pass and soon the ship was in orbit above the fabled planet.

For all its renowned might Maladred from space did not look the part of the seat of inter-galactic terror. The planet was slightly green in color and there was no sign of a military complex. Zoe found a convenient place to land and punched in the coordinates into the landing computer. The ship descended through the atmospheric layers and touched down in the capital city known as Dred. The name of the city led Steve to think that perhaps the people of Maladred were not big on imagination.

The space mobile crew disembarked in what seemed to be a large outdoor market. The shop stalls were all bundled together in a great open space, some of them were empty but without a hint of security for the items. The streets were spotless. The people appeared to police themselves. There was no sense of urgency to the place, everyone seemed to know exactly where they wanted to go and in what speed.

The citizens of Dred wore smart, brown, military uniforms; even the children wore the same style of clothing as the adults. All the people, it seemed, were potential fodder for the grand military machine of Gregos. They were humanoid in appearance except they had a green skin tone, perhaps, Steve mused, to better camouflage themselves in a combat situation. Yet there was no apparent menace to these people, no threat that radiated from their beings. They simply went about their business efficiently. There were no guards, no security forces or military systems of any apparent kind. In some sense that made the place appear a little more sinister than if they had giant guard towers, the imagination created more horrors than reality.

The trio walked through the market towards the largest object in the city, the Tower of Gregos. The citadel so whispered about in legend it became the basis for a thousand myths on hundreds of worlds. The Tower was made of an unusual shiny substance that gleamed silver in the light of the world's twin suns. It was within this tower that the prize the three library workers had sought to claim was held.

The walk to the tower was brisk; the library brigade did not wish to overstay their welcome. The silent Chubba gave off an unintentional wave of telepathic angst that made his companions even more nervous. Soon the trio found themselves at the grand gates of Mighty Gregos, the entrance to the Tower. For a citadel of power there were a pathetic number of people guarding the place, only two soldiers that looked like they couldn't be bothered with the job. It was if after centuries of ruling the universe complacency had set in to the nth degree.

The three stood silent for a moment until Zoe and Chubba both nudged Steve's sides with their elbows. Steve popped forward, turned to give his companions an "all right I'm going" look and quickly asked the nearest solider if the magnificent Gregos was free to receive visitors. The guard thought for a moment, shrugged his shoulders while looking at his companion with a perplexed look then finally said, "Sure," and ushered the three surprised library workers through the gates.

The group walked into the large tower and traveled along empty corridors for what seemed like an eternity until they were greeted by an old man wearing what looked to be a general's uniform. He smiled at the three and said, "My name is General Allan. The master will see you shortly," in a butlery tone, turned, and led them to a massive dining hall.

A large, rectangular table sat in the middle of the room and four chairs, one at the head and three to the right, were situated around the table. Rather than sit down right away the three explored the room. Above their heads was an embellished ceiling that depicted scenes of war and violence that somehow looked beautiful. Everything about the room had some nod to the ways of the warrior but the graphics were so well done that the spectacles didn't look anything but works of pure art rather than scenes of gruesome horror.

The chime of a bell brought the art patrons back to reality, the general re-appeared and proclaimed in a loud voice: "Now announcing the ruler of the galaxy, his majesty Gregos the Seventh." With that address a thin man dressed in a splendid uniform, a large sword strapped to his right side, entered the room. There were the trappings of power surrounding the man but with all that there didn't seem to be much that would impress the unknowing visitor. Gregos was not big, or mean looking, or awe-inspiring in any way. He seemed to be just a normal man wearing a really nice if pretentious outfit.

"Hello, my friends!" the king of the universe said in a friendly voice as if he was greeting long-lost companions. "Welcome to my humble home. It is not often that I have the pleasure of guests." The man motioned for the library workers to sit. "Please, I have had the chef prepare a special meal in your honor. I hope you like Jummies. They are a very rare these days and I only have them cooked on special occasions."

Steve spoke up at the mention of the word Jummie, "Yes, funny you should mention them as Jummies are the partly the reason why…," the rest of that particular sentence was cut off by a kick to the shin by Zoe who wanted to live a little longer before angering their host.

"Why we came. We heard that you serve the best Jummies in the universe," Zoe continued. Steve rubbed his leg as Gregos responded to Zoe's high praise. He informed them that having the best chef and the only supply of Jummies in the known galaxy certainly helped. "But do you really want the secret of how to prepare a really good Jummie?" Gregos leaned closer in his chair and whispered as if he was about to tell a state secret. "You've got to have the right recipes." With that revelation he clapped his hands and the general appeared. "Go fetch the book!" With that the old man turned and was gone once more.

A moment later he reentered the room carrying a silver platter, on the platter was a book. As the general neared the table where the four were seated the title became clear. In large white letters, it read ***The Definitive Guide to Cooking Jummies.*** Steve was about to jump up and yell a great big "Aha!" but Zoe caught him in time and gave him another bruise on his leg. Steve made a mental note to wear armored pads on any future adventure that included Zoe.

Gregos then began to speak about the nature of his power, of how long ago the universe was in great chaos with planet fighting planet and race struggling against race. It was his people, embattled against a race of aggressors that won their war against their foes and struck out into the universe determined to impose peace and order. His ancestors forged an empire that imposed its will on all, his people gave the universe the gift of peace it so richly needed. For centuries the populace of Maladred worked hard to ensure that peace endured.

It was with great sadness that he recently learned that parts of the empire under control for hundreds of years had suddenly erupted into chaos and mutiny. In response he had to send the bulk of his fleet out to suppress the insurrection leaving only a comparatively small force to protect the seat of power. He was quick to add, however, that the planet was surrounded by an energy shield that could hinder any invasion, as long as that shield was up there was nothing to fear. "Damn troublemakers," Steve ventured to say. In his mind there was always some person looking to gum up the works. Of course the irony of the fact that Gregos in his own way had upset the librarian's own small universe was completely lost on the Earther.

Throughout the meal of broiled Jummie, deep-fried Jummie and Jummie Surprise Steve's mental menu was comprised of two things: the first was that it was a shame that Jummies were on the verge of extinction as they tasted really, really great and the second was that for an evil dictator Gregos wasn't all that bad. Gregos had simply inherited the family business, which in his case was the absolute rule of the galaxy. Sure that inevitably took some measure of ruthlessness but in a way Gregos was trapped by fate, playing the role that was his alone to play. Gregos appeared to be lonely, tired of a power that he had inherited and eager for distraction. This is perhaps why he had received his unexpected visitors so warmly. How much contact with people could the man actually have that didn't involve the use of his power?

After the meal Gregos decided to take his guests on a tour of the tower, then he would learn just why these three aliens had come to see him. The tour was only a mere five minutes old, however, when two guards rushed towards the great man. "Your honor, thousands of ships have just entered orbit of our planet! They are demanding freedom and democracy!" The guards, so used to the natural order of things, were at a loss as to what to do. There had been centuries of peace and order in the galaxy, the reality of an actual crisis had been remote at best. The danger had been so remote that despite their training they were unprepared for an emergency of this magnitude.

"Why! Why is this happening? For centuries there has been nothing but peace. What could have happened to change this overnight?" Gregos was visibly distraught over this latest development and rushed to his command center with the library workers in tow.

The command center was a medium-sized complex; a huge view screen dominated the room covering a full one-third of the space. In the back of the room were complicated-looking computers surrounded by a force field. This was the control for the planetary shield, the main defense that ensured the integrity of Maladred. As long as the shield was intact there was nothing for Gregos to fear.

Suddenly a transmission shimmered on the screen; a man's face appeared that seemed vaguely familiar to one of the people in the control room. The person on the screen began to demand that Gregos relinquish his power and return self determination to the galaxy. As the man continued his speech Steve began to experience deja vu. He had heard this dialogue before but for the life of him he couldn't really remember where or when. It was only as he walked slowly towards the view screen and really looked at the face on the wall that he knew that he met that man before and just where. "Hey, you're that guy at the bar!" Steve exclaimed.

Everyone in the control room turned from the screen to Steve as he made that statement but no one's face looked more surprised than the man whose face was on the screen. "Liberator!" he exclaimed. "It is I, Bogatta, your humble servant! Oh, liberator you have inspired a thousand planets, all who yearn for freedom, to strike at the heart of tyranny. I have gathered ships from all over the galaxy to come to wrest power from the wicked tyrant Gregos! Soon the universe will be free and it will be all thanks to you!" The view screen went blank and a bombardment of the planetary shield began.

"Liberator?! I said "librarian" you moron! Damn my faulty translator!" Steve shouted as he shook his fist at the blank screen. Steve's rant about the inherent cheapness of the Inter Galactic Library Board abruptly ended as he noticed the blank faces staring at him in disbelief.

"I've never been so embarrassed in my entire life. Well, I guess it's time for us to go. We'll just be heading off now. Thanks for the wonderful meal and all." Steve clasped his hands and back peddled his way to the door before backing into a pair of guards.

"No, I don't think so," Gregos fumed. "I gave you friendship, a fine meal of rare treats, even a grand tour of my palace, and you betrayed me by inciting rebellion against me!" Gregos exploded into a fit of rage.

"You shall all die slowly! I will inflict horrible agonies upon you all!" Gregos was beside himself with anger. The three library workers slowly moved around the room, Gregos snapped his fingers and guards poured in from the nearby corridor thrusting forward in an attempt to capture the trio.

"Now. Now. Torturing after a large meal has got to be very un-healthy." Steve to no one's surprise was apprehended easily. Too many years of sitting behind a desk and not enough shelving duty had dulled his strength and agility. He made a mental note to become more active if he ever got out of the situation.

Zoe was a more difficult acquisition. She fought like a Zoranian wildcat, beating guards down with kicks and punches until only by numbers alone she was overtaken. At last only Chubba remained, as the guards closed the Gormorian backed up, walked through the energy field that protected the planetary defense control and with a mute cry he fell right into the machinery. Sparks flew dangerously all over the place and the control room went black. The power had been extinguished.

Within a moment the emergency backup system had kicked in and energy had been restored to the tower. Gregos, surrounded by his men, had the library workers' hands bound and stood them up against the nearest wall. The guards formed a line to create a firing squad, their rifles aimed directly at the library team. "This shall be a pleasure after all the troubles you have caused me," Gregos exclaimed as he raised his sword to direct the deadly line of laser rifles. "Guards! Ready!"

Zoe looked over her left shoulder, right into Steve's eyes and said in an angry tone, "Steve, I really, really hate you!" If she could have gotten free she would have killed him herself.

"Aim!" the tyrant shouted.

"Sorry. I just tried to do my job," Steve sadly replied. He was going to die and his final thoughts were of Earth. Despite the fact that there were a great many things wrong with the planet it was still his home and now he would never see it again. He summoned up all his regrets, joys and sorrows into as eloquent an epitaph as he could think of, "Rats."

"Fire!" Gregos's arm fell to his side, laser blasts boomed all over the room and the library staff who fully expected to be dead looked on in disbelief as the tyrant Gregos and all his guards fell to the floor, smoke emanating from large holes in their bodies. Gregos the mighty, ruler of the galaxy and Jummie lover, was dead.

The cavalry, in the form of Bogatta and his troops, had arrived just in the nick of time. The planetary shield had dropped just long enough for some of his ships to enter Maladred. Once on the planet there was surprisingly little trouble in overcoming the remaining military might of a regime that had counted so much on a defense system they thought could never fail and an empire too complacent to put up a fight.

"Liberator, you are alive! I am so happy!" Bogatta exclaimed. He hugged the librarian until his lungs had almost squeezed out all his air. "My friend, we are finally free thanks to you and your inspirational teachings! It was you who disabled the shield so that we could end this tyrant's reign of terror. Come, our troops are finishing off the last of the resistance and soon we will celebrate our historic victory."

"Well, that sounds great but unfortunately we really must be going." Steve sheepishly informed his companion, who still could not bring himself to extricate his hand from under Steve's arm. Steve disengaged himself from the disappointed conqueror and asked if he and his team could have an escort to the space mobile. Bogatta readily agreed although he was clearly disappointed with Steve's refusal to take part in the jubilation. Steve tried to mollify the man by saying that if he was ever needed he'd only be a call away. Bogatta handed Steve a small communication device and made him promise that if he ever needed help he should not hesitate to use it.

Soon the crew was back at the now crumbling spaceport. All the good-byes were quickly said and the three library workers climbed aboard their ship amidst the cheers of their team of escorts. Soon they were once more back in their craft and into space, headed finally for home. "Well, all's well that ends well." Steve exclaimed to his staff in a self-satisfied voice.

"Yeah, you got countless people slaughtered, messed up the entire balance of power in the universe and you didn't even get your stupid book!" Zoe was happy about that last part until Steve, with an 'oh yeah' type of smug grin, pulled out a tattered book from under his seat.

"Oh, didn't I? During that bathroom break I took along the way I had time to head back to the dining room and pick up that item we came all this way for. Sure, I had to step over a few dismembered bodies to get it, but it was well worth it." Steve was happy for the first time since he began his adventure. He was thrilled to be on the way back to the relative comfort of his library with his hard-won treasure sitting comfortably in his hand.

"Come to think of it. Now that I have a closer look at it, this book is so tattered maybe it could be weeded from the collection." The other members of the crew seriously thought about throwing their librarian out the airlock for even thinking such a thing after all the trouble the book cost but the space book mobile kept traveling through space back towards its home without any incident of human slaughter. Soon ***The Definitive Guide to Cooking Jummies*** would once again grace the reference shelves of the space library where it forever belonged.

Chapter Two

Planet of the Vampire Zombie Bunnies

The threat was over; the vampire zombie bunnies had at last been destroyed. Due to the heroic sacrifice of Major Allan Strong the brutal horde of undead bunnies had been eradicated. Snarf had peace at last. Throughout the next few years the planet had begun to renew itself. Humans returned to burnt-out cities and cleared the rubble; they built new settlements on the crumpled ruins of the old. They believed the threat was at last over but they forgot one thing, vampire zombie rabbits burrow!

The lesson that would be learned from the horrific oversight by the inhabitants on Snarf was that zombies may not have any intelligence but they inexplicitly maintain their instincts. This is particularly the case with the lower life forms such as in this case of the bunny rabbit. As we have seen it is quite difficult to kill something that is already dead. It is still more difficult to eliminate a prey that has the innate ability to hide underground. The immediate danger of death and the threat of plague still remain high. All library staff is hereby ordered to stay away from Snarf, or as it is now called New Bunny World, under threat of termination. No one is safe on this now quarantined planet.

From the symposium paper on RFs (Re-In-Animated Life Forms).

"Vampire, zombie, bunnies." The three words were spoken slowly and deliberately. The librarian sitting in an uncomfortable chair simply could not wrap his head around the idea so he decided to forget the thought altogether. Yet he could not. The planet of cataloguers would not let him. He knew he should not have come to the Inter-Universe Library and Information Services general symposium, he knew that it was a mistake yet he went anyway. Now, sitting in an uncomfortable chair in a room full of alien delegates he was unanimously chosen by those in attendance to return the holy grail of lost books.

The Tome of the Lost Ones was a book filled with magical incantations and curses. It had been lost for centuries until recently when a lost star cruiser landed on a forgotten world and transmitted the finding before all communication had been lost. No one wanted to go retrieve the book but it was so important that someone simply had to go, that someone had to be Steve the librarian from Earth who had a reputation for getting in and out of trouble better than any other librarian in the universe.

Steve sat in his twice mentioned uncomfortable chair with the file containing the order in his hand, looked up at the members of the inter-planetary library board and, as none of the members were human, none of them registered the look of utter amazement on their librarian's face. There was a pause as he looked at the aliens in front of him and they in turn waited for his response.

"So…, you want me to take a dilapidated spaceship, fly it to a planet infested with vampire, zombie, rabbits and retrieve an ancient, cursed book that has the power to incinerate the universe?" The librarian waited for the confirmation that quickly came as a matter of fact yes. As the librarian slowly got up from his chair and began to walk towards the exit he vowed to never again go to an interplanetary library conference. Not only had the delegates sent him on a suicide mission, the tote bag of free goodies turned out to be utter crap.

One week later the librarian assembled his team in the launch bay of branch # 6941 of the space library. There were many branches of the space library but his was the only one headed by a human; as far as he knew no one on Earth even had a valid library card for the space library. Earth was still too barbaric to join the universe of civilizations and thus Steve had resigned himself to never seeing another human until he retired or left the space library which he simply didn't want to do. Despite his grumblings he was having too much fun to give it all up for a desk job on good old planet Earth.

The plan was simple: fly to the planet of the vampire zombie bunnies, land, find the book and get the hell off the planet before they were either sucked dry of blood or eaten. Simple. Now he had to convince his co-workers that fighting vampire zombie bunnies was included in the other related duties clause of their contracts.

"Vampire?" asked Zoe the buxom cataloguer.

"Yep," replied the librarian.

"Zombie?!" asked Zoe.

"Yep," replied the librarian.

"Bunnies?!!" said Zoe.

"Yep", replied the librarian as if the last bit was the most ludicrous to believe.

"Ok", the luscious library technician said as she boarded the ship. She was accustomed to the odd ways of the Earth librarian by now and rather than argue an order that came directly from the library command she simply went with the flow. Steve shrugged as he watched her attractive behind climb up the ladder to the flight deck. He imagined he would have had a fight on his hands but no, and to be honest he was a little bit disappointed.

Chubba silently plodded up the ladder after Steve and the trio of library workers sat in their less than comfortable flight seats and prepared themselves for another long, dull trip where danger and possible consumption awaited. A collective sigh went out of the crew as the space book mobile lifted off and into the big dark. Cal, the library automated computer, once again stayed behind and took over the everyday functions of the library. Cal watched as the library book mobile left its sight then closed the hangar's doors. It turned to head back toward the library proper then halted as a light began to blip on its forehead. After a moment's pause Cal rushed towards the circulation desk.

Once more the utter boredom of space travel kicked in and they took time to do their work duties as best as they could via interface with the space library computers. In their downtime the trio kept mostly to themselves as, like many space voyagers, they feared the space crazies. Ever since the terrible incident where a party of twelve happy space travelers broke down on the way to Ork and ended up going crazy and eating themselves, space travelers feared for their sanity. When help finally arrived on that fateful trip only the butler was found alive and he claims to this very day that he didn't do it. Since then people were afraid of going crazy on space trips that had minimal amusements and so the space library crew kept their distance from each other.

Recently, in his spare time Steve had taken to writing stories to keep occupied and although he never thought of them as being any good he enjoyed the creative process. He had no idea where his stories came from but now that these images and words came to visit him he felt compelled to write them down. The stories of the universe were good, some were even great, but the man from Earth could not relate to tales of creatures he had never seen or imagined and references to historical events that meant nothing to him. The images that mystically formed in his mind seemed all so real to him and there was a connection that he did not have with the other worldly written words of regular space library books. Taking out a notepad he began to write a new story to pass the time on the flight to his probably death and digestion.

A Princess, A Dragon, A Knight and A Fool

In a land that can now only be imagined during an age long ago lived a world of miracles. In this world there existed a kingdom so rich, so content that we today could hardly conceive of it. Then that world suddenly, tragically changed.

This is the story of how a wonderful place began its tragic decline into darkness.

In a gleaming white castle high upon a majestic hill lived a very beautiful Princess named Carolyn, whose beauty was so great that the paint defied the canvas when ordered to portray so fine and delicate a face. The lakes stilled themselves whenever she gracefully strolled by so they could embrace her image; no one was as fine, so elegant and as beautiful as her.

Yet this miracle of a woman was not universally loved though the entire world would rage if it had heard of it. For all her immense beauty and innocence and purity of soul she was constantly, unendurably unhappy.

The cause of this great discomfort was her step-mother, the evil Queen Mary who ruled over her step-daughter more harshly than her basest subject. Queen Mary despised her step-daughter. She envied her looks, her majestical charm and the unending love that she fostered in the hearts of the people. For all this the Queen wished desperately to be rid of her.

The evil Queen manifested her hatred in a number of petty ways. She refused her daughter even the most basic courtesies, ignored her whenever possible and created great discomfort to this pinnacle of majesty. This was the cause of Princess Carolyn's constant melancholy and so instead of enjoying the gifts that fortune had bestowed upon her she would spend most of her day crying in her small room lamenting her fate.

There was only one brief instance of true happiness in her sad life, the only time when she would forget her worries and reveal the world's most adored and pleasant object, her radiant smile. This was when the court fool would enter her private chamber and tell the magnificent Princess Carolyn comical stories or perform fantastic magic tricks for her amusement. Only then would she be happy, but when he left her room all her thoughts would gradually return to gloom.

This unpleasant state of affairs continued until one fateful day Queen Mary made a dramatic announcement, Princess Carolyn was to be married to Prince Charles the Blackheart, the most ugly and evil creature in the entire world. Yet despite his horrible reputation and his hideous visage Queen Mary deeply desired the match in order to solidify her power in the realm. The marriage would also forever break her step-daughter's heart which made the evil Queen grin with pleasure.

When the announcement of the engagement was made the Princess barricaded herself in her room, her one sanctuary from the cruelness of her evil step-mother. Yet even there she was not safe, the diabolic Queen Mary ordered the room breached and the royal beauty was thrust out to be prepared for her wedding.

The day of the wedding Princess Carolyn was inconsolable; not even her beloved fool could brighten her dim spirits. Never did so bright a star burn as dimly as she did on that day. All too soon, two of the Queen's guards arrived at her broken door to escort her to her nuptials. As for the people of the kingdom, they knew nothing of the princess's misery. Despite the terrible match the people consoled themselves with the belief that if the wedding made the princess happy then it surely was meant to be. Only a creature of pure beauty of mind and spirit could have seen some spark of good deep within the Black Prince's soul.

It was a dark, rainy morning in which the wedding was to be held. All who attended mentioned how sad it was that the weather would be so horrid on this, the princess's happiest of days. Little did they realize that the world itself was weeping over the fate of its greatest child, so delicate a flower, used so harshly.

Yet despite the downpour the wedding went on, cups overflowed and food was more than plentiful for the wedding of the people's favourite royal. The ceremony was held in the largest hall in the palace, everything proceeded according to plan until the Bishop asked if there was anyone who objected to the nuptials. From outside the largest window came a loud cry ordering the Bishop to stop this travesty.

Outside of the window was a large flying dragon who demanded that Princess Carolyn be sent to him as his bride, otherwise he would destroy all the inhabitants of the kingdom. The creature ordered that she be delivered to him on the outskirts of the forest of doom outside the boundary of the peaceful kingdom at dawn or face his wrath, then without another word its wings outstretched and it soared away.

The gathering was shocked by this turn of events. The wedding was immediately stopped and Queen Mary, terrified of the destructive force of the dragon, readily agreed to give up her step-daughter's life. The Black Prince quickly approved of the decision; he was far too much of a coward to face a fierce dragon. The die was cast. Princess Carolyn, the most wonderful creature in the universe, was to be sacrificed to preserve villainy.

Just before dawn the people living in a small village outside the forest stood quietly by as they watched as Queen Mary's soldiers led the loveliness that was Princess Carolyn to the edge of the forest of doom and then left her alone to face the terrors of the dragon. She was not tied or hindered in any way. There was no question of her running away. She was the bravest person in the entire kingdom; saving herself at the expense of the kingdom and its people was unthinkable. The thought of escape never even crossed her wonderful mind.

At dawn the dreaded dragon flew down in front of the frightened Princess and then slowly advanced. The hot breath of the creature encompassed the Princess's lush body, her long white dress clung to her flesh and her silken hair flew into her eyes. As the dragon drew ever closer the brave princess prepared herself for death.

Suddenly, the distinctive gallop of a horse stopped the dragon's advance. The creature turned its large head towards the sound to see a white knight in shining armour. The angry dragon flashed its large, hideous teeth and flew straight up into the morning sky. It flew over the knight, its gigantic dark shadow nearly blotting out the morning sun.

The knight looked up and showed no outward sign of terror. He stopped his white horse and glanced at the terrified Princess, a mixed look of relief and concern revealed itself in his eyes. Carefully he disembarked from his horse and advanced towards the dragon.

Without warning it spat white hot fire at the hero, wishing to destroy the princess's only hope of salvation. Quickly raising his shield the knight warded off the hail of fire and instantly drew his long, sharp sword. He was determined to end this battle quickly to avoid endangering his dear princess.

Slashing wildly at the dragon he finally succeeded in piercing one of its wings forcing it to the ground. On an even plain of land the bizarre pair faced each other, both prepared to face death for the woman in front of them. A bloody battle of mythic proportions ensued; no ground was given on either side as both combatants fought for the greatest prize of all. Sparks flew into the air as the dragon managed to slash the knight with its razor sharp claws; the knight staggered back from the blow and seemed doomed.

The dragon moved closer and closer for the kill until he appeared directly over his victim and looked down at the seemingly helpless hero. The knight had only the strength within him for one final strike. With a desperate stroke of his blade the knight dispatched the dragon with a fatal thrust to its heart. The dragon surprised and angry, clutched the weapon impregnated into its breast and raised its head to the morning sun as if to protest this cruel trick of fate. With its last gasp of breath the dragon howled out a loud shriek in rage and terror and then it collapsed onto the bloody field and died.

The knight himself fell to the ground exhausted from his battle with the creature. His once shining armour was now covered with both his red blood and the green liquid that had so recently sustained the ferocious dragon. Gashes in his leg and chest revealed the source of the knight's agony.

Princess Carolyn ran to help her saviour; she knelt beside him and lifted up his armoured helmet to reveal her precious fool. The fool who made her happy was the knight that had saved her life, the jester who cheered her when she was sad was the man who loved her above all. Their eyes met as if for the first time and a bond that would last forever forged itself in chains around their hearts. There would be no love created in the history of the world like the love that they now shared with each other.

Before she could open her lips to speak a swarm of the Queen's guards came to take her away from the knight. The Queen, upon learning the dragon's fate, was even more determined to go ahead with the wedding to the evil Prince Charles, who now more than ever was not the princess's true love.

The injured knight was carried off the field by a group of relived villagers who hailed the man as a hero. The body of the dragon, which had rested in the field beside the knight, soon shimmered and vanished much to the surprise of the villagers. Yet as they had never seen a dragon die before, they chose to believe that perhaps that is what they did and no more was thought of the matter.

The knight was treated with respect and honour and was brought to the nicest home in the nearby village in order to recover his health. A warrior who had sustained wounds in many battles, he knew his body would heal in time. The knight's only thought was to be with the woman of his immense desire. The girl who held his heart, the woman who had claim to his soul was foremost in the man's mind. Never a moment would go by from then to the ending of the world in which he could not and would not hold her in the vanguard of his heart.

Back at the castle it did not take the Queen long to recommence the wedding ceremony. The groom, the evil Black Prince, was very happy to have his beautiful bride back by his side without having to go through the effort of saving her. All the attendants were happy to see what they believed to be what the princess had wanted all along, to be united with the Black Prince.

For the princess, she did what she believed to be her duty and did not resist her step-mother's wishes. Although she loved with all her pure heart the white knight she said nothing during the wedding but with head bowed uttered with tears in her eyes the two words "I do," and the union was complete.

The fool/knight, too wounded to help his long suffering love could only listen to the loud bells that proclaimed the consummation of the wedding bands. With each chime his heart would break a little more and his soul which was content had turned to ruin and hopelessness. The happy dreams that he wished for would never materialize and now he would have to suffer the heartbreak that his true love was in the arms of another, totally unworthy man. His world had descended into a bleak nightmare to which there was no waking and his heart shattered at the thought.

The End

The story seemed fine to Steve and the librarian wished that perhaps if he had an illustrator he might even publish it one day. But until that day he simply wrote, expressing himself in words on paper through colourful characters and fantastical adventures. His reality of space ships, alien creatures and adventures to planets to retrieve overdue books only seemed like a job to him and not the adventure that it may have looked like to others. Despite his ease in the head librarian chair he took his duties very seriously indeed and his focus on duty did not give him time to reflect on his unique position in the universe. To his knowledge he was the only Earth inhabitant to fly the galaxy but that was his job and so he rarely took the historic part of his life serious.

Steve picked himself up from his chair and walked to the flight deck where Zoe was making slight adjustments to the navigation controls. He caught her by surprise and immediately apologised. He stared out into the rush of stars on the view screen and took it all in. "Sometimes you just got to take a step back and just remind yourself where you are." He said this mostly to himself as a reminder. Steve continued to look at the stars while Zoe kept on about her business.

They kept the silence for a moment more before Steve pulled something out of his pocket and handed it to Zoe. "What's this? An overdue notice?" she asked only half jokingly. She opened the unmarked envelope and reached for the contents, inside were two first class tickets to the Tiluran planet eclipse, the event she had missed due to their run-in with Gregos the now-deposed ruler of the galaxy. She looked up at the librarian not knowing what to say.

"It's my way of saying thanks and sorry that you had to miss this year's event, but then again you did have crappy seats. At least next year you will actually be able to see it up close rather than rely on those Imagetastic screens that the promoters put up." Steve then turned around and went back to his bunk on the space mobile leaving a happy and slightly confused cataloguer back on the flight deck.

The trip to what was now known as planet of the Snarf which roughly translated to the planet of the lovely fluffy bunnies had been completely uneventful apart from the usual ghosts of librarians past wandering about the decks of the ship shouting out call numbers and book titles at all hours. Steve made it a point to call in an exorcist to see if anything could be done to shut up the annoying deceased bibliophiles. They may have enforced the universal shush rule during their lifetimes but now that they were deceased they wouldn't shut up.

At last the beautiful but deadly green planet beckoned the space weary travelers down to the surface below and even though the planet was dangerous they all desperately needed to get out of the confined space of their ship. All agreed that the best place to land was on the sun-drenched side as vampire lore was specific on those particular creatures disliking direct sunlight. As for vampire zombie bunnies who knew?

The library team left their ship and took a survey around the area. All around them were buildings. It was a deserted city they were standing in, a long time ago the place must have been a sight to see but now the hollow city yearned for a populace that would bring it to life once more but there was only unlife on the planet now.

Steve turned on his book locator device. This was a useful and interesting tool that no good librarian in the space library would be without. It was a small machine that detected unreturned library books but in a pinch could be recalibrated to detect unusual and rare books based upon the scent of musk. Fortunately for the library team books had not been detected on the planet in great quantity and those that were were quickly dismissed as being too young for the type of book the Tome of the Lost Ones was.

All three library workers wore full body armor that were skin tight and left nothing to the imagination but had the hide of a tank. Zoe looked especially attractive as the laser gun that she strapped to her thigh accentuated the curves of her body. The sun gleamed off the black armor and embraced her lithe form as she bent down to stretch as Steve handed the book locator to Chubba who chaffed at the binding second skin.

"You know, the smartest thing to do is to discover where the book is and wait until that part of the planet is in sunlight then go get the book. We'll have little trouble with the vampire zombie bunnies then. We can get the book, deliver it to the Library Board and get back to our usual lives." Steve seemed to be comfortable saying vampire zombie bunnies now and that realization alone spooked him. He was getting too cozy with his odd life that no one would believe back home on Earth and he felt his tether to the planet of his birth slip just a little more.

"Sounds like a sane plan. So what are we going to do?" Zoe asked with only a slight hint of sarcasm. Steve would have stuck his tongue out at the impertinent woman but his shielded helmet hid his face and he didn't want to take it off in case of hiding scary bunny. He would not have had the opportunity to take his helmet off as it happened, as Chubba screamed a silent telepathic cry that rocked both Steve and Zoe to their knees.

Chubba quickly fell straight down head first into the ground cutting off the emotional scream much to the relief of his two co-workers. Zoe was the first one to get up and she immediately rushed over to her fallen comrade. Steve staggered to his feet, shook his head, then walked over to his two companions.

"What the hell was that?" Steve felt a wave of concern rush over him as he knew that whatever affected Chubba had better be resolved quickly or there would be consequences for all three of them. Vampire zombie bunny consequences.

Zoe ran over to their fallen comrade and discovered that Chubba was totally unresponsive. Zoe ran to the space mobile and returned with a medical scanner which confirmed that Chubba had indeed taken a vacation from his body. Neither teammate knew what to do so they simply stood there with their scanners uselessly hanging onto their hands.

"Great, just great! We get the crappiest mission in library history. We travel all the way in a crappy haunted space book mobile and now that we are on the crappiest planet next to the reviled planet of Craptastic our big library technician decides to have a nap just as the sun is about to dip and we are about to be crapped out of some dead vampire bunny's arse!" Steve kicked at the air not even remotely upset at how childishly he was acting. Yes, he was concerned about Chubba but he had also assessed the situation pretty darn accurately.

With a start Chubba flew up and began to emanate a telepathic thank you to Steve. How did he know that a wave of utter anger would trigger an empathetic reset of Chubba's mind?

"Well, that's why I am the head librarian, I guess." Steve turned slightly red under his face shield but even more than embarrassed he was grateful to have Chubba back in the game. He couldn't think of a scenario where carrying a heavy, unconscious giant was a plus. Chubba got back on his feet and began to walk towards the space mobile. Zoe yelled at him to stop but the Gormorian simply kept walking until he reached the steps leading up to the cockpit.

Steve and Zoe rushed towards the giant but neither could get him to halt his advance upward and into the cockpit. Both were unceremoniously pushed down off the ladder and onto the ground. Before either Steve or Zoe could get to their feet the ladder ascended and the ship took off leaving two very upset and confused library personnel.

"What the hell was that all about? We save the guy's life and now he steals our ride and abandons us to the hopping dead?" Steve looked up and shook his fist in anger. For her part Zoe paid no attention to her head librarian. Instead she was busy using a tracking device to follow the space book mobile's movements. The ship was not leaving the planet but instead was flying towards another city not far from the deserted one they were already in. Zoe kept her tracking device in her hand and began to walk towards the ship which by this time had landed.

Steve grabbed a hold of her arm and turned his cataloguer about. "Where the heck do you think you are going?"

"I'm going to find Chubba and our ship. We are going to need both of those if we are to get off this planet." Zoe snatched her arm back from the grip of her library head.

"You are not going anywhere. Take a look around you. The sun is going down and we wouldn't stand a chance at night with those things around." Steve by this time was standing in front of Zoe and was ready to use force if necessary in order to stop Zoe. Fortunately, Zoe was ready to see wisdom, even if it did come from a man whose planet still didn't have an interstellar fast food franchise.

Zoe and Steve decided that the best next step was to find a safe place to stay for the night. Not having the time to make a proper tour of the city they decided that the first place that they came across that looked defensible was the place to stay.

It did not take too long a while to find what looked like an average home with three beds and a bath. Zoe and Steve entered the house and decided to stick together while making a brief exploration. The two story building seemed safe enough so the pair took the task of blocking off the windows and doors. Once that was accomplished Zoe and Steve retreated to the living room where each sat down on two comfortable chairs.

With the house secured both library workers decided to take off their security suits and breathe in the air. Steve struggled out of his suit while Zoe took little time in undressing the tight second skin from her body. Zoe was just getting her body relaxed when she noticed a door leading down towards the basement. She motioned with her head to Steve who was still trying to take off his right boot that she was going to have a look down the steps.

Steve yelled out, "Are you nuts?" falling over himself as he did so. Steve quickly got up and walked over to the door blocking Zoe from opening the door. "Anyone who has any brains whatsoever knows that zombies of all kinds love lurking in the basement. Small basements, large basements, basements of houses, apartment building basements and basements with wine cellars they absolutely love going down there! Don't they have horror movies on your planet? The last place you want to go is the basement. Besides, there are probably otherworldly spiders there and no one wants to have a look at those."

Zoe and Steve got some wood purloined from furniture and barricaded the door so that whatever was down there would stay down. This done, they returned to the living room and sat down once more. A brief silence followed as both library team members collected their thoughts. Then Zoe out of the blue blurted out: "So why did you give me two tickets to the Tiluran planet eclipse?" emphasizing the word "two".

Of course being a man Steve was totally unprepared for this odd question as his brain was occupied with trying to stay alive and uneaten. "I figured you had a pal somewhere in the universe and it sounded like something like the Tiluran planet eclipse was an event best shared."

"So," replied Zoe. "You didn't think of using the other ticket for yourself?"

"Actually, I am busy that week. I got a Library Express delivery ship dropping me off on Earth for a week's vacation. I was pretty lucky as Library Express rarely goes to Earth except on Inter-Planetary loans for Mr. Beeble. I get to visit my family and friends in St. John's then I head back on the same ship once they collect Mr. Beeble's loan materials."

Steve always knew that females could compartmentalize thoughts much better than males but Zoe's question only illustrated that in this case men are from Earth and women are from Cypheria. Yet he could not help but look at Zoe differently for a moment after her strange question. In the light of dusk he noticed, in his old friend Derm Kelly's off repeated words, that she was a festival of health.

Steve took the first security watch letting Zoe drift off to sleep on a couch. Neither person had worn many clothes under their security suits and with those hanging on the hooks over the electric stove getting dried of all the sweat Steve found himself shivering. Zoe had a blanket over her body to keep out the cold and she seemed comfortable. As a matter of safety Steve insisted that they sleep in the living room in case something happened and they needed to get up and out in a hurry.

Darkness fell and Steve's body quivered some more. Someone was dancing on his grave he mused as he complained to himself as quietly as possible so as not to wake Zoe. He looked at the space mobile's tracker and the ship was still stationary. All they had to do was to stay alive during the night then head towards the ship and they would be back in business.

Steve let Zoe sleep for an extra hour before exhaustion forced him to wake her up. Zoe was annoyed that she was allowed to sleep past her time but Steve called out that that was his decision as head librarian and that libraries were not democracies. Zoe strapped on her laser pistol to her slender waist and let Steve fall asleep. It did not take long after this for things to get dangerous.

Zoe peered out the window making sure she could not be noticed. Every minute or so she could see small objects move slowly as if moved by the wind. Not getting a good look she could only surmise that the objects were small creatures that might possibly be vampire zombie bunnies. She was about to move closer to the window when she heard the noise.

Turning about she heard the noise again only louder. At first she could not locate the bizarre sound but as she moved closer to Steve she found that the source of the loud, disgusting sound came from him! Falling into a deep sleep Steve began to snore and it was a snore that was so loud it could wake up the dead, or at least the undead.

Zoe tried to get him to stop by using the tried and true shush method hoping that an automatic response would silence the head librarian but there was no such luck. Then she grabbed a pillow and tried to somehow stifle the noise but it only made it louder and sleepy Steve unconsciously moved his arms to take away the congestion. Finally Zoe half jokingly thought of taking out her pistol when she heard a noise from the basement.

At first there was one shuffle, then two then more. The noise started up the basement stairs until there was a groan at the top. Zoe couldn't figure out which noise was worse, the groaning or the snoring. At last knocking and banging came from the boarded up basement door that increased in sound. Steve bolted up from his sleep, rubbed his face and asked what was going on.

Zoe informed him that multiple bangs were now coming from something down in the basement. She also told him that it was because of his snoring that they were now in this predicament to which Steve responded by saying that it was impossible because he never snored.

While the pair fought a 'you do to snore I do not snore war' another bang could be heard from the barricaded front door. Rushing to the window Steve and Zoe could see a mass of creatures coming directly towards the house. They would be surrounded by a ravenous horde of decaying vampire zombie bunnies if they didn't act soon.

"Upstairs. If we can get upstairs and barricade ourselves in a room all we have to do is wait until morning." Steve said as he bolted up the stairs. Zoe followed and they grabbed every bit of furniture in the room and piled it up against the bedroom door. Only then did they realize their mistake.

"We forgot to take our security suits!" Zoe screamed. She punched a wall creating a large hole. The last time she did something that stupid was when she was ordered to serve piping hot gazpacho soup when she was a waitress working her way through library school.

"It's always the case isn't it?" Steve replied. "You rush off to try and defend yourself against vampire zombie bunnies and you forget your best defense in the other room. Maybe it isn't such a shame after all that our brains are going to be eaten."

By this time wave after wave of creatures were batting hard on the door to get in. It was at this moment that Steve decided to lay down on the bed that was pushed up in front of the door. "What the hell are you doing?" Zoe screamed at him. But Steve ignored her and began looking around the room. After a minute of door-buffeting from the gang of vampire zombie bunnies he shot up and dragged Zoe to the window.

Out and up over the awning they arrived on the roof where below them they could see a sea of ravenous, dead creatures all thirsty to get into the house. A loud crash below meant that the bedroom door had finally been destroyed and bunnies began to tear up the room in search of their feast. It did not take the monsters long to sense just where their prey had taken flight and soon the library duo were facing an army of vampire zombie bunnies advancing up the outside of the house and onto the roof. The pair walked to the edge of the rooftop but there was no where to go without either being killed by the fall or diving headlong into an ocean of killers. It looked like their books were about to be stamped.

Suddenly a bright, searing light fell upon the advancing undead bunnies and a loud hiss came from their dissipating bodies. A ladder abruptly fell from the dark sky and hit Steve directly on the head knocking him senseless. A frantic Zoe slapped the staggering man in the face to wake him up while the sound of hissing, sizzling bunnies screamed into their ears. Both Zoe and Steve quickly climbed to safety.

The machine that saved their lives was unmanned so there was no need to thank anyone. Steve was still too dazed to actually say anything and the fact that there was no need to say an obligatory thank you liberated him from the burden of looking like a complete ungrateful ass. Instead he slowly slumped down to the floor of the transport and fell into an unconscious heap.

When he awoke Steve found that he was alone in a small bedroom. Besides the bed on which he was lying there was actually nothing remotely looking like furniture in the small room. There was a door not five feet from the bed so he gingerly pulled himself up, planted his feet firmly on the cold ground and then went to open the door. A second later he found himself knocked on the floor unconscious once again.

The door that he wanted to use had unfortunately opened and slammed Steve full in the face knocking him out. It took a full four minutes before he felt cold hands over his forehead and a cloth wiping the blood from his nose. Realizing what had just happened Steve wondered just what universal god he had grossly offended to anoint him the Jerry Lewis of space.

Zoe took her hands off Steve and began to explain their rescue. The story went that a group of colonists survived centuries after the Second Vampire Zombie Bunny War or as the people who thought the name was overly long and silly called it VZB II. The survivors took a page from the enemy and burrowed deep down in the ground and created an underground civilization. The bunnies instinctively looked to the surface for food and had no idea, if indeed their minds were capable of thought, that there were people living underground. The people survived through various means and had even taken steps towards eradicating the bunny menace. After all the undead cannot reproduce by themselves and as far as they knew there was nothing left alive on the surface of the planet. Killing one vampire zombie bunny meant there was one less hunting you and they had killed many during the centuries.

"Wait a minute. If these guys are living underground how did they mange to save us and if they have technology like that remote controlled helicopter why couldn't they reclaim the planet or simply get the heck off the world?" Steve asked, his head now pounding like a beating drum.

Zoe explained that the technology was very old and it did little against the menace when it was new. At the time there were too many bunnies to kill but now it seems their numbers have diminished enough that an attack could be feasible, in theory. The helicopter that saved Steve and Zoe was an emergency drone flown by remote control as the survivors did not wish to risk their own lives in piloting the craft. Unfortunately it took a great deal of power to use and could not be sustained in a prolonged combat mission.

Zoe also explained that the survivors knew of the plight of the librarians and agreed to help. In return all they asked was that they return with a fighting force to rid them of this plague so they could return to the surface and rebuild their shattered cities. "Fine, whatever, let's just get this damn mission over with and I'll get the Inter Galactic Library Board to contact the necessary authorities. Once they know the situation, there should be no problem in helping these people." Steve got up from his bed, shook his addled head and asked Zoe to take him to their leader.

In moments, Steve and Zoe were both talking to Vee, the leader of the survivors. She was a distant relative of Major Allan Strong who had won the First Vampire Zombie War and was a capable leader of this strong and proud people. Surprisingly Zoe found herself slightly annoyed at the rapid closeness that Vee and Steve shared right from the first. As Steve and Vee made their plan of attack to rescue Chubba, find the Tome of the Lost Ones and then get to the space mobile where they could contact someone for help Zoe kept unusually quiet and simply faded into the background.

"All right everyone. Let's get this show on the road." Steve's remark didn't really make a lot of sense to an underground dwelling race but they got the gist of the saying. The plan was simple. A group of survivors, Steve, Zoe and Vee would head to the city where Chubba was supposed to be according to his library card. There they would rescue Chubba from himself or whatever had him enthralled, find the book then off to the space mobile all in that order. With a plan that simple what could possibly go wrong?

The helicopter was now of no use as its batteries needed a long time to recharge, time that Steve did not have if he were to save Chubba's life. That, plus a real desire to get back to the space library in time to watch the season premiere of *Survivor*, cumulated in the haste for the expedition.

Steve and Zoe with their tracking device led the way through an underground labyrinth which ended in the heart of the city where Chubba had landed. Fortunately there were no signs of bunnies throughout the long journey. As the group reached the tunnel that would put them very near where the tracking device reported that it would find the space book mobile, everyone's breath seemed to hold as Steve opened the heavy hatch that led to the surface.

Fortunately the sun was bright outside and no vampire would be able to withstand the sun, not even a zombie bunny vampire, so the group felt safe enough to venture out onto the surface of the planet. Steve and Zoe found their craft exactly where the tracker said it would be. Zoe quietly secured the ship so that no fur balls of fun could enter turned back to Steve and then asked what should they do next?

"Easy," Steve said. "We just track Chubba by use of his library card. Every library card has a unique identifying number and in a jam we head librarians can track the card in order to find outstanding overdue borrowers." Before Zoe could ask why on Earth she never heard of that particular library card feature Steve said that only head librarians could use the feature due to the potential for misuse and for privacy concerns.

Steve activated Chubba's unique library ID number and downloaded the map to Zoe's tracker. Instantly she had a fix on where Chubba was located. The subsequent news was not well received by anyone in the group.

"The library? The city's main library? That is where Chubba is?" Steve was incredulous over the news. "Do you know what libraries are? Dangerous! There are all sorts of closed stacks, dark corners where vampire zombie bunnies can fly right at you without warning. There are high shelves where something can jump right down at you! The library is the worst place to go when there is imminent danger of being sucked dry and eaten by a blood sucking, flesh eating fiend!"

"None the less that is where Chubba is and unless you or your partner in crime the vivacious Vee can come up with a fantastic solution to this mess then the scary library is where we have to go!" Zoe seemed almost pleased with her speech as she walked away from the head librarian without another word.

"Okkkkkkkayyyy then," Steve said with eyes rolled. Let's all go to the library." The group collected their things, walked in double formation and with guns ready they found the stairs to the entrance of the old city's main library. "Alright people, listen up. Maximum shush rule in effect from now on. No talking unless absolutely necessary. Ok, let's go find our shelver." For a reason unknown to Steve he reached back and took Vee's hand in his as they walked up the stairs and through the library doors.

The entrance hall looked absolutely beautiful. There were scenes of historical events carved all over the walls and ceiling. It was a type of artwork that could not be given justice by mere words. It was obvious to even the most inartistic that the group who built this amazing library had to be deeply artistic people indeed.

The walk through the library was a slow one for two reasons: the first being that no one wanted to make noise to alarm any other patron of the library and the second was that everyone was marveling at the wonderful artwork that practically came alive. The survivors especially loved the art in the library as it made them proud to have sprung from such a wonderful seed.

At last the tracker indicated that Chubba was in the next room which happened to be the main reading hall, the very large and very, very dark reading hall. Steve nodded to Vee and she pulled out her ultraviolet light rod which emitted the type of light that a vampire simply could not withstand. With this weapon at the ready the group entered the main reading hall.

The majesty of the room was obvious from the moment the group walked in. It was so awe-inspiring in fact that they almost lost their focus as they squinted in the dark. Yet none were so foolish as to miss what was clearly a throne situated where once the circulation desk must have resided. The desk was long gone and one could only imagine how wonderful it must have been.

The rescuers were automatically drawn towards the throne where a furry creature sat in silence. The group stopped suddenly as Zoe noticed the creature but by then it was far too late. "Let there be lights!" the creature cried out and a flood of electric lights blinded the group for just one moment but it as only a moment that was needed to rob the survivors of their most effective weapon. Vee's rod was stolen right out of her hand so fast that she saw nothing. Yet she didn't have to see anything to know one thing. No zombie could have moved that fast.

"Welcome to my domain. I am Lazarus, king of the vampire bunnies though you may call me Your Highness." The king of the vampire bunnies was larger than the bunnies that had swarmed around him. He was heavier and much more alert than the others. He had a red cape that was custom - made for his bunny body which matched his deep, blood red eyes and he held a small scepter in his right forepaw. Here was a king indeed but the question on everyone's mind was:

"Hey, how come you are not drooling all over the place and singing the ever-popular groan song?" Steve asked the monarch.

"Ah, you must be the head librarian! I have heard much about you from my tall and large friend." The king of the bunnies waved his paw, a curtain immediately fell from behind the throne and Chubba was revealed to all. He seemed unhurt but in a trancelike state. Despite his eagerness to see if Chubba was safe Steve stopped himself and waited for the vampire bunny king to make a move.

What followed was a story told by the vampire bunny king of the origin of the vampire bunny. The bunnies originally landed with the first colonists thousands of years ago. They were set free to multiply. Then, as their numbers grew, they were savagely hunted down and eaten by the colonies. The bunnies were helpless creatures with little intelligence and had no defense against the organized killers.

This slaughter lasted for hundreds of years until one night a man with an unusual thirst came upon a defenseless bunny who was plumper and more appealing than most. There under the full moon the stranger feasted and the frightened bunny died, or so he thought. Three days later the bunny rose up from the shallow grave that the stranger had made for him, his paw burst out from the ground and as other bunnies huddled in fear the new race of vampire bunny was created!

"Let me take a wild guess and say that it was you who was the first vampire bunny on the planet," Steve so rudely interrupted. After receiving a loud shush from the entire group, the vampire bunny king continued.

"I was endowed with strength, speed, but most importantly I was given intelligence not just instinct. I could now strike back for my race but I needed more than just myself if I were to rid this world of the creatures that hunted us so relentlessly. I began to feed on other bunnies until I had a small army of recruits all under my will and all who thirsted for revenge!"

The vampire king hopped off his throne to look closer at the men and women who had invaded what was now his library. He examined them closely as he continued his tale. "I was just about to command a war against the evil killers when suddenly an undead abomination came tumbling into our burrow. It began to devour my soldiers, each one it attacked changed into zombies until my group hopped for their un-lives. The war that began soon after was not started by me but by those filthy creatures and we have been hiding in fear ever since. Only the true untainted vampire bunny must live on this planet!"

"Not to point out the obvious again but aren't the true untainted creatures the original bunny without the vampire or zombie added?" Steve so wisely asked.

"To my knowledge there are no true bunnies left alive on this planet and if there are I hope they are safe from the zombie fiends! Now, let Us turn Our thoughts onto matters more relevant than history. Let Us now speak about your timely deaths!"

"Actually, let us, not the royal us, speak on how to rid your planet of the zombie plague instead and for that you need our help." Steve looked into the red eyes of the vampire bunny king and did not waver for a moment. In his mind this creature had perverted the beautiful library that they were standing in by making it a dominion of a king rather than the purview of all. Libraries were about freedom, not tyranny.

For all his knowledge, he could not read or think as higher level sentient beings could, but he understood on an instinctual level Steve's need to protect his own people and it was on that mutual ground that Steve and the king made a pact. The vampire bunny king looked upon the head librarian as another ruler rather than an individual. The two leaders met alone and created an agreement that made sense to both parties.

Steve returned to his small band and began to tell them of the agreement. The deal he made with the vampire bunny king was that Steve promised to end the threat of the zombie bunnies for all time in exchange for the safety of the library party and the survivors from the colony. In truth there was a little bit more to the deal than that but that was all his band needed to know.

With the agreement, Chubba was at last freed from the thrall. Chubba fell down to the dirty floor on the library and Steve and Zoe helped him up. "Hang on there big fella. It is just your luck to be susceptible to the mind powers of a vampire. Well, it just means you can't take all the credit for this caper," Steve laughed as he saw that the old Chubba was returning.

"Now, let's get on to business. We have to find that Tome of the Lost Ones which ladies, vampires and gentlemen is as easy as punch. Why do you ask? I'll tell you why because someone went to a great deal of trouble to make the book invisible and what is the one thing that a head librarian is good for?"

Steve waited for someone to say something but when it was obvious that apart from a nervous cough that only silence reigned in the library he continued on. "A good head librarian can find any book, especially if it is already in the library!" Steve walked up to a small podium in the middle of the room and slammed his hand on a large, dusty old book.

Opening the book a brilliant light shone out of it and he thumbed thought the pages. "Man, this book is much more user friendly than most evil tomes, this book actually translates itself as I thumb through the pages. Ah ha! Here it is! The spell to change dead creatures into undead ones and if I know my indexes correctly then this page must have the reverse spell!"

Even the vampire bunny king was suitably impressed by this amazing feat of librarianship. Sometimes a Masters Degree in Library and Information Science from an American Library Association accredited university can stand you in good stead and this was one of those times for the Earthman named Steve.

Without further ado Steve began to speak the passages that would reverse the spell that had changed the vampire bunnies into vampire zombie bunnies. His body jolted as if reading the written words took a massive physical toll on his ephemeral soul. His eyes turned dark, his voice grew unworldly and his arms rose up above his head unwillingly.

A wave of light came from the book forcing the vampire bunnies present to hide for their very existence. The light continued to spread out until it encircled the globe. All over the world the vampire zombie bunnies turned into dust as the black magic that had kept them moving long after they should have disintegrated left their corpses. The plague of the vampire zombie bunny was at last over on New Bunny World.

Steve fell to the floor as the incantation ended. Vee ran to his slumped form and Zoe rushed to give her a hand. Steve shook himself awake and released his arms from the pair of helpers. This was no time to look weak while in the domain of the vampire bunny king. Steve asked if their dealings were done and the bunny king assured him that it was but they had better leave immediately.

There was little time for fond farewells as even the king of the vampire bunnies could not keep full control over his minions with the colonists present. Steve looked into the beautiful eyes of Vee. Her hair was over her face but he could still see the look of fear in her eyes as she surveyed the massive number of bunnies that surrounded them in the library. She knew her war was one that she might never win.

Steve halted and after a moment's pause he told his companions to go outside. "Don't worry. I'll be with you in a moment." He watched them depart then his face turned cold. He walked up to the bunny king whose mouth was watering at the sight of the helpless colonists. Steve and the king had some private words then Steve and his party was gone from the beautiful library in a long lost city.

Steve, Zoe and Chubba walked to the space book mobile accompanied by the small group of colonists. The sun was beginning to set and the colonists needed to go back to their home before the vampire bunnies came out to hunt. The war with the zombies was over but the vampire bunny war was still at large.

Steve held Vee's soft hand one last time. He looked into her eyes and made a promise that he would return and on that day she would no longer have to be afraid of the surface world. With Zoe looking on from the cockpit Steve kissed his new friend goodbye and reluctantly entered the space mobile. As the survivors watched the ship lifted off the ground and up into space Steve thought he saw a small tear roll down his new friend's face. He promised himself that one day he would make that face smile with joy.

Once the ship had cleared the atmosphere Zoe turned to Steve and asked, "So, how the heck did you really find that book so fast?"

"You mean you don't believe in the magical powers of a head librarian?" Steve said with a smirk. "Well, to be honest it seemed only logical that someone had to have used the book in order to inflict the bunnies with the curse of the undead. Plus if you want to hide anything you naturally put it in plain sight so logically the library was the best choice. Finally, and this was the kicker, my book tracker was going nuts in my pocket telling me the Tome of the Lost Ones was sitting down right in front of me. Still, people like a good show and I gave them one."

"Ok, why would someone want to make vampire bunnies zombies anyway? What would be the point?" Zoe mused out loud to Steve.

"Who knows and who cares? It was probably a wizard with too much time on his hands for all we know. On the other hand it could have been an unknowing library technician that started the apocalypse. A library technician who should have concentrated more on shelving duties and statistics rather than looking at evil tomes might have set the whole thing off."

With a smile Steve relaxed in the co-pilot chair and slowly drifted off to sleep content in the knowledge that soon he would return to the little library he called home. He looked forward to returning to his work and regular routine.

Three weeks later the space book mobile had finally arrived within orbit of the space library's asteroid. After the terrific adventure all three travelers simply wanted to get back to their normal lives. The Tome of the Lost Ones was recovered and with a librarian holding it the universe was now safe from undead bunnies.

The ship slowed as it began its descent towards the library and Steve could already feel the nice, warm bath he was going to have. He was ready to watch his television show which was about to start and he had a case of Quan's Finest Ale in his private fridge. Oh yeah, life was going to get good once again.

Without warning the ship violently lurched up, alert lights and screaming whistles emanated from all parts of the ship. The three library workers were thrown all about the cockpit until they could no longer take the buffeting. The last image Steve saw as he looked out the view screen was the sight of his branch of the space library ripping itself apart and fire exploding out from its crushed metal belly. The space library branch # 6941 was no more.

He did not know how long he had been unconscious but judging by the dispersal of the smoke it must have been a while. Steve lifted himself from the fiery, broken wreckage of the space book mobile and cautiously stood up. Incredibly he was fine. He had discovered no damage physically to his body but mentally he was in hell. He could not find Zoe or Chubba. He tried to move to see if he could find them but his legs did not work. Panic began to form in his heart.

The wreckage of the space library was strewn out but the body of the book mobile, and more importantly its precious oxygen supply, had not failed. Steve looked about but he was entirely alone and that scared him. Where was the rest of the crew?

Suddenly the images changed all around him and he found himself lying on a soothing, incredibly soft bed. Beautiful women were walking around a luscious garden that surrounded his bed, the warm sun shining in a perfect sky. His head was slowly tilted up by warm hands and another beautiful creature started to feed him peeled grapes. He felt that his luck had finally changed for the better. No matter that he had no idea where he was or how he got there he no longer cared, he was beyond caring. He was in heaven.

"We are losing him!" Zoe screamed and slammed her fists on the head librarian's chest. This got a rise from the man whose body lay flat near the wreckage of the space book mobile. Steve opened his eyes and saw the fierce anger and tears run down Zoe's flushed cheeks. He smiled and raised his hand to her beautiful face then his arm fell once more down to his torn and bloody side. The last thing he heard was Zoe screaming on the emergency radio for immediate assistance from anyone who could respond. Then there was silence.

Chapter Three

Discontent

Back on Earth Steve lived a mundane, ordinary life. During his usual weekday morning routine he sleepily got up from his bed, endured a lukewarm wake-me-up shower, dressed in a smart, work-a-day suit and finally, reluctantly made his way to work. Over the next eight hours he would smile at people, sometimes genuinely, as he helped answer their questions in one of the many Manhattan branches of the New York Public Library.

The dumb Inter Galactic Library Association Inter-Planetary Loan pilots simply dropped him off on Earth not really caring where on the planet they put him. The journey was far away as it was and the pilots were in no mood to wander around looking for a particular spot, so Steve was dumped in New York City with a bag of clothes he managed to save from the wreckage of the space mobile and a credit card to keep him from living on the streets his first few nights back on Earth.

In short order he had gotten a job and now Steve was a reference librarian, a breed of librarian that required a great deal of mental stamina, but more and more often he found that resilience slowly waning. A gradual erosion of the soul was taking place inside him and that corrosion felt unstoppable.

Steve never thought of his new existence as being especially terrible. His job was dull but it paid the bills, kept him fed and gave him a reason to get up in the morning. Yet, like most people his age, he had the nagging suspicion that somehow he missed his calling and had instead settled into a semi-comfortable routine that, while he wasn't entirely happy, at least he could live with. Doing the same thing over and over again gave him some sense of acceptance and peace in a world that, if he was truly honest with himself, he did not comfortably belong. Certainly his experiences with the space library left him with some high expectations as to how much adventure a library job should have but mostly he missed being in charge.

His position changed from space head librarian to being a reference librarian for the New York Public Library back on Earth had happened so abruptly that he still couldn't make sense of it all. Why the hell would anyone blow up his library and would they ever be found? The library workers were ordered back to their home worlds until the investigation into the incident had been completed. Steve's broken body had been healed and now he was back on Earth where after three months of living on the planet of his birth he was more than slightly annoyed.

On this particular morning, a sweaty Friday in the middle of August, the librarian prepared to face his job once more. He grabbed his favourite jacket, the one that his mother bought him for his first interview years ago, and fast-stepped his way out of his apartment and onto the street. It was 6:30 am EST and it was the beginning of another long day of commute, work and commute again.

Like most librarians, he was a failure at something else first; as Steve himself once put it: "no one ever dreams as a child of becoming a librarian." Usually the road to librarianship was to try and subsequently fail at something more adventurous or, in some cases, not even bother to try at all before giving up and settling into the role of a librarian. In Steve's case, he had once dreamed of becoming an archeologist like his movie hero Indiana Jones. He fantasized that he wore a manly fedora, cracked a leather whip and had magnificent adventures where he beat up cowering Nazis with one hand while holding a beautiful, sparsely-clad woman close with the other.

Needless to say he fell far short of his ultimate goal. Steve had wanted to do something grand but having never quite put a finger on anything that he was truly good at. He filed his dreams away in the recess of his mind and chose a steady profession that, while somewhat boring to him, at least made him semi-content. Of course his life in outer space was a good library job but his new life in New York was, well, not so much. If life was a game he would have considered his situation of the moment a tie.

His place of residence was a small, sparsely-furnished apartment on Staten Island. While he worked in Manhattan, he could never afford to actually live there, so Staten Island was the closest he could live and still eat on a regular basis. Instead of casually strolling to his place of work which he did at branch #6941 of the space library he now took a long, tiring ride by rail, ferry and subway and then eight hours later he did the same thing again, only in reverse. All told it took an eleven hour a day five days a week toll on him. The cumulative effect was that he was becoming increasingly disaffected with his situation.

Stepping on the Staten Island ferry for what seemed to him the millionth time, Steve stared at the floor of the crowded vessel. The glamour of New York had quickly faded as the world around him gradually beat him into submission. The skyline that had once looked so majestical was now a homogenous mass of concrete towers thrust against one another to become a confusing maze. The Statue of Liberty, that beautiful lady, he now looked upon as one of a multitude of tourist traps instead of a beacon of freedom to the world's huddled masses.

Steve, a Canadian citizen, came to the United States of America via space with the hope of building a better life for himself. He was now a member of the new age of immigrants who looked to the U.S. for an opportunity. This group of young, well-educated men and women who were looking for a new beginning in a different world were replacing the poor, hungry throng of people that had once arrived at Ellis Island.

With the exception of his space library experience his origin story was not that much different from any other new immigrants. He was born in St. John's, Newfoundland, a place so far removed from New York that it might as well have been situated on another planet and yes, he realized the irony of that. Yet here he stood on the deck of the John F. Kennedy ferry, moving past Liberty and Ellis Islands and on his way to work, feeling as if he had been living there all his life.

The nearness of the water gave him a sense of continuity; in St. John's the water is only a window away, in Manhattan it was similar. The big difference between St. John's harbour and Manhattan harbour was the continual presence of the garbage scows, the ugly, rat-infested disease traps that forever moved slowly across the Manhattan River. They were a gross reminder that he was in a different place even more so than all the famous landmarks combined. They didn't have garbage scows in St. John's.

To keep his sanity during the ride back and forth he worked on his novel, a fantasy tale he fancied would bring him everlasting fame and fortune. Of course he really didn't believe that it would; it was just one of the games his mind played to keep him occupied. He had begun his magnum opus on his last journey in the space book mobile right after the virtual chess with the five erased pieces finally gave out. Finding a hard seat he relaxed his back against the hard wood and read over his second chapter of his fantasy novel.

Queen Lenore and the Terrible Tower

Two long, painful months after the titanic battle with the fearsome dragon the White Knight's physical wounds had at last healed, yet his heart remained shattered in a thousand pieces. His one true love, the beautiful Princess Carolyn, had been taken against her will and was forcibly married to the evil Black Prince Charles. He knew that he would never be able to see her beautiful smile or hear her wonderful soft laugh again. This thought was more than the Knight could bear and so he made up his mind to leave the small village that had been his home for the trying days of his recovery and go far, far away in the futile hope that he could somehow leave his pain behind.

As he informed his friends in the village of his decision they begged him not to go. In the eyes of the people of the village he was a great hero for slaying the dreaded dragon and they did not want to see a man such as him leave. Yet the White Knight could not be swayed by their desperate pleas. He was determined to get as far away as he could from the source of his terrible heartache, the evil Black Prince and his wonderful new bride Carolyn. He could know no peace while living so near his heart's lone desire, he would have no rest while he resided in the shadow of their marriage.

The forest of doom seemed to the Knight the obvious choice to explore and he made it known that he would investigate the forest and slay any beast that could endanger the village. This inconsolable man could not be persuaded by the people who feared for his safety in the un-chartered territory for he was resolute. The Knight climbed on his horse and surveyed the earnest scene that presented itself to him. Despite the terrific downpour that mirrored their sad emotional state the population of the village had all come out of their homes to wish the White Knight a good and safe journey. The muddy streets were lined with people in a show of appreciation for the Knight, all who wanted him to remain but knowing his wish to go now simply hoped he would be safe wherever his journey would take him. The White Knight could not suppress his tears and was glad of the rain that hid them as he gently nudged his white horse forward. The steed trotted out of the friendly village and towards the dark unknown.

Not all were sad to see the White Knight leave. Charles the Black Prince on hearing of the news smiled contentedly to himself, believing that he was rid of the one person who could oppose him in his evil machinations. With the White Knight gone he could concentrate solely on solidifying his hold over the land. His love was for power and not for his new bride. As for the beautiful Princess Carolyn, she stared out of the window of the tallest castle tower and wistfully dreamed for a better life in the arms of her one true love.

The White Knight soon had left the friendly village behind and found himself at the entrance of the mysterious forest. Without any hesitation he plunged into the foreboding forest of doom. He did not know where he was going nor did he care. All he knew was that he needed to be far away from the lovely vision that haunted him. It was the wistful dream of an existence with his lovely Princess and the harsh reality of a lifetime without her that spurred him onwards toward the dark interior of the woods. His heart was immensely heavy with the knowledge that all that he desired was in the arms of another and the steadfast belief that a marriage once consummated by God should never be rent asunder by man. All his strength, all his skill, all his burning desire meant nothing to what was; he had never felt as helpless as he did at that very moment. He felt as if he had all the substance of a shadow.

The Knight slowly rode deeper and deeper into the dark forest unafraid of the unknown that lay within. The White Knight had travelled through many parts of the world and seen many things yet while accustomed to odd places still this forest seemed unusual to him. The trees were black with long thin branches that seemed to almost look alive, slowly moving back and forth as if they pulsed with the breath of life. A normal man would have felt unnerved by the unfamiliar sights and sounds of the foreboding forest, perhaps even afraid but the Knight was unaccustomed to terror and gradually moved ever deeper into the trees, ever deeper into the darkness.

He did not fear the darkness, his deepest nightmare had already been realised and now that his heart was broken forever he felt he had nothing left to lose. Sorrow was his companion, a constant throb in his soul that could not be ebbed by something as petty as fear. This was not some demon that he could fight nor was it a raging fever that could be overcome but a colossal sense of loss for something that he never possessed. His was a pain of the heart, a void that could not be filled save for a reversal of luck and the gentle touch of his love's caress. Fickle fate had stolen his Princess away and there was not a sword in existence as strong as the gentle turns of fortune.

The knight stopped in front of a stream of cool, refreshing water. He got off his horse and knelt down and cupped his hands. He lifted the water to his lips even as his horse bowed its head to the water below. Yet even here in the sanguine area of short grass near a beautiful brook he could not be content, for he did not see his reflection in the cold stream but that of his heart's longing and so he added to the fresh water some salty tears.

Lost in the fog devised by his mind he rode ever onward not knowing or caring where he went. It was his horse Victory which woke the Knight from his day dreams as the animal grew tired from the long journey and shook his master with a gentle message that it was time to rest.

The Knight acknowledged the stallion's wishes even though respite was the last thing on his burdened mind.

Soon, the pair entered a clearing in the woods and as the horse and rider both drank from a nearby stream the night stars appeared and it was time at last for the man to lay down his head. It took some time for the Knight to drive his burning heartache from his mind enough to allow him to sleep, but even a hero must rest and so his eyes finally shut and he faded into a fitful slumber. Sleep was to be a scarce commodity that night, however, as eyes both curious and sinister looked upon the sleeping figures with interest.

Nothing out of the ordinary, no sound that was unusual, woke the Knight but it was from a sixth sense created from the necessity of years of battle that forced the man from his dreams and into an instant state of readiness. He grabbed the sword that he kept at his side and his eyes peered into the darkness that was hardly penetrated by the light of the nearby smouldering campfire. He carefully watched as a small figure stumbled out of the trees and into the makeshift camp. A girl no more than sixteen collapsed face first near the fire, gasping from exhaustion and unable to speak, her eyes filled with absolute terror. She looked up at the stranger in front of her in mute surprise and reached out her hand for help.

Rather than immediately help the girl up from the ground the White Knight grabbed a branch from his fire, walked over to his horse Victory, who was by now standing at attention, and reached into a sack that was attached to his saddle. With great care he took out a small blue gem and held it up to the bright moonlight. After looking at the blue stone for a moment as if to make sure it was the right one, he cautiously walked over to the girl, sword still at the ready, and placed the stone on her dirty forehead. Only after nothing extraordinary happened did the White Knight let go a slight sigh, offer his hand to the distressed girl and led her over to the relative comfort of his makeshift bed.

Soon, after sips of water from his canteen and a large helping of bread obtained from the Knight's supplies she began to calm herself enough to tell her story. Her name was Melina, who was in the process of escaping from a wicked man named Alberon who was using her to blackmail her family into surrendering the family farm. She had been held captive for a long time and was sure that her father was about to give in to the evil man's demands. In order to stop that from happening she decided to escape and reach the security of her village before Alberon could recapture her.

The White Knight listened intently to her story and after a brief pause decided to help the young girl reach the safety of her home. A small adventure of this sort would help ease the agony in his soul and offer a reprieve from his dreadful heartbreak. He waited until the girl was finally asleep then once more laid down for the night. All the while a pair of menacing eyes watched the Knight and his new charge while they slept.

The next morning the pair awoke and began to get ready to depart. The Knight, as gallant as he was brave, hoisted the pretty young woman on Victory and then the couple marched in the direction of the girl's family farm. Melina was happy to find a friend in the forest who was brave enough to help her escape the evil Alberon while the Knight was just glad to be occupied; although his thoughts never strayed far from the Princess he had left behind.

It was a long journey through the forest and as the two travelled the Knight learned a great deal about the young girl and her family. Her father had a great interest in bees and kept them on his farm to harvest the honey. She had a sister named Lee Ann and a brother named Martin both of whom the Knight could tell she loved very much. He was content that he was doing something to help this lady become reunited with those that she cared for. He only wished that it was possible that he could be united with the woman that he loved, although he knew that was not to be.

As the sun began to set the pair decided that it was time to set up a camp and rest before the fall of night. The day had gone on without incident and the Knight wondered where this madman Alberon could be. It seemed most strange that a man such as Melina described would give up so easily. The knight expected trouble before the trip was over.

To pass the long nights and lighten her spirits the knight entertained the girl with some tricks, juggled balls and produced bright flashes of light that came from seemingly nowhere. Melina asked where he had learned such tricks; the Knight merely replied that he had picked them up along his travels. Melina could hear the sadness in his voice when he said this but chose not to inquire further. Soon the dark night came upon the land and Melina fell fast asleep near the fire comforted in the knowledge that she would be guarded by her White Knight. The knight lay down beside her and they both entered the realm of dreams together.

All was quite in the forest of doom, too quite it seemed. The Knight whose rest would otherwise be disturbed with a sleepless melancholy was awake for another reason; he knew he was being watched. Standing up from the ground he did not have to wait long before he was proved correct, for soon from out of the forest came a small figure that looked neither menacing nor evil. It was a grey haired man with a kind face that entered into the light and it was this seeming kindness that made the White Knight more on guard than if it was a horrific giant fiend that now approached. It was the face of a man who had no evil in his outer appearance but who could know what was in his soul?

With only a warm smile for a greeting the old man proceeded to sit down near the fire and thrust his arms out to warm himself over the small, crackling flames. The Knight took his cue and sat opposite the man with the still sleeping Melina behind his back and his hand still gripped tight to the handle of his sword. To his right on his horse's saddle his bag of magical gems and amulets crackled as if they were popcorn.

The old man looked directly at the knight and waved his hand indicating the sleeping girl. "It's been a long journey for this poor girl but now it is time to end this game. Melina must be returned to me at once, otherwise I will not be held responsible for what happens next." The old man smiled as if he were talking to a friend who understood and agreed perfectly with what he had just said. The knight was no fool and knew that to take lightly the old man sitting by the fire would be a fatal error. If the girl was frightened by this man then there was much more than met the eye than what was before him. Yet despite the consequences he obviously he could not comply with the request.

"I don't believe she wants to return with you," the Knight replied.

"Her wants are irrelevant young man and before you get all worked up I must remind you that this is none of your affair. I know your sort. You play the hero riding from place to place destroying evil and making the world safe for poor young girls. Well, there is no evil here so please do not make a fuss and just let me have the girl so we can be on our way." This was said such a matter of fact a way that even the Knight had to smile in disbelief. The strange man was either crazed or supremely confident, either way he was definitely dangerous.

"I don't think so. If you want the girl you are going to have to go through me, something that I do not think that you are at all capable of doing," the Knight looked into the eyes of the old man searching to find some indication of the evil that he was sure would exist. Yet, instead the old fellow merely placed his hands on his knees and with some difficulty he raised himself to his feet.

"I don't believe you understand the danger you have placed yourself in, my friend, but you will." The old man then turned his back on the knight and walked back into the darkness of the forest night. His form vanished as if it had never been.

For what remained of the darkness the knight refused to sleep wary that some form of hazard would manifest itself. When none appeared he was more annoyed than relieved preferring to face a fierce foe outright rather than wait for a trap from a devious one. Still the sight of the sun rising over the trees relieved the knight and as he heard the stirring behind him he knew it was once more time to get ready to ride towards the girl's home.

Breakfast was a simple affair, bread and eggs taken from the provisions that the knight had been given by his friends in the village but it was enough to sate the two travellers. Melina washed the pan that they had eaten out of in a nearby stream and soon they were on their way through the forest of doom and towards her longed for home. The girl was very happy that she was on her way back to her loved ones but in the knight's mind he knew that the journey would not be as easy at it seemed.

As the expedition continued the knight grew increasingly tense as if the absence of danger was taking its toll on the man of action. He knew that his quest to see the girl Melina safely home was going far too well and it made him more nervous than if he had encountered a gathering of vicious trolls. For her part Melina was overjoyed that she was nearing the edge of the forest and in just a little while she was going to arrive back home. She thought of her family and friends and how happy she would be once she was in the arms of her loved ones.

At last the forest thinned and Melina could make out her farm in the distance. She was very happy to be finally home and only for the fact that she was riding tall Victory and held by its master did she not bolt the horse and run towards home. It seemed to her as if the horse was not moving at all she was in such a hurry but finally they edged their way towards her home.

She was so thrilled at seeing her home that it was not until Melina had come close to familiar surroundings that she realized that something was wrong. There was no movement in the village. As they drew closer they found that the people of her village seemed to be frozen yet their bodies were still warm. Even the birds and the trees had stilled themselves and the village gave off an eerie feeling that nothing would happen there again. It was as if time had stood still and could not restart.

As they tried to explore, the White Knight began to move sluggishly, as if whatever had frozen the villagers was now affecting him. For some odd reason though Melina was unaffected by the time shift and so despite her desire to explore more she instinctively knew that she had to bring the White Knight and his horse back to the outskirts of town before he had become frozen as well. She grabbed the reins of the horse and pulled as hard as she could. The horse responded slowly but it managed to turn itself and ever so slowly return from whence it had come. The further the horse and its master got from the village the faster the pair began to trot until finally the horse and its riders were in a fast flight from the strange village.

Once they had made it back to the forest of doom and the White Knight was out of danger Melinda broke down and uncontrollably wept. The thought of her people in such a terrible predicament disheartened her and left her with emptiness in her heart. It was apparent that the village was under some sort of spell, in which time had literally stood still. There was no choice but to head away from the influence of the magic and come up with some sort of plan. Melina was crushed by her experience. She knew in her bones that it was the old wizard who had trapped her people in the hope that by holding her village hostage she would have no choice but to return to his evils hands. It was a very sombre trip back to the edge of the forest where once again night had fallen and the two desperately needed to rest.

Sleep did not come easily to the young woman as it had the night before. Her village has fallen under a terrible spell and it looked very much like she would have to return to the evil wizard and stay with him until his demands were met. The White Knight, on the other hand, slept soundly. He knew from bitter experience that worry and tears would not help him overcome his problems and so he took advantage of the night and slept like a log.

The next morning both awoke to a sunny day. Melina awoke with her head lying on the sweet grass. The cover of the forest trees had protected them from the slight drizzle of the night and the glistening drops of morning dew that covered her face had the effect of making her visage seem to be like one of the immortals. The knight looked upon her and for the first time in what seemed forever smiled.

Melina awoke and reality hit her like a vicious slap in the face. She was still in deep dread over what was going to happen to herself and her frozen village. Worry immediately overtook her soul and she could hardly breathe she was so afraid of the future.

The Knight, on the other hand, was full of seeming confidence. Whether this was just for the sake of the girl even he did not fully know but he could not give an indication that there was no hope at all out of her dreadful situation. The Knight knew through past experience that any spell cast would have to have a counter spell and if he could only discover what it was then he could restore Melina's village. Yet despite his bag of mystical tricks he himself was no mystic and it would take a magician of great power to overthrow such a powerful spell.

Fortunately for both himself and Melina there was a person that he knew could help. The woman the White Knight had in mind was a mage called Lenore. Lenore was a good and powerful sorceress who lived in a city far north of the Forest of Doom where she ruled as queen. The Knight had helped the mystic on more than one occasion and she was deeply indebted to him, now was the time to call in that obligation. Laughing out loud he was full of renewed energy. Now he had a plan that would bring some hope to his new companion and that was certainly something to smile about.

It did not take long for the pair to begin their journey towards the northern mountains where the magician Lenore lived. Melina sat comfortably on Victory behind the White Knight and the knight himself steered the course towards their destination. The new adventure had lifted his spirits and while his heart was still broken there was little time for reflection and despair now that a damsel was in distress. His focus was now in the present, the past had to reside in the back of his mind for awhile.

For many days they rode northward towards the mountains. Few people were spotted along the trail that they followed and those that had met the duo told them that it was no longer safe to travel to the sorceresses' castle. They said that her mind had turned and she was now a thing of evil and hideousness. The knight could not believe that his old and trusted friend could have become evil so with a determined resolve and a deepening curiosity the pair continued on their quest to the mountain castle of the sky sorceress.

More days flew by but at long last the knight spotted the familiar guard post that indicated that he was near the castle of his long-time friend. Relief washed over him as he and his companion rode up to the two sentries who were protecting the trail. The guards were unknown to him but he was confident that he would receive a good welcome; he had saved this land many times over from beasts and man alike and was regarded as a hero by the people who lived there.

Stopping in front of the two guards he informed them that he intended to visit his friend the sorceress queen and that he wished to pass. Directly he was told that she would not grant him an audience and that he must turn around immediately or be killed for trespassing. This turn took the knight completely by surprise; he expected a warm welcome and certainly not a death threat. Surely there had to be some type of mistake. The knight tried to inform the guards that he was a close friend of the queen and that she would never bar his way to the castle. In response to this the two cross men pulled their swords and advanced on the knight who sat quietly on his horse.

The ensuing skirmish was over in a matter of moments. The two guards laid down on the ground unconscious thanks to the flat side of the White Knight's sword. He had no intention of killing them for merely doing their duty and there was a faint hope in his mind that all of this confusion could be settled once he met face to face with the queen. Leaving the two men by the side of the road the pair continued their journey to the castle. In a matter of minutes they would enter the Eternal City, a place of absolute wonder and beauty.

Arriving at their destination the town that awaited them scarcely was recognised by the White Knight, the smell of filth was in the air and the people were all dirty and in despair. The Eternal City was transformed into a seedy dive of gambling pits, dens of inequity and places where all manner of sin freely plied their trades out in the open public market, while numb children walked casually by hardly noticing the vile scenes in front of them. The sight was a terrible, mind-numbing thing for sensible people to witness. The travelers were sickened by the sights, sounds and smells that greeted them. This was a very different place than the one the confused knight had once known.

The two walked through the market of flesh and made their way to an open area where they could at last breathe fresh air. The Knight had to pause a moment to absorb all the new sights and regain his bearings after this assault on his senses. He was not prepared for the scenes that he witnessed and still could not believe that such things were allowed to go on within the city walls of a city ruled by Queen Lenore.

Melina, herself frightened, but still clinging desperately to the hope that the sky sorceress offered, urged the White Knight to go forward. The knight shook himself from his confusion and led Melina and Victory towards the home of the Queen, the famous castle in the sky. Ignoring offers both foul and immoral the two soldiered on towards their destination in quiet resolve.

The palace was built on top of a small mountain and was said to be impregnable. To try and climb such a rocky, treacherous mountain face was to flirt with death and to attack the castle by the lone, narrow road that led to its walls was akin to suicide. The only way inside the gates that was sensible was to be invited and as the pair walked up the path the scene that they saw around them certainly did not look inviting. Everywhere they looked they saw the poor, the hungry and the miserable all begging for scraps of food or a pittance of cash. Tears filled the empty eyes of parents as their children struggled to keep them alive, leading their parents by the hand rather than the reverse. The picture of it would exhaust the most hard-hearted of people.

The couple moved on past the squalor until at last they reached the gates of the fortress. The White Knight bellowed at the guards on duty to open the iron gates and let them inside. Immediately the heavy doors were thrown open and a troop of armoured knights emerged from the innards of the castle. They surrounded the couple and led them into the dark rooms of the fortress.

The knight was appalled to see the horrible state of disrepair inside the once magnificent immaculate rooms. There was now garbage everywhere and the stench of death filled the filthy air. The last time he had visited the castle the halls were gleaming in the bright sun, there were art pieces of beauty and glorious colours that reflected the nature of the people and their queen but now there was nothing to admire and the sun no longer shone. The magnificence of the palace had been replaced by an unspeakable dark presence.

Onwards they travelled until they were stopped in the great hall but by the look of the massive room that the two had entered there was there was nothing left of the greatness attached to the room. The large area was a shadow of its former glory, the grandeur that the knight had seen on earlier visits had been completely eradicated. When there once had been majesty now all that was left was dross and decay. If the knight's heart had not already been shattered it would have broken at the sight of it.

The knight's head filled with many questions but the one query that mattered the most to him was what had become of his friend Lenore. In his mind it was not possible for her to travel the pathway of evil. She was a good, noble person at heart and the knight's trusted companion on a hundred dangerous adventures. If something had taken over her mind then he would not abandon her to evil, he vowed to himself that he would save her or die trying.

After some considerable time waiting, at last Queen Lenore walked in the hall trailed by a small retinue of guards and advisors. She did not glance at the knight; instead her gaze was fixed on the throne and nothing else as if she was mesmerized by the seat of power. Sitting down she looked straight ahead as if in a dream, only when her top advisor pointed out the pair of travellers did her eyes focus on the white knight.

There was no hint of recognition in her gaze; it was as if her mind had been stripped off all its memory. She looked very pale, her hair was tired and limp, and her body movement were forced and slow as if she were encased in water. She looked as if at any moment she might die from some horrible malady. The knight moved as if to go to her side but was stopped by a phalanx of spears pointed at his chest. Helpless, he awaited the words of his friend.

Her voice was hollow and her commands were not lucid. One moment she thanked the pair for visiting while the next she accused them of being spies. Her mind seemed distracted as if she was longing for something and that all else was a mere interruption. For their troubles they were told that they were to leave the castle and her kingdom by nightfall or suffer her wrath. The pair reluctantly turned and was herded from her sight with the final warning never to return under pain of death.

The knight and his companion returned outside to the narrow path and slowly walked down the passageway until they reached the end. The guards that had trailed them to make sure that they had left for good turned and walked back towards the castle leaving the pair and their horse alone. The two looked at each other and both instantly knew that this was not the end of the matter; too much was at stake to simply give up and go home. As well since neither really had a home to go to they thought they might as well fight it out, neither had much to lose save their own lives.

Both knew that there had to come up with some sort of plan before they could get back inside the castle walls. Neither thought it wise to climb the cliff and to simply return after being ordered into exile would not have been prudent. So the pair left the kingdom and travelled to the outskirts of the city walls where they could plot a means to get to the bottom of the mystery.

The knight knelt down by the side of a newly created campfire and thought over all the odd things he had witnessed. The Lenore he knew would never have tolerated such depravity in her land nor would she allow such poverty like he had seen. These things were simply not in her character.

Then there was the appearance of the palace and the queen to consider, both were in greatly pitiable condition. Queen Lenore herself was a most desirable and beautiful woman full of life, charm and vigour but what he had seen was a frightening parody of the friend and confidant he had once known. Something was rotten in her state but the knight did not yet know what it was or what to do about it.

Melina strolled over to where the confused man knelt and put her hand on the knight's broad shoulder. She knew that he deeply wished to fix things but was frustrated; she wished she could help not only for her sake and her village but for him as well. Their journey brought them closer together than she ever thought possible and while she knew she could never fill the void in his heart she also knew she loved this brave, selfless man who only lived to help others.

Over the weeks together she had seen the knight help strangers over and over again without asking anything in return. He was a hero to all and a villain to none that knew him and here he now sat wordless by the fire wondering just what to do to help someone again. Where most would simply not bother he stood up time and time again to be counted. This was the true measure of bravery, not the forged weapons or the shining armour but the heart that it protected.

The knight looked up at the young woman by his side and bade her to sit next to him. To amuse and to divert his mind from their problems he began to tell her stories of his childhood and of the games he and his friends used to play. She stared at the man as he relived his youth and wished she could have been there to see how he lived in a simpler time, when heroes and villains could be easily recognised and right was just something that you automatically did.

By the end of his stories he told Melina that in the morning he would look for clues as to why Queen Lenore's kingdom was in such a sad state of disrepair. He would go into town in disguise and search for his answers there. The knight asked Melina to wait with Victory but she refused, she told him that she had a great deal at stake and needed to go but the truth of the matter was that she did not wish to leave his side.

The knight thought for a moment and nodded, he could not refuse her the opportunity to help save Queen Lenore's land and in doing so hopefully her own village as well. With that they both went to bed anxious to begin the new day. He had grown to respect this young woman before him and he knew that she would not falter in the fight that lay ahead of them.

The new morning greeted them with a surprise. The knight awoke to see a grey squirrel perched on top of Melina's forehead staring into her closed eyes. With a start she opened her eyes and looked directly at the animal that had made her forehead his own. Laughing, the knight held out his arm and chirped at the animal that ran immediately into the palm of his hand. He told the squirrel in a soft-spoken voice that it was naughty to step on another creature's head and then let the squirrel run away up to a nearby tree.

With that amusing start to the day the pair got ready for the serious business of the afternoon. They decided to act as travelling merchants who had arrived in town to drum up some business. As the knight was recognisable as the city's former hero it was decided that Melina would do the talking and he would play the role of a mute. They left Victory with the camp as he would attract attention and instead walked back to the city on foot.

An hour later they once again entered the city but this time they were prepared for the sights that awaited them or so they thought. When they arrived there were few things to actually witness. There were only a handful of people in the streets and those that were there stumbled aimlessly around as if in a drunken dream. This was the second time in as many days that the pair looked at each other in utter confusion.

They discovered there was no need for elaborate disguise as no one minded the two strangers that were in their midst. The knight looked about for a plausible explanation but to his chagrin found none. He had encountered flesh-eaters which these people resembled but these were alive while flesh-eaters were the undead. He had never seen the like of this before.

The day waned and the two searched for clues to the dilemma but none were found. As dusk came over the land the town suddenly came to life. The people once more took their places in the market square and began to engage in all manner of depravity. Melina and the knight walked about with objective eyes trying to find some meaning to this utter madness.

They were about to give up for the day when Melina spotted something unusual. She noticed a white shape hovering over a figure in an alleyway and decided to investigate. The pair walked towards the light in the alley and discovered a woman caressing herself as a creature made up of mist and pulsating with light enveloped her body. After a few moments it stopped suddenly, the woman let out a sigh and collapsed to the pavement while the mist shining more brightly rose up from her still form and flew away towards the sky castle.

Here was progress. The couple helped the woman to her feet but her eyes were empty. She had vacated her body and was elsewhere, there was no helping her for the moment. The knight had seen enough and wished to take a close look at the castle at night. The two vacated the town of sin and travelled towards the mountain palace once more.

At night the castle from the outside seemed much more alive and impressive. There was music playing and lights that brightened up the sky. Just as the town had woken up during the onset of the night so too did the castle seem to appear more alive and vibrant.

Upon closer examination they saw that the mists were there too. From out of the caverns of the mountain floated clouds that swept in and out of the castle. Grey mists would enter but bright, shiny mists would depart, as if they had been recharged by something within. The knight suddenly realized what the mists were; he had heard of them but had never encountered one before. They were the energy stealers, the soul takers, they were the succubae!

From the pair's keen observation they discovered that a nest of succubae had infiltrated the mountain underneath the castle. There they could rest hidden until the beginning of the night when they could all go out and feast on the living. Now the odd behaviours in the streets made sense.

The succubae feed off the living energy of human beings; the best way to replenish the supply of energy after an attack was to evoke violent or passionate emotions. If these emotions could be constantly triggered the creatures would have an enduring supply of energy on which to feed. It was only too bad that one day the humans they fed on would become burnt out husks in the process, zombified, living without logic or true emotion. That was something the succubae did not care about as there were plenty of hosts to chose from and like all leeches it was only their pleasure that mattered to them.

Now that the cause of the dilemma was discovered it still left the little matter of what to do about it. The emotional and physical ties between a host and its succubae were strong and while the human would eventually burn out and die it still would be a struggle to get the pairing to break away. Humans almost never did what was good for them.

In order to save the queen and her people the White Knight realized that he would have to return to the mountain castle. He could not destroy the infestation of succubae himself, he simply did not know how, but he knew if he could only free Queen Lenore from her stupor then she could easily rid her land of the evil fiends. Quickly he mapped out a plan in his head, quick thinking and a cool reserve during a crisis was one of the many valuable things his mentor taught him long ago and his teachings once again served him well.

The only way the knight knew how to save a person from a succubus was to sever the bond between them. That meant that the knight would have to stop the creature from feeding off the queen for at least one full night, the queen was strong and he felt that one night would be enough for her to recover. In this way the queen would regain her physical strength and emotional stability and with the outside influence removed she would be able to expunge the evil from her mountain and save her land. In theory the plan seemed straight forward but in practice the troubles began. The first problem being that he had no sane way of entering the palace.

The knight pondered the situation until he remembered that he saw a circus troop travelling to the castle on his way to the bottom of the mountain. He could accompany them and enter the castle disguised as one of the troop. He had to act fast if he was to catch the performers before they arrived at the castle. He told Melinda of his plan and insisted that he must go alone for his plan to work; he did not wish to place his charge in danger. He left her with instructions to travel to their previous night's camp and to await for his return.

With all that said he walked to Victory and took out a small bag that was attached to the saddle of his horse. From out of which he pulled out his old fool costume. A dagger of pain struck his heart as he looked upon the costume and relived memories of happy times with his beautiful princess. Still, he wasted no time but began to dress in his costume until very shortly he was the fool again. Melinda could not suppress a giggle at the startling transformation of the White Knight. It was an amazing change and one that she could only be amused at; her hero was now the ultimate clown.

The knight had no time to delay and wished Melinda a fond farewell; he had to rush in order to catch the circus people. Off he went back towards the sky castle and despite the hindrance caused by his awkward costume he united with the motley crew of carnival folk just in time for the castle gates to open.

Soon they entered the squalor that was once the opulent throne room. Few bothered to look twice at the fool, the castle guests were more interested in the sword swallowers, the fire breathers and the beautiful dancing girls that paraded in front of their eyes. It did not take much effort for the knight to slip quietly away and into the queen's private chambers.

Once inside the knight looked for a secret passageway that only he and the queen knew about. They had used it in a past adventure and now he needed it again, this time to hide himself from view. At last, as he heard the sounds of footsteps coming closer to the entrance, he found the hidden door and entered the secret corridor keeping the entrance open just enough so that he could see what was going on inside the room from where he was standing.

Queen Lenore breathlessly entered the room followed by three of her largest guardsmen in her palace. She kissed all three of them slowly and passionately as she felt her way to her large, luxurious bed. She fell backwards onto the soft, downy mattress and raised her arms over her head inviting the men to do with her as they would. The men needed no encouragement to join their queen but at the last instant she stopped them before they could crawl to her side. She ordered the trio to leave and as they reluctantly obeyed she closed her dazed eyes and waited impatiently for her succubus to feed.

It did not take long for the creature to appear within the room. Sensing her desire it drifted over her lithe body and the white, foggy face smiled at what was about to come. The woman was writhing in passion anticipating the touch of her ethereal lover but just as the monster was about to descend on her form the knight burst out from his hiding place and thrust his hand out at the mist.

The thing reared back in agony for in the knight's hand was a mystic medallion that could repel such creatures of the damned. Queen Lenore moaned in displeasure but the knight advanced on the succubus until it had vanished. The queen flew into a rage! Without her strange suitor to sate her desires she lashed out in violent frenzy. She struck out at the knight who easily defended himself by knocking her out with one blow.

With that all was quiet with the room. The knight placed the medallion around the queen's neck and he waited for what he knew would be a long, torturous night. Without the necklace he was defenceless against the creatures he knew would come. There was no way to hide from the vile things that could fly through walls and he could not leave the queen alone with the evil brutes. The connection they had with the queen would lead them to any hiding place he could think of so the knight did not bother to try. He simply sat on the bed next to the unconscious Lenore and waited for the crack of dawn which would be his only salvation.

The onslaught began soon after. At first the creatures tried to regain their hold over the unconscious woman but the magic of the medallion repulsed them every time they tried to get close to their former thrall. In time they gave up that line of attack and focused their full attention on the knight.

They warned and threatened him but he was unafraid of their villainy. Seeing that bully tactics were useless against such a strong-willed man they tried a new avenue of attack. Peering into his mind they found the means to influence the strong man. One of the creatures transformed itself into the likeness of his true love Princess Carolyn. In the bed chamber she suddenly appeared out of nowhere standing before her knight looking her most radiant. There she was with her long, flowing hair, her perfect body and the face that could make angels weep it was so beautiful. Here was the knight's fondest desire enticing him to rapture.

His knees began to buckle and fail as he slowly made his way towards the incredible vision that waited for him, enticing him to come forward in an unholy embrace. The image in front of him was so perfect in every detail that it truly seemed that his heart's desire had been fulfilled. There she was, his only true love waiting with open arms longing for his body to wrap itself around her. He looked into the eyes of the daemon and with an almost inhuman effort turned away from the figure before him.

He turned because he had looked into her eyes and the truth revealed itself for what it was. The eyes are the windows of the soul and he loved Princess Carolyn's soul above and beyond any of her more earthly charms and while this image could mirror her looks it could never capture her spirit. The creature screamed in anger and faded away into nothingness. Shaken, he returned to the bed where Queen Lenore lay.

Throughout the night hordes of spectres tormented and tempted the knight. How he managed to fend off the attacks no one would ever know and he would never tell. On the first rays of the sun that shone into the bedroom window the creatures howled in pain and were gone. The knight, his torture at last over, collapsed next to the still form of his friend and did not move.

Hours later the knight awoke to the sounds of banging on the door. Both he and the queen were awakened dazed and confused from their rest. Queen Lenore was still weakened but the colour had already returned to her face and the knight knew that she had overcome the worst of her ordeal.

By mid-afternoon Queen Lenore seemed much like her old self but the scars from her addiction to the succubus would remain for a long while to come. Weakened as she was she still had the strength to deal with the evil creatures that had shamed her once magnificent city. As a sorceress she had few equals and it was no task to cast out the succubae that had infested her land. With the creatures destroyed the Queen turned her attention to the needs of her hero, the White Knight.

She mused on the problem that he had given her but by evening she felt she had beaten the curse of the time trapped village. She gave the knight a mystic hour glass to use on the village; this and an enchantment he had to speak out loud three times over would reverse the spell.

Understanding the urgency of the knight's quest she did not wish him to linger. Without any further chat she thanked him for once more saving her life and her land and then bid him a fond farewell. The knight for his part thanked her for the cure and rushed to be on his way, he knew that Melina would be anxious for his return. Now as darkness approached he had descended the narrow path once more and began to travel towards his new companion.

It was dark as he approached his campsite. He could make out his horse Victory but he could not see the girl anywhere. He searched all over the camp but could hardly see by the light of the dwindling fire. There was no sign of the girl anywhere. He looked all over and shouted out her name but there was no reply. Then as he was about to give up for the night he glanced down and found a piece of her garment in the ground. Someone had taken her away and he had a good idea who that someone was. With wild fire in his eyes he vowed to the heavens that he would find Melina safe and alive or he would make the evil Alberon pay with his life. He took off his fool's clothes and prepared himself for war.

End of Part Two

The ferry at last arrived in Manhattan with a pronounced thud and Steve quickly put away his writing, got up and waited. Moments later the walking ramp was in place and the eager throng of passengers slowly moved down the aisle towards their daily activities. Steve trudged along with the rest of the crowd keeping his eyes fixed firmly on his route to the subway. Ignoring the various sights and sounds around him, the inspiring churches, the green parks and all the trappings of the famous city he moved towards his goal.

He sleepily dodged the famous yellow cabs that constantly rushed across the busy streets at a harrowing pace that for some strange reason seemed entirely appropriate for the fast-paced life of the sprawling metropolis. He ignored the mimes' silent pleas for cash and the beggars with their unsteady hands permanently out. It was in this environment that Steve found himself every weekday morning. In many ways his present surroundings were just as alien as his time in space. The only real exception was that he missed his translator which would have worked wonders for him in his present situation. Here in New York City he was on his own.

A brief walk led him to the New York subway system where he filed through the turnstiles and down the concrete steps to await his train. While he waited impatiently Steve always played the game of "Spot the Rat" and he usually found three or four crawling by the rails by the time his train arrived. Then the train would briefly stop, open its doors and he would quickly hop in his railcar and head to work.

The subway was always crowded to bursting in the morning. People interested in their newspapers or a novel sat snug against each other doing their best to ignore the very existence of those beside them. Not wishing to stand out, Steve did the same, closing his eyes, pretending to fall asleep and silently ticking off the stops until it was time to magically arise from his faux slumber and step off the train and up into the blinding light of day to work.

At eight o'clock he arrived in his library, mouthed the perfunctory good mornings to all the staff he encountered and steeled himself for the day. Every morning it was the same; there would be the rush of the first few keen people who had stood outside impatiently for ten or more minutes desperately waiting for a free computer to use the Internet.

Afterwards, there would be the occasional telephone call or reference question to answer, but usually the morning would go by reasonably uneventful.

The workday was divided into two separate sections: the time before lunch was devoted to the reference desk and helping the patrons of the library, the time after was devoted to general workday activities such as weeding books. The morning portion of the day could go quickly or slowly depending upon how many patrons arrived, the type of questions asked and their individual personalities. The afternoon was always the same, a slow, long crawl to the end of the workday.

Steve rarely did reference work in the space library. Cal the computer took the automated calls and because of the distance between worlds and the remote location of branch #6941 few actual patrons actually turned up to ask for books. Those that did were the crème de la crème of the patron universe, beings that truly loved reading and research, who wanted to actually read the books rather than view them on some video screen. They showed up with vigour and enthusiasm and Steve always loved to serve them as their appreciation for the library was always high. Not so in his present circumstance.

A creature of habit, Steve would always take his lunch at twelve and would be back at his reference desk precisely at two minutes after one o'clock. The extra two minutes everyday was his way of protesting the lack of pay he received for the hard work and the added stress he endured due to his dealings with difficult patrons. He detested the fact that he was considered an easy target for every stray lunatic and troublemaker who considered the public library his or her own personal property. Didn't they know he had a Masters Degree in Library and Information Science? Didn't they understand that he was an actual human being with feelings that could be hurt? If he encountered a prick, would he not get angry? No, to the patrons of the NYPL system he was just another dumb clerk behind a desk there only to serve their every whim.

"How the mighty have fallen," he thought as he thumbed through the fast fact files that directed the patrons to various popular topics. Once he was in charge of an entire branch of the great Inter Galactic Library System and now he was a flunky for the NYPL. Steve was not a happy camper.

On this particular morning an exceptionally grimy patron noisily shambled in off the street and headed, as if by instinct, straight to the reference desk. Steve had nowhere to run and after cursing the fickle fates one more time that brought this type of plague on civilization towards his desk, he screwed up his customary smile and waited. He had seen this type of person many, many times over since his return to Earth and he silently prepared himself to take out his metaphorical hand puppets to explain some elementary question.

A whiff of deeply unpleasant whiff heralded the man's arrival. The extremely odorous old man slowly made his way to the large wooden desk, gestured at the wary librarian to come closer, smiled and then without warning let loose, with terrific thrust, a wave of bile from his inner core. The disgusting liquid splashed all over Steve's clothes ruining them for at least the rest of the day.

An explosion of curses emanated at rapid speed from Steve's mouth at the same time as he quickly moved back to avoid the remainder of the gruesome fluid. The old man for his part had now begun to slump down on the desk soiling the paper sheets that explained the rudimentary aspects of the Dewy Decimal System to the public. Steve was stunned at the situation that unfolded in front of him. He never had anyone throw up on him, not even the Knarl Beast from Spittoon who greeting his nearest and dearest with a hurl of the good stuff had managed to spray him. Now here was a rancid man off the streets who in a moment did what alien creatures could not and Steve was furious.

Surprisingly, even with all the noise coming from the librarian this small incident had gone almost unnoticed by the populace of the library. The patrons continued to go about their business as if nothing untoward had happened to the distressed public servant, preferring instead to look after their own affairs. The library staff, for the most part, was also blissfully unaware that anything had happened, engrossed as they were in projects of their own. It was only after two other incidents occurred that anyone actually took notice of Steve's current plight.

The first such item of note was the gut-retching stench that immediately wafted its way from its point of origin, expanding to an increasing portion of the library. The second was the arrival of a small, old lady in fashionable black shoes and a large, grey overcoat. As if immune to the sights, smells and sounds about her, she moved to the right side of the crumpling old man and smiled at the now incensed reference librarian. She waved to the man, continued to smile and then opened her mouth to speak. A moment of silence passed between them after the woman uttered her question on the best way to cure her cat's stomach problem before the torrent of abuse hit.

This little old lady, to Steve, was the personification of all the insensitivities of his patrons. Here he was covered in the foul-smelling puke of his most recent customer and now all this addled old woman that stood before him was concerned about was the troubled intestinal tract of her mangy feline! It was all much too much for the man to handle and he let fly with all the frustrations of the past few months right at the poor old woman in front of him. His arms waved, spittle spat from his lips and some of the sticky substances that had mere moments before resided in the guts of an old drunk now rocketed from his jacket and onto the glasses of the old patron before him.

"What was that young man?" the woman asked. "I forgot to turn on my hearing aid."

The librarian stood dumbfounded. This time most of the people around the library had now stopped to watch the spectacle in front of them. The staff of the library looked on in shock at the events that had taken place. No librarian, no matter what the cause, was allowed to abuse a patron the way that Steve had just done. The librarians shook their heads in disbelief at the out-of-control reference personnel.

Steve, noticing the glares of his colleagues and realizing the line he had just crossed, apologized to the old lady who still seemed totally oblivious to everything that had taken place. Then, with a calm outward appearance, he deliberately moved away from the desk and stiffly marched straight towards the staff washroom.

Closing the door behind him Steve took his jacket off and held it out away from him. It was ruined. There was no way his mind would ever let him wear that particular piece of clothing again. Even if the jacket was washed a billion times, the memory of the old man and his stench would forever remain entrenched in his psyche. It had to be unceremoniously buried.

He hurriedly grabbed the contents out of the pockets and placed them on a small metal shelf by the washroom mirror. Then, after looking over the stained jacket one last time, he sighed deeply and dropped it into the large plastic garbage container that occupied a corner of the room. The suit jacket had survived inter stellar wars in outer space but it could not survive the smelly drunks of New York. There was a sobering thought for you.

The rest of his clothing was thankfully relatively unaffected by the downpour of vomit. It was if the old man had picked a target and struck dead centre. A brilliant shot. A severely drunken Robin Hood himself could not have bettered the accuracy. Steve took a moment to mourn the loss of his jacket then assessed himself in the mirror. He was still upset by the incident, but other than being in emotional distress he was for all intents and purposes ready to go back to duty. After one brief moment to prepare, he whipped one small glob of bile off his tie, turned from the mirror and walked out the door and back into the circulation area.

The reference desk was being prepared by two of his colleagues. With buckets of soapy water and small cloths they were busily cleaning the desk that only moments ago Steve had abandoned. "Two university degrees," he thought, "and they got us cleaning up puke." All was nearly back to normal by the time he neared his station. The unconscious body of the old drunk had been removed and the old lady with goo on her glasses was being attended to by another librarian. The tilted world had returned to its proper axis.

His face tinged slightly with embarrassment as he thanked the two female librarians who were well on their way to finishing up their task. Steve was almost ready to go back to his desk when from behind he felt a tap on his shoulder. It was Loretta his boss and what a terrible, terrible boss she was. At approximately five foot four and over two hundred forty pounds, she was well on her way to being one meal from a Guinness world record. Loretta was the new head of this particular branch of the NYPL and she was the stereotypical nasty librarian.

No one fully knew just how she got her high position, but she flaunted her authority as much as she could. Frequently she would embarrass her staff and would spread rumours whenever she could in order to appease her own sense of chaos. She was a woman that you hated to be around, but one you were always afraid to let out of your sight.

"I want to see you in my office right now," the meaty woman hissed. Steve inwardly recoiled. Entering the Master of Evil's office, a name her associates stamped her with, was something no one enjoyed doing. For starters, it meant that you actually had to speak with her or, as was usually the case, listen to her. Second, nothing good ever came from within the dark, stifling room in which this creature roosted.

It was rumoured she never smiled but one old librarian nearing retirement once was said to have heard the evil one's laugh, remarking, "It was like the cackling of the devil's boss." No one had a kind word to say about this maniacal thing and the worst punishment that could be inflicted upon the staff members of the library was to have a one to one conversation with her in that dingy office, that very same office that Steve had just reluctantly entered.

The office itself looked like it was taken from the beginning of Charles Dickens' *A Christmas Carol*, in which the nasty Scrooge toiled without warmth. It was a soulless, depressing place and its appearance fit to a tee the inner spirit of the occupant. Books were scattered higgledy-wiggly about although it was rumoured that the head librarian never read. Coffee-stained papers littered the thick, cluttered desk that was almost large enough to conceal her girth. Almost.

No one ever sat in the black, comfortable chair that was placed directly in front of the Master of Evil's desk - it was forbidden. On one occasion a high-ranking member of the library board had sat in that seat much to her displeasure, but no ordinary staff could dare sit in the dreaded office. Sitting meant that you thought of yourself as equal to the fiend that was across from you and that would have been a gross insult to her inflated ego.

Steve stood silently as he tried to blot out as best he could the stinging remarks that emanated from the evil one's large mouth and dripped down her drooling chins. To take his mind of this current tongue-lashing he envisioned that he was being told off by *Star War's* Jabba the Hut in drag. For a full ten minutes he nodded appropriately in response to the mantras of his superior. The patrons all come first and you are last. Service is our number one priority. Etc., etc., etc.

Several more of these library truths were spelled out before Steve at last was free to go. Stifling the urge to click his heels and raise his right arm out as he left the den of evil. He opened the office door and entered the hustle and bustle of the library once more. On his way back to his duties he looked up at the large clock that precariously perched above his desk and saw that it was almost twelve o'clock. He cheerfully rushed to his desk, grabbed the tin of orange juice that he kept in his bottom left drawer and immediately hurried away.

Twelve o'clock meant almost as much to Steve as five o'clock when he quit for the day. Twelve o'clock was probably the happiest part of his workday. Twelve o'clock was his lunch break, more importantly it was the same break that he shared with another one of his librarian colleagues. Twelve o'clock was the time when he met up with Melinda Curtis.

Melinda Curtis was by all accounts an attractive woman. She had been an athlete in a previous existence and through the use of a strict diet and regular exercise kept her body in extremely good condition. She was the children's librarian at the branch and on many occasions parents would stay with their children during story time to hear her tales although sometimes it was not the lines of the books being read that was the object of their rapt attention.

Armed with a happy spirit and intelligent mind, Melinda was the much-needed extra spark in Steve's otherwise humdrum day. Steve fed off the positive nature that exuded from the popular storyteller and whenever she had taken a holiday or called in sick he was just that much more depressed with his lot in life. She was his tiny pep pill and unbeknownst to her he was becoming addicted.

This particular high noon Steve arrived in the staff lounge and his eyes immediately scanned the terrain for Melinda. He quickly found her sitting in her usual seat underneath the Gothic painting of Melville Dewey that some patron had long ago donated to the library. She was sitting down on a comfy chair sipping on her small cup of hot coffee casually relaxing after a busy morning of entertaining children, which in Steve's mind was one of the toughest jobs in all of librarianship. How she handled the job so effortlessly he would never know. She looked up and smiled as she noticed Steve's arrival in the staff lounge. It was a smile that checked out a thousand books but had remained as sincere as ever.

"Well, I heard from Janet what happened to you today. You should have been given the rest of the day off to recover or at least time to get a change of clothes," she said. Steve thought that her eyes appeared to sparkle when she talked to him, or perhaps it was just his imagination. Either way he enjoyed the magnificent delusion.

"Yeah, but we both know that the Master of Evil would never allow a moment in her cold excuse of a heart for human compassion. Besides it was mostly on my jacket and I had no choice but to throw that out." Steve felt a tinge of grief when he said this as if talking about a lost friend instead of a well-worn jacket.

"I read your story today and all the children loved it," Melinda said hoping to cheer up the saddened librarian. She produced the neat pages of the story that Steve had given to her. Noticing that they had no effect on the depressed librarian her eyes lit up as she decided to read the story in her famous story-time voice.

Farmer Brown's Problem

Farmer Brown had a problem and because it was such an unusual one he did not know what to do about it. He talked to the other farmers about it, he talked to the baker about it and he even talked to the policeman about it but no one he talked to could tell him how to solve his trouble. It was a problem to beat all problems. Farmer Brown's problem was simple; his cows did not know how to moo.

Oh sure they could talk, in fact they talked all the time. Every day and into the night Farmer Brown's cows chatted with each other. They talked about the hens that were too loud in the morning, they spoke about the sun that was too hot in the afternoon and they talked about the sheep that had the unusual waddle, but they didn't moo.

Instead Farmer Brown's cows quacked like ducks. Quack, quack, quack all day and all night. They quacked to each other, they quacked to the other animals and they even quacked to the other farmers that happened to come by. Yet they couldn't or wouldn't moo.

Farmer Brown was at a loss over what to do. He asked his cows to moo. He begged his cows to moo. He even threatened his cows to moo, but they would not moo. All they would do was quack, quack, quack.

One day while Farmer Brown was buying supplies for his farm at the local store he noticed a sign on the back wall. There was a big competition to be held at the local fair ground and first prize went to the cows that mooed the best. Everyone in the store laughed as Farmer Brown read the sign. They knew his cows had no chance to win.

Farmer Brown left the store in a very depressed mood. He knew that his cows had no chance to win the contest either. He knew the old saying, you can take a cow to a contest but you can't make it moo.

Farmer Brown walked slowly down the road, his eyes welling up with tears, so full of tears in fact, that he failed to notice where he was going. Bang! Farmer Brown smacked into another man walking in the opposite direction. He apologised for his lack of care to the man and explained why he was not paying attention where he was going. The man was very surprised at Farmer Brown's problem but for the first time Farmer Brown was not laughed at, instead the man was very sympathetic.

"Why, I have almost the exact opposite problem with my ducks. They moo instead of quaking. Perhaps we should get them together and see what happens." Farmer Brown was thrilled at the thought of even a hint of a solution for his problem. They shook hands and promised to meet again.

The next day the man arrived at the farm with a large truck filled with mooing ducks. The truck stopped and the man and Farmer Brown immediately decided to introduce these two strange-talking creatures together. The ducks were lifted into the fields where the cows were grazing and were left to mingle.

Hours passed and to the delight of both men the ducks and cows had begun to talk to each other. Sometimes the cows mooed, sometimes they quacked and at other times the ducks mooed or quacked but at least this was progress! The two men decided to leave the animals together for the night in the hope that in the morning all their troubles would be over.

The next morning it was if a miracle took place! The cows were all mooing and all the ducks were quacking. It was then that Farmer Brown decided that it was time to end all the laughter that his problem had begun by entering Carol, his loudest cow, in the best moo competition. Thanking his new friend he quickly walked towards the town with his loudest cow in tow.

An hour later he entered the local store where only two days earlier he was laughed at. He proudly walked up to the sign and jotted his signature down. All the farmers in the store began to laugh and asked where Farmer Brown's mooing cow was. Farmer Brown proudly escorted the other farmers out the door to where his cow Carol was grazing on some small grass. All the farmers gathered around the large cow anxiously awaiting the moo. Farmer Brown knew that this was his happiest moment. No longer would he be laughed at now that his cows could moo.

As the farmers continued to crowd his cow he asked his cow to moo. No moo. No sound came from the cow at all. Farmer Brown asked his cow again to moo and still no sound came from the strangely silent Carol. Finally Farmer Brown shouted with all his might demanding the quiet cow to moo. In response the cow raised its large head, opened its mouth wide and let out a long, loud, QUACK!

All the farmers laughed so hard they fell to the ground. They pointed at the cow and pointed at Farmer Brown and laughed and laughed and laughed. Farmer Brown was so embarrassed he immediately ran away, towing the now loud, quacking cow all the way home.

After a long and sad walk farmer Brown returned to his farm with his still quacking cow. He opened up the gates to his fields and led Carol back to her home. Farmer Brown's new friend was still there picking up his ducks and bringing them back to his truck. Farmer Brown just could not figure out what had gone wrong.

As the last duck was picked up by the duck farmer it let out a large farewell quack to the cows. Instantly all the cows mooed in response. Farmer Brown raised his eyebrow, now knew why his cow quacked, she needed a duck to talk to. Only then would Carol the cow moo.

The next day Farmer Brown arrived back at the local store towing once again his loudest cow, only this time, however, he also had with him a large duck named Steve. All the farmers began to laugh when they saw Farmer Brown. They could not believe he would bring his cow to the competition.

Farmer Brown and Carol the cow with Steve the duck standing firmly on her back took their place in a line with the rest of the contestants. The judge walked up to each one and listened to the cows moo. Some were too loud, some were too quiet but when the judge came to Farmer Brown's cow he knew he had found a winner.

"First prize goes to the cow with the duck standing on its back!" Farmer Brown was overjoyed! No longer would he be laughed at, no longer would he have his famous problem. No longer that is, as long as his cows had some ducks to talk to.

The End

Steve almost wept as she finished reading his tale. Melinda's voice was absolutely perfect for the reading of his work and it moved him more than he thought possible. Over the next ten minutes small talk was exchanged between the two librarians. As always the chat was pleasant enough, the rumours of the day, which staff member was sleeping with whom and all the other day-to-day scandals that every office is accustomed to were bandied about by the two professionals. Then, all too quickly for Steve, it was time to head back to their respective stations. It was now one o'clock and as usual a silent sigh went through Steve's body as he watched the slender, curvaceous form of Melinda Curtis walk away. It was if a dream had simply gotten up from the chair and softly floated away.

After the noon break it became the home stretch for most of the staff in the library. Anticipation ran high as five o'clock approached. The hours of one to three were spent answering the phone but the last one hundred and twenty minutes were for Steve the slowest as he repeatedly looked at the unsteady wall clock above his head and waited for the workday to be done. It was during this time that he usually encountered Dave, the library's security guard.

Dave was a tall, husky individual who thoroughly enjoyed his work. He wandered around the library keenly watching for any indication of criminal activity. Once he caught someone injecting something into his arm, but was disappointed to find out it was only a diabetes sufferer giving himself a shot of insulin. Dave desperately longed for the day when he could make an important arrest so he could proudly tell his friends what a hero he was. This was the vain hope that kept him interested in his boring, repetitive job.

Steve liked Dave's positive attitude, which was a nice change from most of the staff working under the Master of Evil's terrible reign. Dave was simple, honest and, most importantly, he was a raving hypochondriac. Dave was constantly worried about all aspects of his health. If he found a cut on his body he swore it was going to be infected, if he dropped a bit of weight he was convinced he had some terrible disease. Dave was terrified of and at the same time obsessed with all the latest medical news. He subscribed to medical journals such as *Lancet* and the *New England Journal of Medicine* even though he could hardly understand them. All he took from them was a certainty that death in all its horror was diligently stalking him and that it was coming very, very soon.

Steve learned in a short period of time that Dave could never be convinced that he was in perfect health. In fact, the more someone tried to tell him that he was fine the more troubled he would become. Steve eventually gave up trying to assure the man of his soundness of body and instead always mentioned something that would give Dave a good fright. He would tell the muscular guard that he looked pale or that he seemed to be flushed and this would make the nervous guard very happy. His feelings were justified. He was dying and he was very pleased that someone shared his point of view. Dave was always happy to have Steve confirm his theories on his fast approaching demise and Steve took a guilty pleasure in conjuring some affliction for the guard. It was the perfect symbiotic relationship.

The subject of choice for today was the West Nile virus that had been spreading panic throughout the state. Dave talked in a whisper about the troubling effects of this contagion. Steve replied that he would rather have contracted the West Nile virus than the flesh-eating disease any day of the week. As soon as this comment left his lips, the librarian wondered if he had said too much. The bulky guard noticeably diminished and began to turn a deathly white as if he was looking at the spectre of himself being eaten alive by the loathsome pestilence. His eyes widened, his hands shakily went up to his throat and his body began to shrivel.

After a minute of this grotesque pantomime the anxious librarian smacked the quivering man across his broad shoulders in order to physically force him out of his dark fantasy. Dave cautiously returned to the land of reality, the panic that had so suddenly and so firmly gripped him slowly subsided. Bidding adieu to Steve the guard straightened his large frame and silently returned to patrolling the book stacks, ever on the alert for a wicked villain hiding in the shadowy aisles.

The day continued on without further incident until finally, the long minute hand ticked its way to twelve and in a flash Steve was on his way home. With a fast wave, he bid his colleagues a hearty goodbye, walked out the front door of the library and stepped onto the hard pavement. At that moment the real world was full of people leaving their places of toil and heading towards the comforts of home or the excitement of a downtown bar. Friday evenings meant a great deal to the citizens of New York City and this indeed, according to the Julian calendar, was a Friday. It was at this time that weekday plans made for drinks, shows, dinners, dates and all manner of diversions both profound and profane at last come to fruition. Fortunately, the real world had little to do with Steve.

It was a very rare occasion that the reference librarian dallied in the city. Usually feeling drained after the workday and still burdened with the journey back to his apartment, Steve preferred to step on the earliest ferry and head home. Today was no exception and, like an actor familiar with his part, he walked onto his stage and waited to drift away.

It was typical of all Staten Island ferry crossings to have a group of tourists irritating the regular travellers by actually enjoying the trip. Dancing about the deck, laughing loudly and repeatedly pointing to the Statue of Liberty as if it were about to disappear, the tourists were an annoyingly mandatory part of the Staten Island ferry service experience. Before the general malaise set in, Steve was actually pleasant to the tourists. On one occasion he even snapped a few photos of a newlywed couple from Jamaica. However, he tragically dropped the camera and was forced to pay for the loss. This unhappy experience led him to the conclusion that no good deed ever went unpunished and now he avoided the tourists like a cackling band of lepers.

The sound of the ferry's horn made Steve put away his writing and return it to his bag. This particular crossing was uneventful and soon the crowded ferry homed in on Staten Island and the boat was docked and ready to disembark its passengers. Steve waited his turn in the haphazard line that formed at the exit and after a minute or two he left the ferry and walked downstairs towards the train that would take him to his fortress of solitude.

Steve liked trains and actually enjoyed the fact that he could ride them in New York. In his home province of Newfoundland and Labrador the opportunity for a relaxing train ride was non-existent. The trains were wiped out more than three decades ago and with it a big part of the heritage of Newfoundland had been destroyed. As a boy he remembered the whistle of the train and the certainty that one day he would ride the rails to every part of that track. Every time he rode the train to work and back he was reminded of riding the trains back in his true home and felt a small tinge of regret that he never had the chance to make his dream come true.

Not long after he sat down on his seat, the train started with a fit and reluctantly began to chug along the track. Every few minutes the train would stop to let some riders off and then resume its journey. By now Steve had memorized the number of stops it took before he arrived at his destination and could read a book or newspaper before standing up to take leave of the train. This was not to say that he was relaxed; he knew better than to actually be relaxed anywhere in New York. He had seen far too many movies to be comfortable anywhere in the public eye of the metropolis. You never knew just what dangers lurked and letting your guard down was an invitation to who knows what. That kernel of knowledge made him squirm in his seat from time to time.

Head down, a found newspaper held firmly on his lap, Steve ticked off the stops in his mind until finally he stood up, placed the newspaper down on the seat where he had discovered it and exited the train. His workday was now almost complete. Only one task remained before he could finally go to his apartment and enjoy the beginning of his weekend.

Steve had the habit every Friday of going to the supermarket and picking up a 24 pack of beer. Beer in the United States was cheap in comparison to Canada and it was one of the few luxuries that he could afford on a reference librarian's salary. A bonus was that in living relatively close to a supermarket meant he could carry it home without the need for a taxi. Sure the beer on Earth was not nearly as good as the ones he had tasted in his little space apartment in the space library residence but he was on Earth now and it was Friday and he desperately needed beer. He flinched as the thought of the cost of a taxi to the planet Quan to pick up a case of their best jumped into his mind.

The supermarket he attended was always crowded on Friday evening for some reason, which is why Steve usually bought his groceries on Sunday afternoon. Friday was beer only day and so he planned his Friday trip to the supermarket with only this goal in mind. Thus he had formulated early on in his residency on Staten Island an ingenious plan that would take him in and out of the grocery store as fast as possible.

Upon entering the supermarket, he walked straight for aisle twelve where he paused briefly in order to choose which beer he felt like having, picked the case off the shelf and then headed towards the fast checkout. Stopping only for a moment whenever Allison the nubile stock-clerk bent over to retrieve a fallen item, he would arrive winded but pleased in the eight to ten items line. Once at the checkout, there was without exception always someone who had more than the allotted number of items in his or her cart. Steve hated that person, that person in his mind violated the social contract by disrupting the natural order of life on the planet. He hoped that someone up in the heavens was taking careful note.

At last it was his turn to pay. He had the precise amount of change ready to give to the cashier. He refused a bag, as Steve felt that this small act was his contribution towards saving the globe, and then with beer safely clenched under his right arm, he quickly walked out the door towards his domicile. His weekend was about to begin.

Fifteen minutes later, he arrived at his apartment building's front door. Placing his beer down but ensuring it never left his sight, he reached for his key, inserted it into the lock and opened the door. After entering and ensuring that the front door had firmly closed behind him, he took a look in his mailbox, received a slight shock in finding that there was something inside, grabbed up the contents, then walked up one flight of stairs, down a hall and into his small apartment. The last task that needed to be done before he could officially enjoy his break was now fulfilled. He was safe and sound and was ready to at last relax.

The crack of the first beer can opening was to Steve akin to the firing of a starter's pistol to an Olympic runner, it was the start of an eagerly anticipated event. To the tired librarian, the opening of his first beer was the true beginning of his time off, where he could finally shed his work skin and return to his real self, whoever that might be.

With the weekend now started, he got down to what he did almost every Friday night. The rest of the beer was quickly but neatly placed inside his fridge, a call to the pizza deliveryman was placed and the remote control was now firmly in his grip. All was now right with the planet. Free from the aggravations of the work world he could unwind and let his mind wander towards the evening's television schedule.

No matter where you are in the world it seems, *Star Trek* in one of its many incarnations is always on television on one station or another. It was fortunate for Steve that he liked the show and now that he had experience to fall back upon he could laugh at the inaccuracies that littered every episode. If he didn't like his Friday night viewing he would have to go out and rent a DVD and this would also mean that he would actually have to buy a DVD machine. This would enviably lead to other similar purchases until soon the entire apartment would be filled with things that he really did not need nor want in the first place. Steve liked his world uncluttered so his apartment was furnished with only the most basic of items.

A telephone was certainly needed for the obvious reasons, such as pizza delivery, phoning family and friends back home in Newfoundland and, of course, to call in sick whenever the image of looking at his demanding clientele proved too much of a chore. A television was necessary for news and entertainment, a radio/clock alarm woke him so that he could begin his day and a futon made up for the lack of a bed. A stove, a refrigerator, a small coffee table and a sturdy couch had been left by the previous tenant, which was a welcome surprise. All in all Steve's apartment was not very well stocked.

This minimalist approach to his life stood him in good stead when the space library branch he was in charge of was destroyed. He barely had any belongings to begin with and those that he did have which were destroyed he did not miss. It was funny in a way but the only bit he did miss was the people, his staff. Chubba in particular was very distraught that the library had been destroyed. The tall Gormorian had to be sedated in order to leave the wreckage. Oddly enough Cal the computer was relatively unscathed and it was just as the same as always.

Zoe was hurt in the crash but managed to keep it together in order to save Steve's life. Steve was fortunate that she knew something of the human body and could apply her knowledge adequately enough to keep him breathing until the emergency crews arrived from a nearby star system to save his life. Steve felt lost without his right hand cataloguer; although at times they were at odds Steve never told her that he respected her. Despite giving her tickets to the Tiluran planet eclipse, he knew that Zoe and he weren't close enough to actually say anything much other than work related issues and now looking back he wished he had. It was the same old story. He was from Earth and she was from Cypheria, the planet of cataloguers.

After the crash of the space mobile and the destruction of the branch library the Inter Galactic Library Board felt that all those involved needed to go to their home planets and await word of the investigation. In Steve's case, however, he was from a world that was out of the jurisdiction of the Board and thus returning home meant never coming back to space. He did get a nice t-shirt that read: "Best Branch Library Closure, Runners Up," however, before being shipped back to Earth.

Through the haze that came with relaxation and alcohol came day-dreams of a life not chosen. Steve once wondered what it would be like to have a real home of his own, with a wife, children and a well-stocked pantry. What would he have been if he had taken on a different path in life, married a girl and settled down rather than subsist on pizza, beer and a poor-paying job? Would he have been happy or would he have simply been incarcerated in just another level of hell? Life in New York was about the same as in space save for the poorer quality beer but better pizza, but in either life he was alone just taking it day by day.

A knock at the door woke Steve up from his daydream and jarred him into the real world once more. Walking to his door, he looked through the peephole at the image of a pizza deliveryman tapping his feet on the hall's dirty carpet. Unlocking the multiple locks, Steve opened his door and quickly thrust some money into the waiting hand of the pizza man. Steve had recognised the large, black man as his regular delivery person, but he had never spoken one word to him in the numerous occasions he had opened his door. He knew from previous experience the exact amount he had to pay and added a one-dollar tip for the muscular man who held his evening repast. After the cash was exchanged he took possession of his pie, nodded to the deliveryman and retreated back into the comfort of his abode.

Placing the hot box on the table in front of his television set he walked over to the fridge, opened it, grabbed another beer from its innards and walked back to his supper. With one twist of his hand the box cover was lifted and his world was filled with the smell of a fresh pepperoni, cheese, hamburger, green pepper and mushroom pizza pie. The one thing that could be positively said about Steve was that he enjoyed a good pizza and while he knew that his waistline would exponentially expand with every morsel of the tasty goodness of fresh, thinly crusted, mouth-watering New York style pizza, he really could not help himself. Too soon all that was left of his medium-sized pie was a still warm, gooey, empty box.

Staring at the empty pizza box and the half dozen of empty beer cans that littered his coffee table he knew that he was not a contented man yet he also felt that there was little he could do. He was alone and it was about this time every night that the realization came back to slap him in the face. He had trapped himself in a world of his own making and it would take a great gust of courage to whisk himself away from it. He wished that something, anything, would happen to change the mundane pace of his drab existence. Life without the space library was driving the Earthbound librarian slowly mad.

Rather than think of things he could not change the frustrated man decided to look once again at his novel and checked over chapter three for errors. It lacked something he knew, but he did not know what. There was a block that kept him from seeing his story entirely clearly but he kept banging away at it. His fingers unknowingly caressed the pages as he read the words.

The Nightmare Place

Sleep did not come easy for the vexed man but after his recent ordeal with the succubae in Queen Lenore's bedroom tower he knew his body desperately needed the rest. Reluctantly he lay down on the ground, his thick blanket tucked tightly under him. He closed his eyes and gave himself over to the dark. In his dreams bizarre creatures, battles with dragons and the face of a famous king all warped in and out of his unconscious mind. Then with crystal clarity he saw an image of Melina and in a flash he was up in the real world once more.

It was morning and the sun had risen over the trees. Waking up the knight packed his things and prepared himself for a trip to the unknown. Experience told him not to rush headlong into danger and instead he took his time and searched for clues to the girl's disappearance. With the sunlight now over his head he noticed an interesting clue and that clue was that there was indeed nothing to discover at all.

This in itself was odd. The reason was that if someone had been forcibly taken from a wooden area there would at least be some sign of a struggle. The campfire would have been overturned or some foliage would have been disturbed but there was nothing to indicate that there had been a struggle of any sort. Indeed there was no sign of anyone even coming or leaving the campsite.

This was telling in itself. If there was no sign of struggle then there were only two logical conclusions. The first was that there had been no struggle at all. This was unlikely considering Melina's abhorrence for the evil wizard Alberon. The second was that she was taken by surprise and that an unusual means of transportation was used. If this was the case then it was possible that magic has been used to transport the girl and her abductor. The knight was not prepared to come to this conclusion, however, without the inspection of the site from a more knowledgeable person than himself. That meant that he had no choice but to return to the mystical castle of the sky sorceress and ask Queen Lenore for help.

Without further delay the White Knight mounted Victory and rode towards the Queen's palace on the mountain. Eager for the exercise Victory made good time and soon the knight was once again in the presence of his friend Queen Lenore. The queen looked very weary. Her once bright, brown hair had noticeably fizzled with the strenuous efforts that had been placed on her over the past few months. Yet she readily agreed to help her friend look for his companion and without much delay she, the knight and a retinue of guards made their way back down the mountain and to the campsite where the missing girl once rested.

Upon arriving on the spot Queen Lenore ordered everyone to remain still as she began to look for mystical signs. She out-stretched her arms and spoke in a strange tongue, chanting the names of forgotten gods and beings too old to be remembered by man. Soon a vision appeared out of the air that seemed so lifelike that the guards unsheathed their swords. But there was no corporal existence to the shades; they were simply a reflection of things that had happened in the past.

The shapes took on human forms and began to re-enact what occurred the night before. What the past projected was disturbing, the phantoms told a horrifying tale of woe. They showed how a man in dark robes stole up from behind Melina as she tended her campfire and struck her to the ground. The man raised one arm to the sky and shouted while clasping tight Melinda with the other. With a flash both were gone and the vision abruptly ended.

Queen Lenore swooned as the spectacle ended and would have fallen save for the White Knight's quick action. He held her close as she gathered her strength enough to stand on her own. It would take hours before she could recover sufficiently to try and help the man recover his friend. The White Knight waited until the queen was ready to get to her feet. He was concerned that she had not yet recuperated from her experience but he did not know how to help. He talked with his ally until she felt she was ready to try the same spell the robed man had done to transport himself and his captive away.

It was now dusk and the beautiful queen ushered the anxious knight and his horse into the exact place where Melina had been taken away. The knight sat on the back of Victory and closed his eyes as Queen Lenore directed. She began a chant and in a moment he felt a shiver go up and down his spine. Then there was silence. He opened his eyes to discover that he was no longer where he once stood. He had been taken from one place and brought to another by way of enchantment. The man hoped that this strange journey had brought him to the place where he could find and rescue his lost friend.

The knight did not recognize anything familiar about the place he was now in; there was nothing to indicate that it was any place in particular. There was only a well-traveled road which led it seemed to infinity. There were no marking posts, no buildings, just an open space that contained grass on either end of the long road. There was no choice it seemed but to follow the road and discover where it led.

The White Knight urged Victory onward toward the unknown. This was his only opportunity to find his missing companion and he was eager to be on the way. The knight traveled forward down the road searching his surroundings for some sign or clue to the lost Melina. He could find no sign of the girl and strangely not even anyone or anything else on his journey. All that was before him was a long, winding trail with no end in sight.

At long last the road made its way to a large water well. On four sides of the round, brick well were signs that pointed in different directions of an intersection in the road. Another sign, this one placed on the well itself, simply had one word attached to it, that sign read: "DRINK".

Feeling oddly thirsty the knight pulled up a gourd that was attached to a rope and drank deeply from the water of the well. Rather than slake his thirst the water instead increased it and with every drop the knight poured down his dry, cracked throat his thirst increased. Finally he choked, grasped his throat and fell down, down into the well.

There was enough water at the bottom of the well to save the knight from serious harm. As he slowly got up from the bottom of the well he found his curious thirst had gone. He looked around, the water up to his chest and instead of total darkness he spied a light coming from a cavern. He walked towards it.

The water level dropped as he continued on towards the light until at last there was no water at all. The cavern he found was no underground place but an entrance to the surface. The brightness of a giant fire blinded him for a moment but as his eyes adjusted he saw three young, beautiful women laughing amongst themselves. They were scantily dressed in long, silken robes of different colours, one in dark red, one in deep purple and one in a shallow blue. The trio was frantically dancing by the light of the flickering fire, twirling around and around the caress of the hot flames. Their shadows played with each other from behind, desperately trying to catch each other all in the hypnotic rhythm of the dance.

The women stopped their gyrating and came together as they spied the knight. "Welcome," the women said one after another. The knight slowly walked towards the three temptresses and halted directly in front of them. They circled him like wolves all the while smiling and staring directly into the man's eyes. The knight found he could not move, his limbs were cold and he could not focus his mind as the three robed women continually traveled around him. He tried to summon his entire strength to move but he found he had none. All he could do was stare blankly into the eyes of his mesmerizing captives.

"Come," the three sang in turn and led him gently to a large stone altar where they made him lie down, his limbs no longer under his command. His armor was stripped and he lay frozen, now unable to move save for his eyes. He saw the women as they transformed from beautiful maidens to creatures with sharp, long fangs. Smiling as they licked their thick, ruby lips they advanced on the helpless knight on the stone altar.

With all three kneeling by the man they each smiled, lowered their heads, opened their mouths and bit deep into the body of their helpless victim. The knight could immediately feel his life slip away as the three drank deeply of his blood, sucking the life force out of him. He felt no pain, no fear as the blood flowed from his body, just a vague numbness and the sadness that he would not be able to rescue his friend. His life was a thing that he would not miss too badly but he grieved over the fate of his poor friend.

Just when he felt that he could lose no more blood and live the three disengaged from their feast and began to wretch. Screaming, cursing they all gasped their throats. They shivered with a strange intensity, then with a final cry, they erupted into flames and fell away leaving only ash and dust.

With the three dead the knight was now free of their power and could move once more. Staggered from the blood loss he still managed to get to his feet. The glow of the fire helped him locate his armor. He slowly dressed and with an amazing feat of strength smashed the stone altar with his mighty sword. No one would ever be sacrificed again on that pillar of evil.

With no clue as to where he was and no light save for the fire, his mind and exhausted body told him to rest until it was once more day. As he laid down his head on the ground he inwardly thanked the great foresight of his mentor of old who made him get his blood blessed by an oracle so long ago.

The next morning the knight awoke to find his horse Victory licking his face. Dazed, the knight slowly got up and looked about at his surroundings. There were strange ruins that he could not recognize. The ruins were of buildings that he had never seen before, they were made of metal and steel that had one point must have been tall but now they had fallen and were no longer either impressive or even recognizable. The knight unfortunately had no time to explore the ruins. He was focused on returning to his search in the hopes that it would lead him to his friend Melina.

The knight decided to ride towards what looked like a town high on a hill that overlooked the ruins. He did not know what type of a reaction he would face but knew that he had little choice but to continue onward if he were to find the girl. Soon he was on his steed and traveling toward the town, hopeful that some clue would present itself.

The town that the knight entered seemed innocent enough. There were trees, some homes, a market and, of course, a castle where the lord of the town resided. He rode directly to the castle's gate and asked who the ruler was and if he could have an audience. The response he received was cordial and soon he was before the child-king Solon who heard the knight's tale with great interest and sympathy. Solon had not heard of the wizard that the knight spoke of but he did know of a man who knew of all things magical. If anyone could help it would be the wise man that lived in the caverns of the unknowable. It would be a three day ride to find the wise man so Solon supplied the White Knight with twice the supplies of the journey and wished him success on his quest.

The knight thanked the gracious king and left to find his friend. He struggled to keep his emotions in check as he traveled to find the wise man. Each day that he spent searching for Melina was another day of horrible captivity for the girl. He urged tired Victory forward and on the second evening of travel the knight at last found the home of the wise man who lived in the caverns of the unknowable.

The knight walked toward the wise man and was about to say hello until he saw the face of the man opposite and pulled out his sword. What he saw was the face of the man in the forest of doom, the case of the man who held Melina hostage; it was the face of Alberon. The knight raised his sword and struck the man, cleaving his head right off the shoulders. The body swayed then collapsed in a heap on the cavern floor. The quick victory left the knight suspicious, there was simply no way a formidable magician could be defeated that easily but the proof of it lay in front of him.

The man did not delay in his thoughts but began to search the caverns for Melina. He crept through cave after cave until finally he found what he was after. There, in a dimly lit bedroom rested Melina. He walked over to her and turned her face towards him, the scene that presented itself in front of him filled him with a horror previously unknown. It was the visage of an old man projected onto the pretty face of Melina.

The knight recoiled as the twisted face screamed. "You'll never have her, never, never!!! Hahahahahahhahahhahahahaha!" The body vanished and the confused knight was alone except for a presence he felt behind him. He turned to see the body of Alberon holding its head under the right arm.

"Well," the head sighed. "You've really done a whole lot of good this time haven't you?" The body replaced the head on top of its shoulders, twisted it and snapped it in place. "Now, before you go all crazy with that sword again let me introduce myself, I am Eldrad the wise man and you have made a terrible mistake."

Eldrad sat the confused knight on a nearby chair and began to tell his story. A long time ago he was given a vision that a girl would be born who had the power to bend time to her will. That power could be turned towards great good or great evil. It was his destiny to find this girl and help her on the path of good. He knew that if other, more sinister, magicians caught wind of the girl's power they could force her to do their bidding. He had to discover where the girl was before anyone else did or the entire world would be in danger.

Unfortunately he did not. The evil wizard Alberon found the girl and kidnapped her. He used the ruse of holding her hostage for the family's farm so that she would not suspect his true purpose that of turning her mind and her power to evil. Eldrad was about to rescue her and bring her to his home to instruct her on the use of magic when he found the knight in the forest of doom. He decided to let fate play its hand before revealing his identity to the knight. Yet when he found the girl alone in the woods unprotected he decided it was best to take her away. She was fine in his caverns until the knight interceded and ruined it all.

The knight was greatly suspicious of this story but chose to ignore the flaws in his logic for the moment. For now the main problem was to find Melina. There was no sense in arguing with what was obviously a powerful wizard. If indeed she was in the clutches of Alberon then it was best to have another wizard on your side rather than have two against you. The knight was confident that all would reveal itself in time.

The knight, led by Eldrad, walked through cavern after cavern going ever deeper into the mountain of the wise man. Ever now and then they would travel up a bit before walking straight once more. When asked why they couldn't simply transport to Alberon's lair, Eldrad's response was that Alberon would detect the magical energy and raise his defenses.

On the pair went until at last an opening filled with light could be seen. They went through to discover that they were on top of a mountain range. The knight had never seen this range of mountains before and glanced down from the edge to see the sight below. It was scenery he would get a closer look at all too soon. Eldrad seized his chance and pounced; he ran towards the knight and tried to push him off the cliff. The knight was fortunate to be wary of his traveling companion and was much too intelligent to fall for such a trick. They clashed and in the ensuring struggle Eldrad fell off the cliff and into the abyss.

The knight was pleased to have disposed of one adversary but still he needed to find Melina. With no other option he continued on the hazardous path the wizard had set out in the hope that the trail would lead to his friend. Onward the knight traveled, slowly oh so slowly as he armor weighed more heavily around him. He fought the wind and the snow in the hope of finding something in the blinding light.

Ever forward the man searched, feverously looking for any sign or a small clue to where his companion might be held. Onward he went looking for any indication that would lead him to hope. At last he came across a home. There was smoke coming from a tiny chimney and the knight rushed towards this private oasis on top of the cold mountains.

He entered unbidden and found a round man sitting on a large wooden chair reading a long list and smoking a pipe. He had a huge white beard and he seemed to recognize the knight even through his armored face. He bid the knight to sit down near the fire so that he could rest and the knight did just that. He took off his helmet and looked at the smiling face opposite him. There was nothing menacing about the man, he simply seemed like a polite, friendly fellow that had a vague air of familiarity about him.

The man smiled and asked the knight about his journey. The knight, feeling oddly relaxed in the man's pleasant home, told the tale of how he was looking for his kidnapped friend and how the wise man of the mountain had tried to trick him. The large man smiled and said that the person who tried to trick him was not the wise man of the mountain, but that in fact he was now in the company of the wise man.

The knight smiled and thought to himself that of course this man was the wise man. A truly wise man has little evil in him as this man obviously had. The wise man told the knight that he should rest in his house for the night and that the next morning he would help him with his problem. The knight, tired and with nowhere else to go, took the kind man up on his offer and let himself be led to the guest bedroom where he discarded his armor and quickly fell into a deep sleep.

The next morning the knight woke to discover that his armor, which had been tarnished by the many battles and months of travel, had been cleaned and looked as if it were new. He also found a note on the foot of his bed reading that there were new clothes for him to wear in a chest under the bed. The knight got up and found the chest which indeed contained new clothes for him to wear.

The knight quickly got dressed in his new clothes and looked to find the wise man. He found him in a kitchen area where he was cooking eggs on a small stove. He bade the knight to sit down and help himself to some food which he gratefully did. After the meal was over the knight inquired about his armor and was told by the wise man that he had helpers that would do requests for him. A knight's armor should be shining after all, the wise man observed.

The wise man had also been busy finding the hideout of Alberon. The wizard was located not too far from where the knight was. After he felt completely ready the wise man agreed to show him where the evil wizard was. In short order the wise man proved to be true to his word and soon he and the knight had located the lair of the evil Alberon.

The knight, in all good conscious, could not let the wise man go any further. He had come to like the short, round fellow and it would have been wrong to let him help rescue Melina as he had offered. Seeing that the knight was resolute the wise man wished him the best of luck then with a wink and a nod vanished.

The knight had no time to wonder as to the nature of the man, he had work to do. The knight steeled himself for battle and entered the lair of the evil wizard. The large mansion was well lit. Every hallway had many torches on either side. All doors to the rooms were locked. Some doors had noisy growls behind them. The knight explored the building searching for the missing Melina.

Finally, deep within the large building he found Melina chained to the wall of a large bedroom. Her hair had fallen all akimbo over her face, her eyes were tired but still defiant, her clothes were torn and her boots were gone. The knight was enraged over the spectacle before him but knew that rash action would endanger the girl and he had to wait. The evil wizard was standing in front of her, telling her that soon she would give up her struggle and give him access to her power. Soon she would become like him, pure and unadulterated evil.

The knight had the advantage of surprise thanks to the wise man and now he had to play that card wisely. He waited until the wizard had left the room before cautiously approaching Melina. For her part she at first believed the knight to be another trick of the terrible wizard. It was only once she had been freed of her chains and in the arms of the strong man that she knew that her dream of rescue had come true.

There was no time to reacquaint themselves. The knight had to get the girl out of the clutches of the wizard and to a place of safety before he could turn his attention towards ridding the world of his filth. Finding she did not have the strength in her legs to walk the knight lifted her up and easily carried her towards freedom.

The knight retraced his steps and soon he was once more outside the lair. Standing on the same spot as the wise man had, the knight winked and nodded and he and Melina were transported to the wise man's mountain home. There the wise man had been waiting for the knight and was very relieved that nothing had happened to his new friend. Melina quickly found herself in a bed, given a healing potion by the wise man and very soon despite her fear she was asleep.

Both the knight and the wise man understood that there was little time to waste before Alberon discovered the girl missing and would begin to look for her. They had to act quickly to destroy the wizard once and for all to ensure the safety not only of themselves and Melina but the entire world.

Fortunately for them both the wise man had lived up to his name. He had prepared for the advent of war and had amassed a collection of weapons, shields, mystical potions and armor that would have embarrassed the finest war monger. Accoutered in the best of his weapons the pair took a pause to look in on the newly rescued friend. They found her resting comfortably under the influence of the sleep draft they had given her and once they were satisfied she was fine the pair set off to exterminate Alberon.

Using their teleportation spell once more they found themselves at the entrance of the evil wizard's lair. Ready for battle they entered chamber after chamber until finally arriving at the same room that once held Melina in chains. He had just discovered that his prize had been stolen from him and he was raving against the world when the pair entered. A look of hatred shone from the visage of the evil warlock as he saw the wise man and his friend. Screaming at them he fired a ball of fire from his left hand. The shields of the two heroes protected them from harm as the fire licked at their hardy, mystical steel.

Seeing the look of utter determination in the eyes of the White Knight the evil wizard began to feel fear.

He halted his useless train of fire and concentrated on conjuring daemons that would hack the pair to pieces. He summoned large monstrosities that were ferocious in nature and appeared from their looks to be nigh unbeatable. Yet no matter how many the now frightened wizard conjured the two advancing men kept hacking them down until at last only one creature was left to kill before coming to the master himself.

Tired and now nearing a state of panic the desperate wizard put all his efforts into one final spell. He summoned Sutra, a fire demon that ate souls and bodies alike. Commanding the creature to attack his enemies Alberon laughed, so sure he was that this mighty creature would destroy the two men in front of him.

Yet he was badly mistaken in his estimation of the courage of strength of the two warriors. Rather than fear this deadly creature the two understood that Alberon's power must be waning to conjure such a beast. They took heart at this thought and ran full speed ahead at the monster. Despite its size and strength it was slow and the small room made the creature vulnerable to attack.

Alberon's face sunk as he saw the inevitable outcome of the fight. While the pair was occupied in defeating his monster he slipped away from the room. It took some time but the soul eater was at last defeated and the two tired men looked to find the instigator of evil had vanished. They searched throughout the lair but could not find Alberon.

Suddenly it occurred to them both that the crazed wizard might take his revenge on Melina who was all alone and helpless. The pair rushed back to the teleport spot outside the lair and made it back to the wise man's home just in time to catch the evil wizard about to strangle the helpless girl.

The two rushed towards the would-be killer as Melina woke up and screamed. Once again the two heroes waded through mystical fire as they surged forward to dispatch the evil one. The sorcerer shouted out in anger and fear, hurling obscenities along with his flame. Claiming his next attack would be the one that would finish the two off once and for all he thrust his fists out in front of his body. A massive ball of energy formed in front of him when suddenly all movement stopped.

Melina, looking back at the two heroes, had used her time power to halt the wizard and she had surrounded herself and him in a ball of frozen time. The white knight told her to get out of there but she explained that she could not if she was to halt the deadly flame. The pair of heroes protested and told her to come to her senses but she refused. With one last look she turned her power inward and both the evil wizard and Melina vanished in a blast of energy and flame.

The knight rushed to the spot that once was occupied by Melina but there was nothing. She was gone. With nothing left to fight for the White Knight collapsed to the floor in pain and in misery. Once more he had lost someone close to his heart and there was no solacing him. The wise man knew it was best not to interfere and so he let the man have some time alone.

All night the White Knight wept as he reflected upon his failure to save his companion. By dawn he made up his mind to quit this land, find his horse Victory and travel back to Melina's village to remove the curse that had confounded it. At least he could do that much in her memory.

The wise man provided the knight with as much goods as he needed. After some rest the wise man took the knight on a journey in his magical flying sleigh where, with the advantage of flight, soon they spotted Victory grazing in a field and looking content. The knight thanked his new friend for all that he had done and then after loading up his horse with supplies he was about to depart when the wise man stopped him.

In his hands was a small shield made of the finest material known in the world. He handed it to the knight as a gift and made him promise that one day he would return to that strange land that had only given him trouble and grief. To that the knight replied that at least he had made a friend, and that was gift enough. He accepted the shield and went on his way, his heart filled with misery but with still a mission to accomplish. At least that was something that would keep him going into tomorrow and for many of the trying days ahead.

End of Part Three

At last, tired from his day at work and bloated from his excess of pizza and beer, with a grunt Steve rose from his couch, turned off his television and got ready for bed. One quick change of clothes and a brush of his teeth later he was ready to slip into the arms of Morpheus. A brief pause to pray for all the things that mattered to him and he was ready to engage in one of his few true pleasures in his existence, unconsciousness.

On a table on the right side of his couch rested his unopened mail. It was the usual fare of bills, junk and advertisements, items informing him he could already be a millionaire and that he could lose twenty pounds in twenty days. All was normal, except for a small letter that teeter-tottered on the edge of his small, brown table. Little did he realize that the thin envelope contained a missive that was to forever change his life.

Chapter Four

The Decision

Saturday morning in Staten Island, New York meant for Steve that his weekly chores were about to begin. All the accumulated mess that had somehow been strewn about the apartment during the past six days had to be cleaned, swept and reassembled into some sense of cleanliness and order. Straining to get out of bed, Steve sighed inwardly. He loathed the details of life, all the boring minutia that was necessary in order to keep his dreary existence going. In the space library apartments things were so much easier and it still did not sink into Steve's stubborn mind that there didn't exist on Earth a magic machine where you could leave your room, hit a button and when you returned all your cleaning was done for you.

Steve hid beneath his covers a little longer than even he wanted to on Saturday mornings, hoping that if he stayed under there long enough the mess would just go away. Yet restlessness would soon mercilessly prick at him as if somehow a mean-spirited porcupine had slid underneath his wrappings with him and inevitably he would slowly roll out of his warm, comfy bed and reluctantly begin his day.

Once he had arisen, his usual Saturday morning routine would begin. Breakfast was always created first, two English muffins, a cup of tea, three hard-boiled eggs and a large glass of orange juice. Cooking was never a chore, but was something that he did with an easy heart. The pretence of being a famous chef always played out in his mind and even something as simple as toast could be elevated into a work of gastronomical art if he thought about it hard enough. The simple swipe of the knife as it bathes the bread with sweet butter was done with all the dramatic flair of a culinary maestro.

Breakfast finished easily and after a quick scour of his teeth and a change into casual clothes, it was time to begin with his domestic duties. The preservation of time was the key factor in the decision to create an unbreakable routine for the chores so that they could be done as efficiently as possible. First all clothes had to be put into a laundry basket for the weekly trip to the downstairs laundry. It took precisely ten minutes to locate, gather, and herd all his clothes into the awaiting basket. Steve tried to get his time from ten to seven minutes, but somehow there was always a sock or shirt that eluded the initial search and the goal could never be reached.

The second task was to sweep the apartment of all dust bunnies that lurked almost everywhere. At least, he thought, they were not vampire zombie dust bunnies. Third was to put back all the items that were misplaced throughout the dwelling during the week. Tasks four, five, six and seven all were done in order until the morning was gone and it was time to go to the laundry. Picking up the red laundry basket, he left his quarters and made his way towards the downstairs emporium The Whirl and Twirl.

The downstairs laundry was always busy on Saturdays. This would sometimes mean that Steve had to wait for a machine to become free but he accepted the hurdle as part of his routine. Once and only once he had decided to do the laundry on a Thursday evening and much to his everlasting regret he found himself trapped alone with a man who muttered to himself for the entire wash cycle. The man, who looked a heck of a lot like Steve himself, kept up a continuous mantra of "Carol why did you leave me? Carol, Carol, why did you leave me?" Disturbed by the experience, Steve concluded that only strange, exceedingly lonely people did their laundry on non-Saturdays and so he vowed never to do his laundry on a weeknight again.

Today luck smiled upon the reference librarian and soon he was watching his socks chase after each other in a bizarre flight of fancy. For all the time that he spent sitting doing his laundry watching his clothes perform, Steve never spoke to anyone. Rather he looked about hoping to find a discarded newspaper to occupy himself with. People weren't like those in his beloved St. John's. They rarely talked to you if they didn't know you and to introduce oneself was sometimes taken as a crime in itself. Rather than try to make friends, Steve simply took the easy way out and sat silently saying nothing to no one. He was safe that way and that was all he cared for. He sat back and took out his writing once more looking for ways to improve his story. He almost felt compelled to write and he hoped that if his soul told him to write that at least it might be good.

King Chronos and the Death of All Things

Legendary King Chronos stood on the summit of the tallest mountain in his small, prosperous kingdom. His strong heart beat proudly as he slowly surveyed the majestic city state below. His was a peaceful country but on this morning his thoughts traveled back to a time when it had not always been so.

He had to fight hard to obtain his land, the glorious kingdom that stretched out before him. A fierce conflict against the ruthless dictator Khan had to be fought and won before the rule of law and order could at last be established in a place that never before had known justice. All fear of authority had slowly vanished after the tyrant Khan's defeat and a happy people emerged from the husks of the old. As a result of the victory King Chronos' deeds were now etched in history in story and song and his country had prospered under his benign reign.

This day was the 20th anniversary of the final night of the last glorious battle and the victory of good over evil. The king on this morning had traveled to the top of his largest mountain to pay his silent respects to the fallen heroes of that long ago conflict and to re-dedicate his soul to the welfare of his people.

Ascending the mountain had been more of an effort than the King had liked. His heavy beard had become flaked in grey and his large muscles were beginning to show telltale signs of fatigue. Time had taken its harsh toll even on the legendary ruler but he was more than satisfied with the outcome of his life. Twenty years of hard work had resulted in the creation of a city state that was the envy of the known world. Alas, unknown to King Chronos and his people it was the vast, unknown world that would soon threaten his kingdom's existence and his very life.

The sky was unusually clear and the sunrise brightly shone down upon his happy land. The king, content that he had given a proper tribute to his long remembered fallen comrades, had looked down for a brief moment to plan his descent from the mountain. When he had raised his head once more to enjoy a final glance upon his land the scene had drastically changed from tranquility to terror.

A veil of darkness magically encroached upon the cloudless sky and a gruesome shriek of horror seemed to emanate from the newly formed firmament. Thunder and lightning crashed from the dull atmosphere and sharp bolts of death splintered the city below. Buildings fell, people died then as quickly as it had begun the lightening stopped just as suddenly and a torrent of hard rain poured from the heavens striking the city with deadly effect. Streaks of fire began to smash into the city and King Chronos could hear the anguished screams of his people even from the height of his mountain retreat. Leaderless in his absence they all looked to him for courage and guidance as this new crisis emerged.

Shaken by these unlikely events King Chronos quickly started down the mountain eager to return to his beloved people. Descending down the rock as fast as he could manage he discovered upon his arrival a horde of courtiers, soldiers, and ordinary citizens anxiously awaiting his return.

The King looked into the helpless eyes of each of those who had come to him and he could offer nothing but the silent assurance that no matter what foul circumstance had happened and no matter what dark enemy had plagued them it would be fought with and overcome. His people had seen that grim look before and it was his determination and leadership that gave them the strength of will to fight foes both natural and unnatural. This instance would be no exception.

The King set out at once to return to his palace and investigate the recent events. His train of followers grew as he carried on towards the innards of his city. As he arrived near his castle's walls and walked down its long, rocky pathway the crowd of people that had huddled near the walls for safety parted to let him through. A swarm of soldiers took their place around their King looking more for security in his presence than he in theirs. He motioned for the guards to let everyone into the safety of the castle walls and a thong of people entered the gates as he continued on to the castle proper.

The palace was an extraordinary example of how ambiance and karma can change the entire feel of any particular place. In the dark times before King Chronos the palace was a place of fear and chaos where anyone who valued their life stayed well clear of the cold castle. Now the court was a haven filled with majesty, truth and justice and despite the transformation of the atmosphere Chronos had never even bothered to change the carpeting.

The King entered his throne room and walked towards his large throne. Outside confusion reigned but here his majestic seat was a source of comfort and his people expected him to be the strong leader he always was. Only this time he had little clue as to the cause of such wanton destruction and suffering. Was it a natural occurrence or a prelude to an attack? He did not know but he was determined to find out. Somewhere out there the answer lay.

The White Knight had woken up to a deafening roar. He was unused to sleeping soundly but for some odd reason the night had been unusually pleasant and so he was greatly irritated that while enjoying a rare sound sleep a bright flash followed by a piercing thunder woke him from his rest. The infant dawn had barely emerged to shoo the elderly night away when the cacophony began. Little did he realize that the loud noise was merely the clang of the first round bell in a twelve round match of danger.

His white horse, wary but unafraid, was already alert and staring down into the weary, half-open eyes of its sleepy master searching for reassurance. The world was akimbo and as his senses sharpened the White Knight rose up from the ground to witness the strange event. Streaks of light flashed across the sky and ended beyond the horizon with a smash and a crash. He had never seen such unusual sights from the sky before and wondered how nature could go so far astray.

The streaks of thunder appeared to point towards a spot far off in the distance. Even so the White Knight had to shield his eyes from the bright light that had erupted in the morning sky. The Knight took a moment to think then he chose to break camp and ride towards the danger. There might be someone in trouble and he would help if he could.

Putting on his shining armor was a chore but a necessary one. Once he was encased he was ready for action and by the unearthly feel of the weather he was sure that action was what was soon to be called for. He rapidly dressed then mounted Victory and headed off in the direction of the odd lights.

King Chronos did not have any time to reflect on the attack on his city state. The people and the terrible crisis demanded immediate action. Fortunately for all concerned he was a man of action and was very used to it. He had ordered all his people who were still in the city to evacuate their homes and leave their property and assemble in the courtyard of his castle. There within the thick walls the people huddled close together afraid and confused, all the while watching their city die a violent death.

The onslaught lasted until the blackened sun was high overhead. The last bombardment hit their sacred temple, effectively destroying the last place of solace outside the castle's walls. Smoke from the debris wafted upward and began to drown out the remainder of the sun's rays. The people soon grew cold and shock, disbelief and fear filled all their hearts and minds.

King Chronos watched helplessly from the height of his tallest tower in his castle. He surveyed his frightened people, his shattered city and he felt a tidal wave of anger. This was no natural occurrence. Someone somewhere had deliberately done this to his precious city and that someone he vowed was going to pay a dear, dear price. Yet vengeance would have to wait until the needs of his people were attended to. Chronos called his most valued advisors together to help map out a plan to help the victims and rescue those who had the misfortune to remain trapped in their homes.

Meanwhile, on the far edge of King Chronos' once proud city, the White Knight had arrived on the scene and had begun to search through the remaining homes standing in the hope that someone was still alive. That hope seemed lost as the While Knight found only empty shells of homes and the broken dead. He had seen destruction before but the seemingly senseless carnage that was spread about before him was novel even to this veteran of war. The crumpled remains of ordinary people lay scattered around him and as the Knight looked upon the damage and death, it made him very angry.

Some time later the dark clouds had dispersed completely and the bright, warming sun returned to the land. The White Knight walked out of yet another shattered home to discover that five soldiers had taken up defensive positions before the entrance of the crumbling building. Their spears pointed directly at the White Knight's armored chest.

The Knight was confident that he could disarm his assailants but he knew that action in this instance would end up being useless and unproductive so he raised his arms in the air. The men led the White Knight on a trek through the ruined city, past the destruction and pungent stench of death as he passed the crumbling, weakened buildings. As he walked the Knight took mental notes of the utter devastation. Clearly the objective of the attack was not to conquer but to completely eradicate the city. This indicated to the Knight that this might be a revenge attack rather than one of simple maliciousness. No matter what the motive whoever caused this much damage was clearly a power to be reckoned with.

The small procession continued through the city and into the large outer walls of the fortified castle. The group marched past the huddled, cowering mass that looked at the White Knight with blank, lost eyes. Finally the soldiers and their prisoner walked in through the inner walls of the castle and onward to the royal hall where King Chronos stood with a group of his advisors planning their response to the massive attack.

All fell silent when the White Knight was halted a mere five feet away from the angry king. Chronos was a man of action and he felt the urgent need to do something to retaliate against the horrible crime perpetrated on his people. Now a stranger who was garbed as a soldier had been presented to him under guard and it took all of his mental strength not to strike the man down where he stood.

King Chronos breathed deeply and took a step back from the prisoner to study the figure in front of him. It was obvious that the fellow was a military man and from his bearing a considerable one at that. Here was a person who could supply some answers and Chronos was the man who could get them.

The questions that came from Chronos and his advisors were spiced with anger and desperation. The White Knight tried to explain that he was a friend and not a foe but his story was too simple, too neat to be believed at face value. Here was a stranger dressed in armor arriving in the city just as the place had been ruthlessly attacked by some unknown force. The circumstance weighed heavily against him. The Knight was quickly sentenced to the dungeon with the threat of torture and death if he refused to tell the truth.

The White Knight was stripped of his armor and led away to the dungeon that was deep underneath the castle's walls. The first thing that the Knight noticed once shoved inside the dungeon was that this was the cleanest prison he had ever been in. It was not at all damp, it was not smelly or vile, instead it was well lit and above all it was empty. This indicated one of two things; the dungeon was either newly built or few were ever sentenced to the place. The Knight hoped for the latter as it would indicate a fair and forgiving monarch.

Outside the castle's walls the unpleasant process of cleaning up the rubble and recovering the bodies had begun. The people were organized as efficiently as they could be under the circumstances and they, with the help of soldiers leading the way, systematically began to comb the city for survivors. As time went by their hopes diminished and at the gruesome sight of their loved one's charred and broken remains their anger grew. Rumors had sprung up that there had been someone captured and their thoughts began to rush towards revenge.

King Chronos spent all night and the next day organizing his ruined city's defenses against a possible further attack. His troops covered all entrances into the city and patrols were organized in case more strange knights appeared. His ministers took charge of the details of the rescue effort and the caretakers of the food stores of the city-state had begun to distribute rations to the people. The castle guards had to be reinforced to halt a mob who were determined to stone the prisoner but they had been sent back after a plea by the King himself that no harm should come to the man before all the evidence was clear. By the end of the second day after the assault the city had amazingly begun to slowly return to the calm state before the attack had begun.

The White Knight had spent the past two days in the confines of the dungeon and had now tired of captivity. He initially thought that if he allowed himself to be captured he could get some answers to his questions and prove that he was only there to help. Instead he had been tossed into the clink and had been relatively ignored. He had little fear that his beloved horse, Victory was ok. It had been on its own for long periods of time before but now he feared that he had gravely miscalculated and was in danger. The knight had no intention of rotting in prison forever. He resolved to escape the dungeon and search for answers on his own.

In the throne room, high above the musing Knight, King Chronos was asleep. He had been reacting to the attack on his kingdom for two whole days non stop and now he had reluctantly drifted off into the arms of Morpheus. In his dream that followed he found himself in a small, pretty village. The sun was shining brightly and the people seemed happy and content.

A girl dressed in flowing white robes suddenly appeared from the far side of the village and slowly walked toward him. She called herself Melina and she tried to speak to King Chronos but her words were soon blotted out by the loud crack of thunder. Clouds had miraculously begun to form and now a dark and foreboding presence seemed to overcome the land. A hail of fire poured down around the people and haunting laughter filed the putrid air. The girl looked up at the now blood red sky and screamed.

King Chronos bolted up from his throne and quickly looked around his court. Besides the two guards by the door there was no one else in the room but this did not make the crown rest any easier on his head. Chronos knew all too well that dreams could be a gateway to the answers for puzzles in the realm of the waking. He thought if he could somehow find that girl perhaps that she could help him in his quest for knowledge but he did not know how or even where to begin.

Chronos got out of his throne and casually walked over to the White Knight's armor that had been placed on a large, round table at the far end of the court. It was gleaming from the light of the candles and something about this armor had sparked a memory of long ago but it was far too distant to be remembered. All these puzzling pieces had been laid out in front of him but nothing seemed to fit into place. It was time to talk to the White Knight again.

Shortly thereafter the guards who had been sent to retrieve the knight returned with some startling news. The stranger had escaped and no one had seen or heard him go. Chronos was furious on hearing the news and ordered his men to search the castle and find the escapee. The sharp prod of steel from behind him immediately told him not to bother.

The hardest part of being a famous king like Chronos was living up to the expectations of all those around you. He had in the past been given all sorts of titles such as All-Wise and All-Knowing and when you get those titles you just had to live up to them or risk disappointing people. In this instance King Chronos really had wanted to get some information from this unknown but now with a sword poking directly in his back he felt he had no choice but to kill the man holding it.

The king turned with lightning speed and faced the knight. The quickness of Chronos had surprised even the White Knight. It was obvious that Chronos was a powerfully built man but his spotted, grey beard had spoke of a man whose prowess has slipped. The imposing figure in front of him though looked like one of the most powerful individuals he had ever faced. The White Knight surveyed the situation, looked the king squarely in the eyes and thought that it was a shame that he had to kill him.

King Chronos shouted at his men to stay back and not to interfere in the coming battle. He grabbed one of the guard's swords from his hand and faced the stranger. Both men's eyes locked as the deadly contest was about to begin in earnest.

At first the two slowly moved around each other, testing their defenses with their keen battle-hardened instincts, hoping to reveal a weakness in their foe. When neither man found any, their eyes betrayed a glimpse of curiosity and grudging respect for their opposition. Suddenly and at the same time both men chanced to strike a blow hoping to quickly end the conflict. Their swords clashed and the clang of steel upon steel rang throughout the throne room. Neither men cared that their present struggle would become a monumental clash that would produce many songs and legends for hundreds of years to come; they simply wished to survive it.

Again and again their swords smashed against the other, both men desperately trying to inflict a wound but neither man could manage to exact a blow that would decide the conflict. The courtiers, guards and noblemen who had arrived to watch the fierce battle worried that perhaps this was the day that their fearless king would be at last vanquished. All in the now crowded throne room stared in worried fascination over the spectacle that was being played out in front of them. Their king had finally met an enemy that had his measure and their world, which had been forever changed due to the recent attack, might yet further be altered forever.

For over an hour the two men fought, each reigning blow after blow on the other, every one which would have easily destroyed a lesser opponent. Yet both still stood in the middle of the crowded room, weary with sweat pouring down both their brows, eyes filled with fierce determination to topple the other and win the day. With swords raised above their heads they advanced on the other determined to finally end the conflict when suddenly the entire left wall of the room exploded with a violent bang.

Each man stopped their attack and looked at the haze of smoke and rubble. The crowd turned its attention to the opening and wondered what new horror had begun. It did not take much time for them to find out. Within the smoke was a dark figure covered in black robes. It was a man who smiled a menacing smirk at the occupants of the throne room. All seemed to instinctively know that this man was evil and that he was somehow the true cause of their misery.

The White Knight instantly recognized the man for who he was. It was the dark wizard Alberon who he thought was destroyed. This man was dangerous and if he was the blame for the cause of the destruction of King Chronos' city then Chronos had a formidable challenge on his hands. The White Knight stared at the wizard and, as their eyes briefly met, there was no hint of recognition in the evil man's gaze which surprised the Knight.

The Wizard gently stepped over the fallen rubble and apologized for interrupting the people's amusements. He had a proposition for the King and he refused to wait any longer. The bargain was simple. The king was to relinquish his crown to him by the end of the day or his castle and all the people in the kingdom would be destroyed. His powers, as demonstrated by the city's ruins, were too powerful for all his army to stop and there was no choice but to accede to his demands or his people would suffer. With his ultimatum made clear the wizard disappeared in a flash of smoke.

The gathered crowd muttered to themselves as King Chronos mulled over his people's fate. The wizard seemed on the surface to be all powerful but his vast experience with such tricksters told him that all he needed was time to defeat this new one, but to his anger it was time he did not have. Swallowing his pride he knew what he had to do.

With this new enemy to contend with he had no inclination to continue his battle with the White Knight whom he felt now that he had wronged. Sensing that a man who could fight as well as the Knight had could not be evil he told the Knight that he was free to leave his kingdom in peace. For his side the White Knight found in his heart a great deal of respect for the troubled king. Only a valiant warrior could have defended himself as well as he could. Feeling that he could help the cause of justice he offered his services to help restore his kingdom and defeat the evil wizard.

King Chronos was very pleased to accept the warrior's offer and he repaid the man for his generous help by returning his armor to him. Chronos decided that since there was so little time that he had no choice but to feign acceptance of the wizard's demands. He would formally give up his kingdom and leave the city at once. After he had left the city it was up to his spies in the castle to discover any weaknesses that the wizard had and to come back later to exploit them.

So came the dark day when King Chronos, after twenty years of ruling his people wisely and well, had to give up his throne and leave his beloved land and people. The citizens all came out of their hovels and cheered the King. Many of them realized just how horrible the King felt but knew that he had no choice but to leave in order to save what was left of his people and city. From the tower of the castle the black wizard smiled. He was confident that now that he had a base in which to plan from soon the entire world would be his for the taking. No one, he firmly believed, would be able to oppose him, especially after the world learned of how easily he defeated the famous King Chronos.

King Chronos left his city by himself. He refused to let anyone share in the shame of the exodus that was his alone to bear. The king loved his people and would do anything for them, including save them from a useless fight. He knew that only with a well-thought out plan could he hope to defeat his enemy and restore his shattered kingdom. Until then the shame of exile would be his to bear alone.

After traveling for a way down a long road he met up with the White Knight. The knight was a man much like himself, willing to face all sorts of danger for the sake of the general good. He was greatly pleased that this man whom he had mistreated was willing to let bygones be bygones and help him in his quest to regain his kingdom. Once together they traveled to a wooded area and began to wait for the opportunity to destroy the evil wizard.

Weeks later the White Knight and King Chronos had become good friends. Each told the other stories of the adventures they had enjoyed and the many dangers that they had overcome. The White Knight had even shared with him the tragic tale of Princess Carolyn and the Black Prince and their forced marriage. Chronos, with eyes tightly closed as he heard the sad story, understood only too well the utter pain of heartbreak. He himself once had a queen who had died during childbirth and his heart still sang her name. His own twin children had died during that same awful night and he vowed never to marry again. He could defeat mythic monsters and terrible villains but not the savage pain of a broken heart.

It was on the fifth week of their exile that the knight had heard rumbling in the woods near their encampment. It was a dark night and he could not see the approach of the visitor but his keen, trained ears told him that someone was near. The shuffling sounds of feet on leaves indicated that stealth was not one of the intruder's attributes and that worked to the knight's advantage. In a manner of moments the trespasser had been toppled and flung face down on the grassy carpet of the forest floor.

King Chronos, who too was alert had been awake the whole time of the confrontation, took some embers from the dying campsite fire and brought them over to where the other two people were. The face revealed by the fire light was that of Commander Cody, one of the finest officers in King Chronos' army. Once the White Knight had gotten up from Commander Cody's behind the three walked to the dying fire, re-stoked the flames and talked about the previous week's events. Commander Cody had informed the two men that the city had begun an amazing transformation. Thanks to the wizard's powers the process of rebuilding the city had been virtually effortless. Buildings had erected themselves seemingly overnight and food had been miraculously grown in places where no crop had ever grown before.

King Chronos listened to the tales of miracles and grew ever more concerned. It appeared that the evil wizard had discovered the Chronos Stone, a stone that could make time do the welder's bidding. With it a man could speed up, or retard time giving him the ability to do seemingly impossible things in the wink of an eye. The magical stone had been placed in a secret room in the depths of the castle. There the stone was to be left forever. King Chronos had won the stone from the she demon Zeta who had placed a curse on all those who used it. King Chronos had hoped that he would never see the stone again but now it appeared that he would have to contend with its powers once more.

The White Knight listened intently to the story of the Chronos Stone. He had wondered why the wizard did not recognize him from their previous encounter in the forest of doom but now he realized that the wizard must have somehow traveled back in time to fight him. Thus the wizard knew him earlier but not now. Now the tables were turned and he hoped that he could somehow use this knowledge to his advantage.

From Commander Cody's story it appeared that the wizard was also using the power of the Stone to summon demons from the past and dragons from the depths of time to become a part of his new army of conquest. The entire sky was sometimes filed with creatures diving up and down, looking for things on which to feed. Even the innocent citizens of the city were not safe as there were occasions when a horrible creature would swoop down and pick up a terrified inhabitant and carry off the poor soul. The city may have been dressed up to look glorious but it was a city of terror and fear. Something desperately needed to be done to stop the madness.

King Chronos became very angry over the news of how his city and his people were being so mistreated. It was obvious from his actions that the wizard was up to something and he knew that he had to act soon before the wizard's preparations were complete. The time to strike was now before the wizard's power grew too strong to oppose, but he still needed a plan. Rather than simply attack and fail, stealth and cunning would be required in order to restore his rightful rule. The three decided to sleep on the problem and hope that in the morning inspiration would strike.

As King Chronos shut his eyes and fell into the misty haze of unreality the girl from his previous dream came to him. She was wearing a white, flowing gown and she was trying to speak to the king but her words were muffled by the cries of hawks overhead. Once again the pair was in a beautiful village whose occupants seemed to take no mind to the girl's cries for help. The king began to shove people aside in order to stay with the girl and at the moment when he came close to her again the wizard appeared for one brief instant and looked shocked and angered over the sight that befell his eyes.

Before he could do anything the wizard faded away and took his anger with him leaving the pair alone. The girl Melina took the king by his hand and led him towards the edge of her village. There she pointed to the source of all her woes, the Chronos Stone. Here was a way to defeat the wizard but at the cost of the very thing the user would hold dear. It was a risk the king would have to take to help save his people from the fiend that now enthralled them. By now Melina had begun to fade and she bid him a wordless farewell. She was gone but now the king had his answer, the key to destroying the wizard forever.

King Chronos woke up speaking the name Melina over and over again. This shook the White Knight to the point that he feared that the fates were playing some game against him. He urged the king to tell him why he had called out that name. The King gave him a full account of his dreams and the solution that Melina had proposed in them. The beautiful Melina had now spoken twice to King Chronos and the White Knight was inwardly disturbed by this strange turn of events. He had witnessed the horrible death of Melina after the defeat of the wizard by her hands. Had she now somehow come back from the dead in order to once again thwart the wizard's plans once more? As the White Knight rose to begin the quest to return King Chronos to his throne a multitude of questions filled his mind. Yet these had to be answered another day. The time for doubt was over; it was now time for bold action.

The plan to destroy the evil wizard was simple and straightforward. Commander Cody would go into the city first to rally the troops for an offensive action against the demons and dragons, King Chronos would challenge the wizard to a duel to the death and the White Knight would sneak into the castle, retrieve the Chronos Stone and hand it to King Chronos who would use it to end the evil reign the of wizard king. Chronos knew that in using the stone there was a possibility that he would be cursed but he realized that this was the only way in which to save his kingdom and thus he was resigned to do what he must.

The time had come to force the issue with the evil wizard. It was still early in the afternoon when all was ready to begin. A disguised King Chronos stepped out of a crowd of people in the market square and cried out for all to hear that the wizard was a filthy coward who dared not face him. The people in the square stepped back in surprise at seeing their beloved king. The last time they had seen him he was leaving the city in shame and now he had returned and their hopes were buoyed. They longed for their torture to end and their King, they prayed, had finally arrived to save them.

The wizard soon learned of King Chronos' announcement in the market and laughed heartily. Who was he to make such a threat? Chronos' kingdom was now his and his former subjects were now the wizard's unwilling slaves. What could the feeble ex-king do now to him, especially since he had in his possession the powerful Chronos Stone? The wizard decided to call King Chronos' bluff. He would meet him in the market and end the charade once and for all.

The White Knight, spying from outside a window, had witnessed the wizard's lack of respect for Chronos and inwardly smiled. He knew that the wizard's overconfidence would be a great asset to his plan and as he watched the evil villain depart for the market the knight had the freedom necessary to search for the Chronos Stone.

The market was packed with people all eager to witness the events that would soon become legend. In the middle of the marketplace the heroic King Chronos stood, his hand firmly gripped on the handle of his sword. By this time horrific demons that the wizard had conjured up from the depths of hell had surrounded the brave king waiting but for a word from their master to tear into the flesh of the lone man that dared oppose the wizard.

Suddenly, storm clouds filled the air and the rasp of thunder filled the sky. The wizard, riding a large fire-breathing dragon, appeared high in the dark sky. A more dramatic appearance could not seem possible and the sight of the leathery demon and its master spread immediate panic in the streets. Yet King Chronos was unmoved. His steel heart refused to allow any hint of fear to escape from his bosom. His thoughts were only of his people and the task at hand.

Angered over Chronos' lack of respect, the wizard swooped down from his high perch and landed not ten feet away from the stalwart king. The wizard looked into the steely eyes of the king and laughed. He knew that there was no way in which King Chronos could harm him. The wizard had an army of the most fearsome creatures from the netherworld at his beck and call. Within a second he could order his beasts to exterminate the pretender to the throne. But first he was going to have a little fun at the former king's expense.

While this was happening outside the White Knight had slipped past all the defenses the wizard had to offer. His artistry at stealth had once again come in very handy. While the demons that the wizard had summoned were frightening to look at they were not at all gifted with any great amount of intelligence and thus simple tricks to avoid detection worked like a charm against them. So it came to pass that the White Knight faced the heavy door of the room that housed the Chronos Stone. King Chronos had informed him of the stone's whereabouts and now all the knight had to do was to open the door and obtain the stone.

The door, although thick, was surprisingly light and there was no trouble in opening it. Through the haze of the castle light the knight caught a glimpse of the object. There, sitting on a big, purple pillow, was the largest gem the knight has ever laid eyes on. The Chronos Stone was beautiful but it was not for its beauty that the knight needed it.

The knight approached slowly, looking for any traps and once he decided there were none he reached out and picked up the stone. Staring into its wonderful form he seemed to fall into a trance for a brief moment. Knowing the tricks of magic he put the stone in his leather pouch by his side then quickly turned around to face a hundred snarling demons, one more ferocious than the next. It looked like there was no escape for the White Knight.

The King was faring no better at the marketplace. The evil wizard had him surrounded by the denizens of hell. Laughing, the conjurer was about to call upon his creatures to at last dispose of the brave king when a great cry from seemingly every direction sounded throughout the market. Thousands of well-armed soldiers thundered into the square hacking to pieces the demons and creatures that were threatening the king. In an instant the wizard's forces were scattered and running for their petty lives. The threat to the king for the moment had been vanquished.

The wizard was furious over this turn of events and began to rant in an ancient tongue. Once again the sky began to cloud and thunder rattled over the city square. Vowing to never let control over the city vanish he cried out that he would rather destroy the entire population for this betrayal. King Chronos looked up from his place in the market and knew that if there was ever a time for mystical intervention then surely this was it.

Seemingly from out of nowhere the White Knight appeared with the Chronos Stone in his gloved hand. He lifted it over his head and said the magic words that were inscribed on the stone itself. A hum began to emanate from the stone and it began to glow. The wizard looked down upon the scene and immediately understood the danger. His winged beast swooped down to grab the stone but by the time he had neared the White Knight it was too late.

Time had frozen and only the man holding the Chronos Stone had been protected by its immense glow. The Knight asked the Stone to send the wizard to a place and time where he never again could trouble King Chronos' land or people. With a loud whooshing sound the Chronos Stone glowed even brighter until there was only a blinding white light. The White Knight closed his eyes from the radiance and when he had opened them again the wizard had vanished.

In the market place all the demons were gone and only King Chronos and his people remained. After a brief explanation from the White Knight, the King announced that the danger was past and that there would be a glorious celebration in honour of their victory and especially for their great friend the White Knight. The knight handed back the Chronos Stone to the king for safe keeping and walked with him back to the palace where they both could rest after such a difficult day.

It took a week of laborious searching for the army to conclude that all the dragons and daemons that had been conjured had all vanished. Their lasting legacy being the pain and loss of those left behind with a son, daughter, father or mother missing. The White Knight stayed in the castle during the search and did his part to help restore order to the kingdom. His experience dealing with such matters proved useful and he became admired for his intelligence as well as for his fighting skills.

The day came when King Chronos declared an end to official mourning and announced a holiday to celebrate the people's victory over evil. It was during the planning of the special day that the White Knight made the decision to leave the kingdom and travel the world once more. With peace and stability the ache in his heart returned and if he stayed in one tranquil spot with time for reflection it would make the pain unbearable.

During the night of the celebration, with the people feasting and music whistling through the streets the White Knight gently informed the king of his decision. Chronos, while unhappy his friend was leaving, understood the reason why and gave him provision and a large bag of gold to help him on his travels. He also swore to him his eternal friendship.

With that and a few last goodbyes to new friends the White Knight mounted his horse Victory and rode into the night. His heart was at once heavy with the knowledge of what he had given up but also eager to see the unknown and all the adventures that awaited him.

The End

Steve got up from his seat, gathered up his clothes and filled his laundry bag, another chore biting the dust. Returning to his apartment with the fresh laundry emanating cooling heat from the basket and into his arms, he immediately placed his bundle on the floor and plunked himself down upon his worn couch. After a brief momentary sigh, he looked about his small, tidy abode. The last thing to do on his Saturday ritual was to open his mail. This chore he saved last, for as long as he had unopened mail he could imagine that inside the envelopes were letters from long-lost friends who had sought him out or a missive from someplace else that would take him away from his current life and install him in a much better one.

Unsurprisingly, nothing like that was ever in his mail. Instead of letters from long, lost acquaintances, rather than urgent calls from libraries in some distant part of the world that needed his skills, there were bills. Bills for all sorts of things that Steve needed in order to make life bearable in his solitude, bills for the cable, heat, light, charge card and a host of others but nothing more. Today, though, was the day in which all that would change, for today there actually was an abnormal item in his pile of missives. On the bottom of the tiny stack of mail there was a letter, a communiqué that would change his life forever.

The correspondence was from a small private library in St. John's, Newfoundland that Steve never even knew existed. The letter said there was a need for a librarian to run the downtown branch operations of their company library. Apparently the manager of the library had heard from a friend of a friend that Steve was interested in returning to his native soil and that if Steve was willing to return he could have the job. The man who held the letter in his hand was astounded. At last here was a new opportunity to go home and finally re-establishing his life, his real life that he had abandoned two years ago to go on some insane adventure. What the hell was he going to do?

Even in his bitterness and despair, life had taken on a routine that was comfortable, and habit defined Steve's existence. To return to Newfoundland would mean a great upheaval and new routines would have to take the place of the old ones. Although this was everything that he wished for he would need to think about this offer. One does not just throw one's life into upheaval just because opportunity knocks. No, time needed to be spent on reflection before making a spur of the moment decision.

After his weekly chores, the lonely librarian usually took a walk about his neighbourhood in order to get some fresh air and exercise, a leisurely stroll to the supermarket where he would buy his grub for the week and this day was no exception. His pace was quicker than usual. The arrival of this exciting news jump-started him and it took less time to arrive at the store. Once there he hummed and hawed and eventually bought nothing. If he were to return home to St. John's why would he waste his money in buying food that would only be left over for the next renter to eat? It was best to save his money, walk through the supermarket isles and pause briefly only if the buxom Allison presented herself.

Today the lovely Allison did indeed present herself. She was once again stocking the shelves with tins of soup and since this was possibly the final time Steve might be in the presence of such a lovely creature as this he decided to pretend to read the labels of the tins near her. He caressed the hard cans and cautiously glimpsed down on the beautiful girl going about her work. Her lovely, large yet delicate breasts clung precariously to her loose-fitting white blouse and with every breath of her body Steve clutched the tin of chicken soup just a little more tightly. He could have exploded in his overwhelming desire for her as he gazed down on her perfect, sensuous body swaying in her own unique rhythm, keeping in time to only her own internal music.

"Excuse me young man," a loud, cracked voice said from behind. "But can you reach up and get for me a box of chicken broth?" It was a tiny, old woman and she was pointing up towards a brown box that was out of her reach. Slapped back to reality Steve was slightly embarrassed but nodded to the woman and tried to reach up for the elusive broth.

Unfortunately, the height was too much for his five foot ten frame and so the box remained unattainable. The woman then advanced toward Allison who by this time had stood up armed with a gorgeous, helping smile. Steve waited as Allison found a step ladder, reached up and snagged the elusive box. It was the most amazing sight Steve's eyes had seen since returning to Earth.

After his visit to the grocery store the rest of his Sunday was spent walking and talking, walking around his neighbourhood looking for some reason to say no to the offer and finding none. Talking to his family and friends who all told him to come home to the greatest place on Earth did not help matters. Of course, they wanted him to return but did he? New York for all its hustle was a status symbol for Steve. Just being there said something about him. It said that he could survive in one of the harshest jungles on the planet. It was an ephemeral, but powerful attraction.

Yet the lure of home was incredibly strong. Home meant for Steve a place with clean air, a world virtually free of violent crime. It was a place nicer, cleaner and more natural than his present environment. At home he could feel freer to be himself. At home he could be more natural. Being in New York felt alien to him and giving it up meant that once and for all he would never again have that feeling of being on a different world, even metaphorically again.

Despite the emotional tug, a decision had to come quickly and Steve decided that tomorrow would be the key day on whether to stay in New York or to return to the land of his birth. He made up his mind that Monday would be the day he would decide the future course of his life.

Monday morning arrived slowly for the restless librarian. Steve had stayed up all night thinking of the letter sitting on his small brown table. Images of home danced like drunken sheep through his head and scenarios of what might come next paraded in and out of his mind. He was grateful for once when the alarm sounded to begin another workweek. Perhaps the busy duties of the reference desk would take his mind off thoughts of home and bring clarity to his dilemma.

The morning did not begin smoothly for the troubled librarian, as the crowd that boarded the Staten Island ferry was unusually pushy, forcing the man to be thrust up onto the rails of the ship. The precariousness of his predicament was not lost on Steve. He knew that only the sliver of chain that connected the railings together protected him against the threatening tide and certain doom. One slip of that chain and his life would be over and that thought was not a pleasant one for the nervous man.

Fortunately for his sufferings the trip was over unusually fast. The ferry stopped with a thump and the crowd was herded back as a ferry worker arrived on the scene to open the gate and let the throng out. Steve, whose life was spared for the nonce, ticked off strike one against the Big Apple. Three strikes and he was outta there!

After the usual travels he at last arrived at the front of his library. Rather than immediately walking through the doors, he paused for a moment and looked up to assess his physical place of work. The building was not very striking and there was nothing at all glamorous about the concrete mass, but this was not grounds for strike two. So he sighed a little and walked into his place of work ready for a Monday-type workday.

Mondays meant that you had to talk to your co-workers about your weekend. Some variation of "How was your weekend?" was the question of choice that inevitably sprang out of the lips of those people whom you bumped into during the day. Of course, the question is purely perfunctory. Yet it is mandatory that the questioner receive a reply much like "Oh a little of this and a little of that," usually as one is walking away from the person who oh so politely asked. If either of the two, the inquirer or the inquired, actually took the question seriously the rules of the universe would slightly change. The questioner would be forced into actually listening to the answer and then search their brain for an appropriate response. This would in turn begin an actual conversation about how their weekends actually went and no one, neither the questioner nor the asked, really wanted to do something as silly or time-wasting like that.

This Monday morning the library workers were unusually animated. Instead of the after-thought-knee-jerk "Good mornings," there seemed to be an actual conversation going on between staff members. Steve took this chitter-chattering as a sign that something of monumental impact had transpired. What could have happened that would upset the routine of a normally coldly efficient library? Had a war broken out? Did someone erase the library catalogue? If something affected the library Steve wished to know. Who knows, perhaps it would help make up his mind.

Hesitantly, Steve walked up to a group of four library workers, two librarians and two assistants and before he asked the question he knew that the news would be bad. Librarians rarely talked to library assistants except to bark orders at them and while Steve never adhered to that particular custom he made a point to never overly fraternized with them either. One does not chew grass at a tobacco chewing contest. The four turned to Steve, and Joan, the redheaded clerk with a tendency for over-stamping the date due stickers, informed him the bad news. Dave, the security guard, had passed on.

The shock that hit Steve froze him to the spot. Who knew that there actually could have been something wrong with delusional, hypochondriac Dave? The man was a mountain, a tower of strength, a superb physical specimen that should have easily lasted for decades to come. He could have fought in the death arena in Maladred and come out a winner. If the man had a best before tag attached to him it would have been good for a long time to come. He searched back to the final time he saw the hulking man. Could it have been something that he said that aided in his demise? Did the friendly teasing that Steve enjoyed with the man go too far? Was he somehow an unwilling murderer?

Steve felt ill at the thought that he might be a murderer, a cold-blooded killer who frightened away the life of an innocent human being. Small short jabs emanated from his stomach as if invisible people had begun punching him mercilessly. A cold wave of nausea came over the guilt-ridden librarian and he felt the need to sit before he collapsed. Seeing his distress, the four library workers tried to console the man. "It was all over with in a second for him," Judy from periodicals quickly said. "The bus that struck him was going so fast that he probably never had time to feel a thing."

"Bus? Dave was killed by a bus?" Steve had to get confirmation that he was not a killer.

"Yes, he was killed by a runaway bus," one of the women repeated.

"Oh thank God!" the librarian crowed. "What a relief!" Standing up straight and noticing the blank stares he was receiving Steve quickly added, "Well, I think it is at least some small comfort that he did not suffer." Steve bid his adieus to the four women and walked to his work area where soon his mind wandered towards Dave, the unpredictability of life and death, and his own predicament.

Dave, for all his nonsense about his health, was just about the closest thing Steve had to a friend in the library. Without him the only reason that he could think of that could make him want to stay in New York was the hope of a romance with a certain children's librarian. That one hope was the silver that remained in the back of his dark cloud. That was the lone possibility that could keep him in the big city; for undoubtedly Dave's untimely departure from this Earth was strike two.

The day was filled with people's chatter about Dave's death and Steve could not help but feel depressed about the whole thing. Time lurched by in a dense fog; the patrons who asked their questions received only perfunctory service. It was only when the clock struck twelve did Steve show signs of any real life at all. If anyone could turn his funk around it would be the sight of Melinda, the woman on whom he hinged all his hopes.

Steve walked down to the break room where Melinda sat with two of her friends. Strangely, they looked excited rather than depressed or sad. Could it be possible they didn't hear the news about poor Dave? Steve walked over to the table where the three sat and joined them. Melinda smiled her usual cheerful smile, but there seemed to be a hint of extra happiness in her eyes, as if she had somehow tapped into a spring of joy that had hither been left dormant.

"Did you hear about Dave?" Steve asked. Melinda replied, "Yes, and it's terrible. In fact if I had known right away this morning I never would have blurted out my news, but I guess good news travels as fast as bad."

"What news?" Steve inquired.

"Oh, you don't know? I'm getting married," Melinda gleefully said. The sudden pain in Steve's stomach came so quickly that he thought he would like to literally drop dead just to make the agony go away. Here was not only strike three but four, five, six, seven and on up to and including any given very large number. Without Melinda to fantasize about Steve was packed, on the plane and drinking several pints at his local pub in downtown St. John's before Melinda could say another word. Unfortunately though, not having the super speed powers of the super hero The Flash, Steve could only do his best to squeak out a congratulatory reply.

"Why, that's great," Steve said in his best William Shatner impersonation voice. "I am so happy for you."

Steve squirmed in his chair, his testicles rose up into his body; he desperately needed to get the hell out of the room but knew that if he just up and left it would look suspicious. So he stayed while he listened to how Bill, her newly minted fiancé, proposed. It was such a charming and wonderful proposal with lots of flowers, sweet romantic music, gushes of tears and heaped with all the Harlequin fixings that Steve wished for a moment that an errant bus would smash through the wall behind him and hit him too.

At last the longest lunch break in the history of breaks was mercifully over. Melinda and her friends got up, wished Steve a good day and left, still huddled around the sparkling ring on Melinda's hand. Steve, on the other hand, found that he could not move his body. The shocks of the day proved to be overwhelming to the sensitive soul from Newfoundland and it took a good five minutes before he could lift his heavy frame off the wooden chair and slowly begin to move upstairs and back to his workstation.

On his way to the reference desk a horrible sight awaited him. It was the Master of Evil and she looked to be headed in his direction. Fate, it seemed, had chosen this day to be one of the worst days of Steve's life and it was not going to get any better until he was at last in bed having the dark nightmares he knew would surely follow his time in the conscious part of the day.

"You," the blubberous one spat out pointing her finger. "You should have been at your desk a full seven minutes ago. Just where do you think you are working?" The Master of Evil had both her hands on her large hips, challenging him to explain himself. Steve looked at the thing in front of him and fumed. In no mood to be congenial and with a guaranteed job back home, he saw no need to be polite.

"Go to hell, you rancid cow," Steve spurted out for starters. "I am sick to death of you and your Nazi ways. You can take this job and stick it where you can't reach it, in other words your arse!" Steve could have gone on but he was too piping hot to speak. Instead fuming, nostrils flared, he walked around the startled woman, grabbed his coat and stormed out of the library and into the crowded streets of New York City. His days as a poorly paid New York Public Library flunky were now over.

His abrupt departure was purely an emotional response brought about by the death of his closest acquaintance and the shocking announcement from the woman whose mere glance brought joy to his mundane existence. Now both his reasons for sticking it out in a library managed by a modern equivalent to Hermann Goering were either dead literally or buried beneath the knowledge that his last chance at happiness in New York had found joy without him. It was a harsh blow and one that needed to be immediately numbed.

In a daze, Steve sauntered past teems of people all seemingly more happy than himself down to 915 Third Avenue, East 55th Street to PJ Clarke's Saloon, the bar where Ray Milland began his lost weekend. Steve entered the establishment, walked up to the broad, wooden bar and ordered a drink from a large, dark haired bartender who had seen the dazed, hurt look in Steve's eyes a million times before. In moments a pint of the bar's best bitter was sitting in front of the former New York Public Library librarian.

With refreshing beer came some clarity and a restored calmness. The cascade of soothing froth gently flowing down his throat was a salve for his troubles. It was a tonic for the list of his ailments that were growing exponentially in number. First and foremost he has just quit his job. No problem, he had another one already lined up. Second, he had lost his only true semi-friend in New York to a horrible albeit quick death. Oh well, these things can't be avoided and he could always meet another friend/acquaintance. Last, his heart had been broken, that was the tough one. Carrying a flame for a girl is always tough, but having it extinguished in such a shocking and sudden manner was cold cruelty. She didn't know it and never would but she had inflicted a terrible blow, the kind of dreadful shock that demanded copious amounts of beer to dull.

With alcohol came sadness, a depressant for the depressed. Steve had just raised his fourth beer to his lips and mouthed the words, "hmmm, beer foamy," when his sharply honed survival instincts took over. The cruel hard fact of urban life is that no one gives a sweet damn about you. Life is cheap and there are sulking vultures willing to take advantage of any weakness. They hide in the shadows and are everywhere eager to pounce. So Steve, one nudge short of miserable, but still capable of reason, decided it was best to simply go home and drink about the day's events.

Chapter Five

Ready to Go

When Steve made up his mind to do something that something was usually done in very quick fashion. Now that his time with the New York Public Library was over, he was ready to move on towards his new goal. After a night spent with twelve of his coldest friends, he arose the next afternoon slightly dazed, but ready to go forward with his life rather than dwell on the recent past. Baptizing the cobwebs away with a thorough dousing of his aching head in the sink he paused only slightly to look in the small bathroom mirror at his red-eyed reflection before saying out loud to himself, "All right pally, let's get to work."

Work meant giving the number on the letter he had received from St. John's a call to ensure that he still had the job that was offered to him. The phone shook slightly in his hand as the last digit was punched and the ringing began. "Hello, Joe Simon's Archive and Museum," answered the call. Steve informed the woman on the end of the line who he was and soon he was transferred to a Mr. Stan Cleary who was in charge of human resources. Yes, indeed, the job was still open and it was Steve's for the taking. Apparently the last librarian had to quit due to an unfortunate occurrence and someone was needed quickly to fulfill the position. The director heard that Steve was looking to return home from a friend of his and that he might be interested in a position. Rather than go through a lengthy interview process it was decided to contact him first to see if indeed he was interested in the job.

It was only a matter of minutes from the time of Steve's enthusiastic acceptance of the job to the working out of the minor details. The salary would be reasonable in comparison with other librarians' wages in Newfoundland and he would have to be ready for work in two weeks, more than enough time to clue up any outstanding business he would have in New York.

It was like a dream come true to Steve. When he hung up the phone he was on cloud ten, even cloud nine was too low for him. Imagine, a job in his hometown! Now that it was real all the soul-searching of the past two days seemed ridiculous. The decision had been made and he was as happy as a cat in an occupied birdcage. He was about to go home and that was something few Newfoundlanders did once they had left the province. Hell! He had to leave the planet to have gotten his last job.

The many minute details of his quick removal from his life in New York now flooded his mind. Fortunately he had the foresight to ensure an opt-out option in his lease that he could invoke at anytime. This was unusual in a lease, but he claimed that he needed it as he had an ailing mother back home and that he might be called away to take care of her at anytime. The landlord, an elderly woman herself, sympathized with the man and ensured him in writing that whenever he needed to leave he would be accommodated. After a brief call the woman was true to her word and he was free to leave. Steve knew that while New Yorkers displayed gruff exteriors many of them had hearts of gold.

The next step was a trifle more harsh. The plane ticket to St. John's was going to be harmful to Steve's thinly-packed wallet. A one-way trip to St. John's proved much too expensive; however, a trip to Toronto was reasonably cheap. A few phone calls later to friends in Canada's unofficial capital informed him that it would be cheaper to buy his ticket to Toronto and then take a plane to St. John's from there. Overall it would save him a couple of hundred dollars and as well he could visit a few friends in the bargain. In the end that is precisely what he did.

Soon all the arrangements he needed to make were made. He would fly to Toronto in three days time, which was just long enough to take care of all his last minute details in New York. In Toronto he would stay with friends for a couple of days before continuing his journey to St. John's where he would quickly re-establish his life back in his old homestead. It was a brilliant plan if he did say so himself and indeed he did.

With his plans for the future already taken care of Steve decided that he might as well take care of some of the remaining loose ends. First he decided to formally quit his job rather than merely leave in a huff. Steve thought that he couldn't hurt his image with the head office of the New York Public Library if he explained just why he felt it necessary to leave immediately rather than give the nominal two weeks notice. He would simply state that he was an orange is a city of apples. While it was with some unease that he left his apartment to go off to Manhattan, he hoped that this was the last unhappy experience he would have to deal with in his last days in the city of dreams.

Surprisingly, Steve found that he had arrived just in time to meet the train which had been just in time to greet the Staten Island Ferry which was just in time to coincide with the subway train to the stop where the head office of the New York Public Library was. It was an amazing alignment of public transport. He mused that only if he were headed to the dentist would the journey be any faster.

The nervous librarian walked into one of the many tall buildings that permeate downtown Manhattan and entered a slow-moving elevator that emptied him out onto a hallway, which led to the human resources hub of the N.Y.P.L. Steve was greeted by an attractive secretary who, after listening to the reason why he was there, motioned for him to sit down while she got someone who was able to help him.

Steve looked at the photos on the wall for a moment or three until finally the first woman arrived with a second woman who looked like a librarian's version of television's Murphy Brown. Tall, well-dressed, attractive but with the typical hair bun and glasses that makes stereotypes out of all librarians, the woman ushered Steve into a small yet comfortable office.

"Well, we have heard quite a lot about you of late," the woman said. "Very seldom does the human resource department get such heated calls from one of our head librarians." The woman gave a slight hint of a smile when she said this that was off-putting for Steve. He wondered what kinds of things she had been hearing. The closed world of librarianship was populated by many gossips and rumormongers.

"I must apologize if my departure seemed abrupt, but the thing is I was greatly upset over the death of one of my friends in the library. That coupled with the fact that I have never gotten along with the head of the library made me boil over to the point where I couldn't hold back my displeasure any longer. I now wish to formally quit my position from the library where I, until yesterday, worked." Steve wished to add that the Master of Evil was the nastiest piece of work he had ever encountered and that perhaps she was the result of a failed military experiment, but he decided to forgo the colourful depictions and stick to the facts.

The woman seated across from him seemed very sympathetic with the disgruntled librarian before her. She had heard complaints before from other disenchanted staff workers at that particular branch and so she decided not to give Steve too much of a hard time. Obviously he would lose any benefits or pay that would be coming to him if he was to work the normal notice time and she mentioned that it would be better not to have the New York Public Library on his future reference list. Beyond that she considered the matter closed, made the man sign the proper forms, held out her hand and wished the newly freed librarian good luck in the future.

Steve turned his back on the attractive library official, hesitated, then decided to ask a question. "Excuse me. I just have to ask, just who the hell would hire a lunatic like that mad woman to run a branch library anyway?" He did not add that the Inter Galactic Library Board would never hire someone than nasty, and they hired T-Bad the Abominable Terror from the planet Nova.

The woman replied that she was not involved with that decision and did not know who hired the woman. That seemed unusual now that she had to actually think about it but explained that she must have been on holiday that week. She shrugged her shoulders and once again wished the man good luck.

Steve left the office gladly and felt that the spirit of liberation had suddenly come down upon him and set him free. He never had to look upon his doughy boss again. No longer would he have to take that terrible three hour trek back and forth to work, never again would he be ill-treated by an unruly patron looking to heap unwarranted abuse on a public servant. He was free, free to choose a new direction in his life and he chose to go home.

The return to Staten Island was uneventful and Steve spent the rest of the day cleaning his apartment. Knowing that he had received a kindness given to him by his landlady he wanted to make sure that he would leave his present home in immaculate condition. He scrubbed, dusted and polished every portion of his apartment. By the end of the day, dirty and exhausted, he was only too willing to visit his shower and go to sleep.

The last time a person knowingly does anything somehow increases every little thing's importance, so it was with Steve's last full day in New York City. It was hard to believe but this was the last full day of his life in the grand city. Sure he might visit the place again but this was the last day he could say he was a New Yorker and that was a big thing to him. To many people in St. John's going to New York was the same as saying you went to the moon. The grand metropolis was another world to them so Steve prepared in his mind for his final day as if he was Neal Armstrong looking at the lunar dust one last time before taking off to Earth.

There was nothing he wanted to see on Staten Island itself the island was a quiet place compared to the nearby sprawling metropolis. New York City, the place of John Lennon, Tiffany's, Radio City Music Hall, the United Nations, King Kong and so much stuff you'd think that the entire world started and ended in New York, that's the town Steve wanted to see for the final time. For the first time in a long time the ferry ride to the big city didn't seem like a chore. Steve actually held his head up high looking around at the scenes and people around him. He even obligingly took photos for the early morning tourists. Yes, Steve was a jolly fellow indeed that morning of his last full day in the Big Apple.

After the familiar thump of the ferry Steve set out to walk the city, or at least as much as his feet could stand. He walked up the section of streets known as Alphabet Soup where he paused to see a large, disheveled man swaying unsteadily back and forth near an outside wall. The urine than streamed out of him struck an ironic chord as it splashed on a single word etched on the concrete - that word was Hope.

Walking on and upward Steve witnessed life, not the dull, listless life he had been leading but a potpourri of zest and vigor that he had not, or refused to, encounter. A fight between an Asian shopkeeper clashing with an upper class businessman over reading a newspaper without paying strolled out into the sidewalk. "You mo pay! You mo read!" the screaming shopkeeper screamed, wildly waving his fist at the man with a crumpled newspaper in his hand.

Onward Steve went, strolling along seeing a giant picture of the Amazing Spiderman on a building wall, watching the police guide traffic with unchallenged authority, buying from the billionth hot dog stand that he saw. Life; vigorous, extravagant and alive was exhibiting itself along the streets and byways that Steve walked by, lost in his own world.

On his wanderings he chanced upon, either consciously or not, the branch library that only two days before was his employer and his existence. It was not until he was almost past the library did Steve realize where he was and he stopped suddenly when he saw the sight that laid itself out in front of him. It was Melinda coming out of the large doors arm in arm with a somewhat portly gentleman who at first Steve thought might had been her father. On further inspection, or, in other words, when the man's drooling tongue snaked its way down her pure, downy throat, he changed his mind about the status of the man and assumed that this might possibly be the fiancé. Steve's first thought was that he had only previously seen tongue action like that on an Aldorian troll and even he had to work hard to match the maneuvers that Mel's fiancé was achieving.

This was too much of a blow for Steve to take. He turned away before the delicious Melinda could see him and as the happy couple turned left and he turned right Steve did his best to stifle a tear. He didn't know if he ever truly loved that magnificent girl but he regretted that he let the opportunity to know go by.

Despite this disturbing episode the day was still not quite ruined for Steve. He walked on and after a little spell of inner grief he began to think that perhaps it was all for the best. He had little to offer that glorious flower and she deserved the best. Perhaps with her gnome she could have all the things that money could buy, a nice house, a sensible car and many other things that a poor librarian could never afford. Yes, perhaps it was all for the best, but that would never completely nullify the pain in his heart that would sting whenever he thought of his beloved Melinda.

Soldiering on, he made his way to Central Park where he saw what seemed to be the world playing and laughing in that carefree way he thought reserved only for soda commercials. He went through the large grounds surveying the statues and watching the girls go by. Standing by a statue he tried to take in all in, one final day in one of the world's most famous parks; but, in the end, feeling empty, he sighed a defeated sigh and turned to slump towards home.

On his way back he once again saw the two lovers come out of what looked like a party store. "No doubt planning the big event," he bitterly thought. Still trying to be cautious he did his best to cross the street before he was recognized but this time he had ran out of luck. Traffic in downtown Manhattan is notorious for its delaying effect and it had halted the anxious man in his tracks. "Rats!" he shouted to himself as he saw her motioning for him to come over.

"Steve! My goodness there you are. Where have you been?" Melinda observed him closely for a moment as if she were looking for something.

"Well, I've been wandering around just killing time," Steve replied as he wondered just what it was she was staring at.

"At least I got to see you before you went in," Melinda said. Steve had no clue as to what she as talking about, his only interest was to end this conversation as quickly as possible so he didn't have to bathe any longer than necessary in the couple's infinitely irritating happy glow. "The wake is almost ending so you better get in quick. By the way, let me introduce you to my fiancé. Steve, this is Bill."

Steve unwillingly shook the chubby man's hands, he wouldn't have liked to faced off with the fellow in a pie eating contest but he assumed there must have been some good qualities in the man, perhaps an ample wallet to go along with his ample frame. Yes, he knew that just that thought was unjust but he was bitter and depressed damn it! Give him a break! "Well, I better get going," Steve said after a few seconds/decades pause.

"Yes, you better be going in if you are to say goodbye to David." Melinda flashed one last drop-dead gorgeous smile at the man she never knew and continued on arm in arm with the man she loved. Steve watched as the two walked down the street, turned a corner and out of his life. Steve was about to go on again when a tapping on his shoulder made him turn around. It was Joan, another former co-worker from the library. "Man, I am seeing more of these people a day after I quit then I ever did in my time working with them," he mused.

"Steve, so glad you could make it. Come in and pay your respects to David's poor family," the annoying woman wearing a crisp black dress said. She waved the bewildered man into what he thought to be a store for party supplies but once inside he realized how wrong he was. He was shocked to discover upon looking at a sign over the door that read 'Time's Up Funeral Parlor' that he was inside the most bizarre funeral home he had ever had the displeasure to be in. For a start the interior was painted in odd colours with reds and deep blues everywhere. The lighting was bright and happy and the atmosphere was creepily cheerful for a funeral parlor. "David is in room number three," the thin woman said.

Wishing not to be impolite and a tad curious over what he would discover the man walked to room number three and peered inside. There he saw festive lighting, recliner chairs with coffee holders in the arms, party streamers hanging down from the ceiling and a miniature bar in one corner of the room. In the middle of it all was a shinny, bright blue coffin with the body of Dave the security guard inside. He had forgotten about Dave's funeral, with all the confusion as to his quitting and plans for leaving the final voyage of his friend had been all but deleted from his thoughts. Now fate had put him and his only quasi friend in New York City together one last time, he could not help but feel a little bit guilty at his absentmindedness.

He walked slowly over to the coffin and looked down on his friend. "Holy Mother Goose! Is he smiling?" an astonished Steve asked out loud.

"Yes, it's the policy of the funeral home that all customers must be entirely happy, or your money back" a nearby mourner said matter of factly.

"But, but his face looks like something the Joker would be proud of." Steve was referring to Batman's arch enemy whose victims would acquire grotesque smiles as they were murdered. It was unnerving to see Dave's face, which was always in a state of grimacing or worry, now looking as if he had laughed himself to death. It was a total misrepresentation of the man and it was if Steve had not known him at all, which to be fair to the funeral home operators he really did not.

Steve stayed for a while talking to some of Dave's friends and family, many of whom talked about how David always spoke about the kind man from Newfoundland who talked to him in such an honest fashion. "David was truly grateful for your friendship. He thought of you as his best friend in that library," David's weeping mother told the now obviously embarrassed man.

With all the love and regard that was apparent for the recently departed Dave Steve wondered why was he being waked in such a gaudy and unsuitable setting? Steve posed the question to Dave's buxom cousin Cindy who despite the solemn occasion still felt it was necessary to show off her more than ample assets. The answer he received was that he had won the funeral with all the trimmings a year or two earlier while surfing the Internet late on another lonely Friday night. Apparently a new variety of funeral home was having a promotion for their business. David won by creating the slogan "We'll put the fun back in funeral." For coining such an inventive phrase he won his own funeral with all the fixings. "Most people obsessed with dying don't get a thing out of it but not our dear David," the tiny girl proudly squeaked into a moist handkerchief.

After a polite amount of time elapsed Steve paid his final respects to the family and exited the colourful establishment. He shook his head a little as he walked down the street trying to figure out if anyone but him thought that having a farewell party in a place like Time's Up! Funeral Parlor was a little odd. Still, there were all types of people in New York City and that was something that was special about the place. Steve began to walk towards the ferry and home both glad and sad that he was finally leaving this wonderfully bizarre city.

Walking out the door it suddenly hit him that he never really had a chance to say goodbye to the space library he called home for almost two full years. It all had happened so fast that he only now realized that he was still suffering from shock from all that had happened to him. One day he was living a dream life of space librarianship then all his co-workers get blasted, his library gets blown up and he gets investigated by suspicious library board aliens then gets unceremoniously deposited in a new city at night with nary a cent to his name. Yeah, that's something that could screw you up for some time.

Once home he found that packing up his life was simpler than he would have thought. There was little to it in the end, some books, some nick-knacks, some clothes, a phone and a clock radio. Steve decided to leave his small television because in some small way he felt a kinship to the previous renter who had been either kind or in too much of a hurry to take his possessions.

The next morning he took his bags in his hands, reached the front door, turned and looked about once more. It was the end of an era for him. He had lived through his New

York experience and was about to go on a new journey to an old land. He smiled for a second, and then closed the door on his living in America experience.

Chapter Six

Toronto

You can be forgiven for the panicked thought that you had gotten on the wrong flight when going through customs at Pearson International Airport. Everyone working in the area it seems has a long beard and sports a turban. The greetings of "Welcome to my country," in Indian dialect that come from the genuine and smiling faces of the customs officers do not help to alleviate such fears and it is not until one actually leaves the confines of customs and walks through the exit towards the luggage carrousels that you at last accept the reality that you are in fact in Canada, or to be more precise, in Toronto.

Toronto, Ontario is the multi-cultural hub of Canada and it accepts all manner of colours, creed or gender. Whatever it is you are you will accepted and it is more than likely that you will find another one of you in Toronto. It was in this smorgasbord of humanity that Steve found himself the day he arrived back on Canadian soil.

Canada, the United States' younger sister, has a great personality, but to all other nations seems is a little on the dull side. Canada, the politest country in the world, if there was one country you could take home to meet the folks, Canada was definitely it. It is such a nice, quiet country.

Canada is a place of ice hockey, 'pleases', 'thank yous' and 'pardon mes', quite the opposite of where Steve had left.

Standing outside the airport terminal Steve inhaled his first taste of fresh, Canadian air. Tasty. Now it was time to head into the city. Airport Express is a bus service that heads into Toronto proper every 15 minutes, so despite the occasional prodding of the taxi drivers lurking about hunting for rides, Steve sauntered up to a youngish woman in a Plexiglas booth and purchased a return ticket. He held the ticket in his hand and thought about what would happen next.

Three days, that's what he had given himself to meet old friends, fellow refugees from Newfoundland who had to go elsewhere to find gainful employ. It was not that he could not spend a year, or even the rest of his life, spending time with the vast tribe of Newfoundlanders that inhabit the city and its boroughs. There were plenty of comrades he could visit here but the urge to get back home was strong and he needed to grow roots and enter into a new routine as soon as possible.

When it arrived the large Airport Express bus was half-full with people of all shapes, colours and sizes. Most of the occupants were people returning from someplace else and were visibly tired from their various travels. Others like Steve were arriving for a quick visit to friends and relatives, to attend a wedding or some other special affair. Steve searched and found an empty double-seat and, after placing his travel bag on the cozy seat next to him to dissuade fellow travelers, claimed it for his own. The bus door shut and with a sudden lurch the ride had begun to Toronto proper.

The view along the way to downtown Toronto is not impressive. Large rows of traffic and even bigger rows of still more traffic greet those driving in to the metropolis. Some days you might get lucky and see one of the many accidents that pock the highway and block the lanes creating congestions and angry noise of blaring horns and screaming people always in a hurry. Gray buildings hurl by at a rushed speed, objects that might be advertisements of one sort or another blur into one big mass of nothingness.

Whatever else the trip may be it is also fairly quick and soon Steve was dispatched outside the Royal York hotel, a fancy, large, impressive hotel, one of the many in downtown Toronto. Steve surveyed his situation for a minute then proceeded to take action. He had in his side pocket the name and phone number of one of his closest friends and at once he fished it out. Searching for change and finding some he headed for the nearest pay phone and quickly punched in the number.

"Hello, Neal. Yep, that's right I am finally back in Canada. I was hoping you'd be free tonight for a few beers. All right, I will see you tonight at eight at the Friar and the Firkin." Steve hung up happy in the knowledge that he was going to see one of his friends again. He had thought about asking Neal to put him up for the few days he would be in Toronto but decided he would not impose. Instead Steve decided to head for the Toronto youth hostel located on 76 Church Street. Church Street was near the heart of the homosexual community but as Steve had no prejudice in that regards he soon was in a taxi and taken to the hostel's front door.

The hostel was busy; a lineup had formed in front of a large desk manned by two young people, one man and one woman. The couple appeared jaded by their tasks as if the sunny pamphlet that enticed them to their jobs had somehow intentionally misled them and now having giving up on being friendly merely worked to stifle their inevitably growing disappointment. The people who they served suffered under the tyranny of indifference.

In any lineup there is always one person whose responsibility it seems is to hold up progress. This particular line was no different and the person whose job to engage the desk attendants' time was an overweight man with a harsh German accent. The complaint was a minor one, something to do with check out time, but as with such people who make such minor complaints an explanation must be long, totally satisfactory and repeated over and over again to ensure every nuance is captured.

So people fumed, the lineup got longer and Steve patiently waited. Hostels were cheap and relatively secure. Sure some are better than others but in Steve's opinion they were the best bang for the buck anywhere in the universe. At last the needy, bitter man with the thick German accent had his answer and the line moved once more. Steve quickly got the key card to his room and after a brief stop to drop off his luggage decided the best thing to do was to re-familiarize himself with the city.

The streets of Toronto have little in common with the streets of Manhattan. The streets in Toronto seem dirty and it is accepted to see homeless people sitting down begging for change or simply lying in a dark corner with their sleeping bags curled up in an uncomfortable manner, signs of various proportions near their person pleading for passers-by to bestow a trifle. The love for your fellow man is in short supply in the cold, unforgiving city and it seemed to Steve as if the hard face of capitalism that he would have expected to see in New York City had made its home instead in Toronto.

Steve wandered through the streets watching life unfold around him. Young Street is the longest street in North America but to Steve the tiny Young Street in St. John's had more vigor in it. There were Taco Bells, McDonalds, department stores, bookstores and a potpourri of other places designed to take you away from your money. Above the shops and trinket stores are offices, many, many offices teeming with people who all seem to be wearing the same set of clothes. But there was no true vitality there, no real signs of humanity. It was if a copy of life had been made, and a poor facsimile at best.

Rather than go into any of the stores Steve walked on until he spied the banners for the Royal Ontario Museum, one of the most spectacular museums in Canada. Steve's love of history led him up the large steps and into the museum. What greeted him was a gift store, an empty restaurant and a large reception desk eager to take your admission. Steve sauntered up to the desk where he paid the exorbitant $18.00 fee to the smiling uniformed ticket seller and after being given a small, red, tin badge to show off to the world that he had paid his fare he entered.

The collection in the ROM is jam-packed with artifacts from around the world and from all periods of time. Steve marveled at the large Buddhas around him; then he began to view the exhibits. He walked through the rooms and the floors and sensed the history that unfolded around him. Ancient civilizations called out to him yearning to tell him their secrets. Faces chipped in stone looked at him, figures in paint and oil called to him, armor and dresses enticed him with tales from their previous owners. The past shouted out to him demanding attention and for hours he lavished upon them all he could.

Steve had once visited a museum on a small asteroid nearby his library but he got little from the visit. Looking at old laser pistols, energy sabers, transporter rooms and all sorts of technology that to the universe was so old and useless but to Earth would have been wonders. But to Steve there was no connection as all the artifacts were from other species, other worlds to which he had not belonged. The ROM though was nothing like that.

Along the passageways through time he encountered many people both famous and forgotten. Caesars of long ago, Kings and Queens of yesterday, farmers, politicians, warriors, mothers and daughters and fathers and sons all stared at the visitors walking aimlessly past. The world of history revealed itself in every room calling to people to come, begging for its story to be heard.

As he wandered Steve encountered the typical school groups in one of the most popular exhibits of the ROM, the dinosaur room. Here in this large showroom creatures from millions of years long gone by are gawked at by over-excited children and by bored teenagers everyday. This day was no exception and the peace of the pottery exhibit was nowhere to be experienced here. Steve never enjoyed school trips even when he was a boy except on the one occasion that his class went to the Pop Shop back home, never in a billion years would any child disapprove of free pop.

The presence of children ruined the atmosphere of learning. Screaming, shouting, running around the loud, snotty-nosed youths tainted the dino-experience for Steve. He hoped for a moment that the dead, flesh-deprived creatures would suddenly sprout to life and begin eating the unruly beasts. With a sigh the disturbed man decided to go to a less crowded room where surely there should be some sign of peace.

The Egyptian exhibit was one of the more interesting ones for Steve and probably for most people who visit the museum. Here are real dead bodies to gawk at. Steve studied the dried-up corpses and thought out loud. "What the hell were you thinking?" The mummies did not answer. Hundreds, perhaps thousands of people milled their way through the glossy coffin staring at the body inside. Steve thought that this was not the way the man or woman inside the tattered cloth had imagined the afterlife.

Hours of cheerful exploring and learning later, Steve looked down at his watch and with a sigh realized that his time in the museum was about done. He had to meet his friend at the pub and that coupled with the rumble of his stomach forced his mind away from history and to his present day hunger. With a bit of reluctance the faux archeologist walked down the stairs and out of the museum pausing only to return his tin badge to the ticket attendant.

It wasn't a long walk to the Friar and the Firkin but to Steve's yearning stomach every step was too short. Soon he was practically sprinting to the pub and at long last when he did arrive he had a warm trickle of sweat running down his forehead. He made a mental note to lose a few pounds when he returned home to Newfoundland. He inwardly promised to begin a diet right after he'd finish a few burgers that night. Down the five concrete steps he went, opened the heavy door and entered the dark pub.

It took a few moments for Steve's eyes to adjust to the dim lighting but when they did so he discovered that besides the staff and a few people sipping on a beer he was alone, his friend was not there. Rather than worry over the fate of his pal Steve sauntered up to the bar and ordered an Upper Canada Rebellion Ale. Finding a seat in a quiet corner of the pub that had a good view of the front door, he sat down, gulped his beer and waited.

Twenty minutes elapsed before his friend appeared in the front door. Twenty minutes in which Steve thought about his new life in his home city, his new job that he so far knew nothing about and many other unrelated things. Twenty minutes can be a long time when you are alone in a dark pub waiting for someone.

Neal had been a financial planner for a major corporation and had been living in Toronto for the past ten years. An ex-patriot of Newfoundland, like so many others he received his degree from Memorial University then went off in search of a job. Eventually he found one in Canada's big city and there he had stayed ever since. He sat down at Steve's table and ordered a round, the night was about to begin. The burgers were big, the talk was fast and furious and the time was quick.

After the small talk had ended Steve and Neal got to the important business of drinking copious amounts of alcohol. Round for round they went until their heads were spinning round and round. Soon the pub they had been in began to grow tiresome and they headed out for excitement.

Sometimes, men who have been drinking together for a while get an urge to go wild and this night the two friends decided to do just that. First on the agenda was more booze and with all the lighted signs showing the way it was not hard to find a suitable place. Walking in the doors of a dance club the two men were hit with a wave of sound so loud they couldn't decide if it was the alcohol or the deafening sounds that staggered them.

The flashing lights, the pounding, drumming noise and unintelligible chatter all combine for the experience of the typical nightclub scene. Maneuvering their way through the crowd the pair made it to the long, thick bar and waved to the tall, attractive woman bartender for service. Once their order was taken and cash exchanged they were once again plowing through the throng and to a reasonably uncrowded portion of the club where they could observe the action around them.

Clubs can be a lot of things to a lot of people. Some people go to simply dance and have an enjoyable evening, others try to find a companion for the night or forever and still others are celebrating an occasion. For the two Newfoundlanders overlooking the events from a corner of the facility who had no reason to be in a club besides the fact that there was booze for sale they quickly became bored. With glances to each other they downed their drinks and walked outside once more.

After mulling it over for a moment there was only one thing they could think to do. "Strippers?" Steve asked Neal in mock innocence.

"Strippers." He replied as if that was the answer to a profound question and off they went in search of attractive women who dance without clothes for remuneration.

The Brass Rail is one of the more popular exotic clubs in Toronto. Clean and relatively unthreatening, it is a place where people who wish to be entertained by the fine art of exotic dancing go to enjoy the centuries-old tradition. There the talented artists perform for paying customers who are among the most vocal and enthusiastic of all audiences in the world of entertainment.

The men stood outside in line waiting for their opportunity to enter the popular club. Soon they were herded inside; surprisingly, there was no cover fee. They sat in a nice table and watched a beautiful woman wearing a cowboy hat and gun holsters dance for a hollering crowd. The attendance for the show was made up of mostly men though there were a surprisingly significant proportion of females in the audience as well. This was a sign of the times, where today's tuxedos and burlesque have taken over yesteryears' seediness and bump and grind.

It was in an exotic club's interest to project a veneer of elegance. By doing so management encourages a "better" crowd who will pay more for drinks than the lusty mob of the past and, as the owners know, the cash is in the drinks. With this in mind attractive women prowl the pack of customers continually asking them to "freshen" their drinks at exorbitant prices. It is always this way in an exotic nightclub and all who enter such an establishment should be aware of this trick.

With bosoms bouncing everywhere and drinks flowing expensively, Steve was in the perfect mood to be victimized by trawling lap dancers. Soon, in a dreamy haze, Steve was led away by a dancer, who looked exactly how he imagined comic book reporter Lois Lane to look like, to a small corner of the bar where the more intimate dancing was held. As the woman jumped on the librarian's crotch he wondered if somewhere overhead in the night sky he was getting into deep, deep trouble with Superman.

"So where are you from?" the pseudo-heroine inquired.

"Newfoundland," the man murmured while maintaining his focus on her ample bosom.

"What part of Vancouver is that?" she innocently asked. Steve cringed and was grateful when the music began and the beautiful woman started to gyrate on his lap most agreeably. He had hoped the DJ would play the lengthy "Stairway to Heaven" but in what seemed like to Steve two seconds the song was over and the disappointed man was passing a twenty-dollar bill over to the pleased artiste who pleasantly took the money, quickly turned and looked for more men to entice. Steve staggered back to his waiting friend who, feeling a tad peckish, wanted to go looking for food to quiet his now ravenous hunger.

Out the pair went in search of chow. It didn't take too long to see a closing McDonalds and the two entered, courtesy of an exiting patron, into the fast food emporium. Sighing but not wanting any trouble from drunken people the young girl behind the counter quickly asked for the two men's order. The menu must have been placed in a precarious position because the sign moved to and fro as the men tried to make an order. Soon there were many hamburgers placed in front of the hungry men and the ravenous began their feast. The Cookie Monster would have in comparison seemed to have more delicate eating skills then the two gentlemen sitting down in a small stall. Pieces of burger flew out of their mouths, ketchup ran down their chins and Coke drooled from the sides of their mouths.

Finally, tired and satiated the men decided that they had enough for the night. Neal and Steve left the restaurant and bid their adieus under the stars wishing each other a good night. Steve decided that he was well enough to walk back to his hostel. He spun about a couple of times then went off Northward.

On he strolled past chilled to the bone prostitutes begging to be of service; by dangerous looking characters in dark corners and past trembling children hidden on the streets with yellow, hollow eyes. He continued on witnessing all manner of sin and disorder, walking past both filthy rich and cleaned-out poor. Saints selling salvation and degenerates pimping innocence, the night belonged to them all.

Steve made his way back to his lodging and, with a wave to the uninterested man behind the thick reception desk, went inside the elevator and up to his room where he then went to sleep. His rest, alas, was not a peaceful one. Something haunted him, an image that was all at once beautiful and frightening. The image burned in his dreams all night but once he had awoken he had forgotten it had even existed. The thought of ham and scrambled eggs moved the specter from one side of his mind and into the dark recesses on his memory.

Breakfast, so the saying goes, is the most important meal of the day and Steve believed in that cliché with a passion. It was a rare day in the librarian's life when he did not sit down next to a plate of eggs, toast and tea in the early morning. This was not one of those days. The communal showers were thankfully empty when Steve entered to engage in his wake up cleansing, most of his fellow hostlers were young so they were either sleeping in until late or had already gone exploring. Exploration was not on the man's mind at the moment rather it was the first taste of ham and eggs that filled his thoughts.

Breakfast can be cheap, reasonable or expensive in Toronto, but it had almost always been Steve's experience that a cheap breakfast can be just as filling as an expensive one and far more satisfying. So with that thought in mind the man quickly got dressed and headed out onto the streets to find the perfect breakfast for a reasonable price. It didn't take too long for the man to find what he was looking for and in a manner of minutes he was seated looking at the breakfast menu of a small, tidy diner.

During his wait for victuals, he began to overhear a conversation between two men drinking coffee in the booth behind his back that whiffed its way through the restaurant and into Steve's unwilling ears. "So, did you see her last night?" asked the first man excitedly.

"Yeah, I saw her last night." the second man replied. "Man, she was hot in her tight sweater, mini leather skirt and big tits." Steve could almost feel the lust emanating from the man behind him as he continued on for some time in his admiration of his girl's apparently very generous attributes.

"So, what did you do?" the friend asked excitedly.

"Well, I took her out on the town to show her off, we had a few drinks, and I pretended to listen to all her wacky troubles. Man, can she whine! Then it was back to her place for a good, no I mean fantastic time, if you know what I mean." The man chuckled and almost choked on his gulp of coffee.

"So, are you going to see her again tonight?" the interested second party asked.

"No, I better stay home tonight and spend some time with the wife and kids. My wife's stupid but she ain't THAT dumb." The man laughed heartily at his little inside joke, and then as the laughter subsided the pair called for the waitress to come over with their cheque. As the waitress came over to the men the brazen adulterer threw some cash on the table, paused and trickled a couple of coins on the table. "Here's a little something for you too sweetheart."

The snickering men got up and as they began to leave Steve's curiosity got the better of him, he turned and tried to get a look at the two men. At first he could only see their backs but when one of them turned to his friend, cupped his hands to his chest and laughed Steve saw the full face of both men. He was not impressed, rather than a smarmy man or a short man or an evil looking man or any particular type of man to whom could be predicted as a cheat on his wife and kids Steve saw only a man. He was not too tall or too short, he was neither thin or fat nor young or old. Instead he was just an ordinary-looking man with nothing seemingly unique or special about him. Steve looked away, brushed the face from his mind and his thoughts returned to his longed-for eggs.

After a long wait his eggs at last plopped unceremoniously in front of him. He was visibly disappointed. Eggs to Steve were akin to stamps to a stamp collector. He wanted them to be in pristine condition and unlicked. So when the eggs that the waitress plunked down looked like something Satan puked up, Steve had no choice but to say something. "Excuse me miss but…"

"Yes!" the waitress yelled in such a way that anything negative mentioned about the food she had just served would result in an uncontrolled emotional explosion. The look on the woman's face, as if she was about to beat the living daylights out of the next person for upsetting the delicate balance of her fragile world, stopped in an instant Steve's notion of opposition to his mangled, soggy, nauseating eggs. Steve cowered behind his breakfast and re-established his gaze from the girl to his plate.

Next to his troubled eggs were cold, limp-like things that tried but failed to pass as hash browns, next to them were two slices of very white soggy things that pretended unconvincingly to be toast. Steve was not impressed, but, fearing the wrath of the waitress from Hell, decided that it was in his best interest to sit still with his head down and try his best to get through his increasingly memorable-for-all-the-wrong-reasons breakfast.

Feeling downtrodden and still hung-over from the previous night's carousing he picked at his faux breakfast. Two minutes and three sips of his cold tea later he stood up, placed a five dollar bill on the table for his breakfast and another John A. MacDonald as a tip for the frazzled woman in the apron in thanks for the worst breakfast he ever had in his life. Waving goodbye he left the diner and walked onto the streets once again.

This time he knew exactly what he wanted to do and where he wished to go. He wanted to go to the Hockey Hall of fame to see the trophy known as the Stanley Cup. The subway station was mere feet away and so after checking his pockets to ensure he had a tiny, gray token he walked down the concrete stairs past the violin player playing "Moon River" and down into the depths of the TTC.

Hockey, that wonderful Canadian pastime, is deeply imbedded into the Canadian culture. The eminent writer and former goaltender Ken Dryden described it as Canada's national theatre and so Steve on his last full day in Toronto wished to see the shrine of the game, the Hockey Hall of Fame located in the BCE building with the nearest entrance on 10 Front Street.

Paying his admission, he walked into the museum and wandered through the exhibits. He saw the Canada Cup whose legacy was tainted by a corrupt businessman, he saw jerseys from the Soviet Union that reflected the nature of their cold regime and he saw masks painted to scare the opposition. But the one thing he really wanted to see was the Stanley Cup, which rested on the second floor.

Walking up the stairs, he passed the immense Lester B. Pearson trophy. Now he understood why that one never got presented at the NHL awards ceremony. Steve finished climbing and turned right to see the holy grail of hockey, the Stanley Cup shining in all its glory. He almost couldn't believe it was real and as he approached the famed prize he had to hold his breath as if he were afraid that a quick exhale might wake him up.

An employee of the Hockey Hall of Fame stood a few feet in front of the Cup with a tripod and camera. "Wanna have your photo taken with the Cup, pal?" he enquired sensing a sale.

"Yeah!" Steve answered as if the question he was just asked was "wanna sleep with Nicole Kidman?" The awestruck man put his hand on the Stanley Cup and the photographer took a picture. "It'll be waiting for you in the gift shop on your way out."

The ploy was a good one. Everyone wanted to have a photo taken with the Stanley Cup and if you had to go to the gift shop to get it well that was a bonus for the Hall. Steve spent some time walking around the upper level of the Hall. All the NHL trophies were there: the Calder for best rookie, the Vezina for best goaltender, the Conn Smyth for playoff MYP and so on.

Standing in the Hall looking at the Norris trophy was a man that Steve had the strange feeling that he should have known somehow. He had the inexplicable urge to go say hello and with that he did. "Hello," Steve said to the man still peering in at the trophy. "Best defenseman, that's a heck of a trophy."

The man looked up and smiled, "Yeah, it's a pretty hard one to win." Rather than go back to looking at the award the man began to talk to the librarian. He talked about hockey, how important it was to him and how important it was to the country. He spoke about how a young man from anywhere in the world could become a hero to people all over Canada just by having his name etched on a silver trophy. The man continued on in this vein, expounding how much the game of hockey meant to him and the people of Canada.

Steve listened intently. Sometimes you can tell when someone is trying to impart some special wisdom to you and this tall man beside him was trying his best to say in words what really could only be understood with the heart. He was insightful and generous and simply a pleasure to listen to. The man seemed like he could wax on forever about a topic he loved, but a young boy about ten years old came up to the man, raised a piece of paper and a pen and asked him for his autograph. The man smiled warmly, asked to whom he could make it out and then handed him his autograph.

The boy smiled and said, "Thanks Mr. Dryden!" before walking away. Steve knew he had been out of Canada too long when he couldn't recognize Ken Dryden, the former star goaltender for the Montreal Canadiens.

"Well, I better be going. I have a meeting soon. It was nice to talk with you." Mr. Dryden shook Steve's hand and with a smile he walked down the stairs and out of the Hall of Fame. It was nice to see that fame had not given airs to the eloquent man from Ontario and it was a reminder to Steve that despite some reservations he might have about the city of Toronto that there are good people as well as bad wherever you may go. Hell, even on the planet of Maladred where everyone wore military attire, might have some good people on it. Then again, maybe not.

The rest of the day went by quickly. Steve met some friends that he had not seen in years and was invited into one of their houses. They talked about old times, they talked about what they were doing in the present and they shared their dreams of the future. Many of them were jealous that Steve had an opportunity to return to the motherland. Jobs were the key factor in making them stay in Ontario, some regretted the fact that their children were becoming like mainlanders, to the point that they were saying "Eh?" instead of "B'ye" None of them understood "What ah ya at, b'ye?" It was disappointing to these reluctant exiles that they were somehow losing the very essence that made them Newfoundlanders.

The night went by with the help of beer, during the night one of the byes who had recently been home to visit his sick aunt revealed a case of Dominion Ale. This was a great luxury for the fellows who could not get this brand of beer anywhere else but in Newfoundland. With the aid of this treat another man decided to get out his flask of London Dock, another Newfoundland item that cannot be had in Ontario.

Very early the next morning Steve was greeting by a parched mouth and a swirling head. He had a good time with his friends but now he had to pay the penalty. Hangovers were the currency you had to recompense for hours of late night drinking fun. Fortunately the hostel he stayed at was a 24-hour affair and upon returning from his friend's home he had little trouble getting in the door. He packed his things, paid his bill and walked out of the doors where he would take a bus to the airport and home. Home where his new life would soon begin.

Chapter Seven

Librarian on a Bench

St. John's International Airport is vastly different than the airports at Newark or Pearson; there exists a small town atmosphere. The workers walking about appear less jaded than their counterparts in larger cities and are certainly more willing to help lost strangers find their way. There are always relatives and friends waiting patiently for friends, family and lovers to return from abroad. Throughout all the activity there is hardly a rush, no buskers looking for bribes to go away, no hustlers in your face wanting to deprive you of your loot, just folks looking for folks.

At this particular moment Steve was looking for his own folks. "Where the hell could they be?" he wondered? Looking about he saw neither hide nor hair of his brothers who had promised him that they would be at the airport to pick him up. What at first was an inconvenience became a worry as thoughts of horrible car crashes filled his head. It was the gruesome image of decapitation that flashed before him when Steve spotted a familiar face in the crowd. It was his friend, also known as Steve, his head moving from side to side searching for Steve.

"Steve, what are you doing here? Is everything all right?" Steve immediately asked.

"Yes, everything is fine. Your mom just asked me to pick you up at the airport," Steve replied. "Let's just get your bag and head."

Steve was all in favour of that so after waiting for twenty minutes near the merry-go-round that is the luggage carousel, the two friends exited through the large glass automatic doors and into a car that would lead Steve towards home.

The scenes that greeted Steve were as welcome as any he had ever witnessed. As familiar sights rushed past his passenger window, Steve felt a wave of relief come over him. In the urban jungles and hostile planets no one is your friend, no one truly cares about you and many will take advantage of you however possible. Here in St. John's it was different. People talked to you when you were waiting in line at the supermarket, people said hello with a genuine smile as they passed by on the street and it seemed you were a part of an actual community rather than a sole survivor leading a bothered existence in a metropolis of millions of equally bothered people.

Soon the car stopped in front of a small house and Steve almost broke the car door handle in the attempt to get out. He was finally home, back to where he truly belonged and now finally he could begin to live. Steve got out of the car, opened the trunk and helped Steve with his luggage. In a flash the front door of the house was open and his family greeted him with a chorus of "You're back" all round.

Steve was elated to be home again. Here in the loving grip of family and friends he could finally find the peace and contentment he had been longing for while in the wilds of New York City. "Why did I ever leave this place?" he thought. The answer to that question would be coming sooner than he would realize.

The next day Steve had settled in, sleep had been good and restful except for the one instance in his dreams when a somehow familiar image appeared in his mind that threatened to disturb his peace. With the beginning of day the dream had faded from his imagination and with the coming sun he was still in a period of deep, deep sleep. Deep sleep, that is, until the noise began to intrude upon his morning.

"Boom, boom, boom!" the thunder struck. "Boom, boom, boom!" it again shattered the containment field of dreams. Continually the onslaught of noise assailed the sleeping librarian's senses until at last the cacophony had done its work and eyes that were once shut tight were now wide open in confusion.

Jumping up and out of his warm and comfortable bed Steve rushed towards where the dreadful noise was coming from. He found it downstairs where his brother was busy pounding nails into an errant piece of canvas. "Well, you're finally up" his brother said annoyingly.

"What time is it?" Steve sleepily asked.

"It's eleven o'clock in the morning," came the fast reply.

"Well, it's only nine thirty in my time zone," Steve countered.

"It's your time zone no longer now is it?" came the response.

Steve refused to be bated especially in his hazy condition, so he retreated to his bedroom where he opened up his bags and got out his clothes for the day. It was his first full day in his old home and he was ready to acclimate to his new/old world. The ringing of the phone sent the man back to his reality very quickly.

"Hello," Steve said.

"Whatayaat?" the voice on the other line shouted.

"Sean! Whatayaat man!" Steve enthusiastically said.

"I heard you were back in town and wanted to give you a call," Sean enthusiastically said. "I was wondering if you were free to drop by the house for a few beers sometime the week?"

"Sure, I can manage that," Steve replied. After a few minutes of idle chatter Steve hung up the phone and smiled. He was glad to be back home with friends and family. It was a nice sunny day in the city of St. John's and Steve decided to get re-acquainted with his capital. Bidding his mom adieu he went outside in the sunshine and walked towards the harbour.

St. John's is the capital city of a province in Canada named Newfoundland and Labrador. It has a population of, according to the 2006 census, 174, 051 and it can be reasonably told that all 174,051 in some way or another know each other. For example, you may have never have heard of

Patrick O'Toole, however, you know Lee Ann Rogers who knows Ed Henderson who is familiar with Penny Moore who once dated a friend of Patrick O'Toole. It is a great deal like that Kevin Bacon game only on a grand scale. The scary point of it is everyone knows you in some fashion in St. John's and if they personally don't they know someone who does. Thus everyone knows your business sometimes even before you do yourself. It was armed with this knowledge that enabled the strolling Steve to be prepared when he encountered Ronnie O'Leary as he walked down Long's Hill.

"Why hello, Steve. I heard that you were coming back. We just weren't sure when."

Ronnie was a librarian working for the Public Library system and more importantly was a well-known gossip. Steve disliked talking to Ronnie. She went to the same library school as he had and he made the mistake of being honest with her once. It was a mistake that he would never make again.

"Oh, hi, Ronnie," Steve said unenthusiastically. "What do you mean you heard and what do you mean we?"

"Oh, everyone knew you were coming home. That job on Duckworth Street is a plum post especially since it is downtown."

"Yeah, unlike the public library system that doesn't seem to think a downtown library is a good idea, just another thing that makes our capital unique I guess." Steve never hid the fact that he thought the St. John's Public Library system was pretty awful. There was no downtown library, which for any other city in Canada would be a no-brainer; as well librarians were not allowed to serve at the reference desk because of union rules. All in all Steve thought that the literary-minded public in Newfoundland and Labrador suffered under a fairly poor library system. No wonder literacy levels were so low in the province.

Ronnie went on to talk about the lives of fellow classmates, the troubles at work and through her long speech she posed leading questions to Steve looking for some slivers of gossip to spread to her friends, co-workers and even people she didn't even know. Steve refused to take the bait and once the sly one realized that she wouldn't be getting any morsels of news she gave up, looked at her watch and said, "Well, I must be off, things to do you know."

"Sure, have a nice day Ronnie," Steve chirped sarcastically with his version of have a nice day interpreted to mean please get hit by a bus. Off the woman went and Steve hummed the Bob Dylan tune "Positively 4th Street" which he hummed after every encounter with the Weasel. Humming along, Steve walked down the hill to Duckworth Street where he began to search for his new place of employ. Surprisingly he was still looking after a few minutes. Duckworth Street was not a very long street, but the address Steve had in his hand must have been in error. He certainly didn't see a building that appeared to house a library. He continued until he found the building that matched the number to the paper he held in his hand.

The building was an old semi-Gothic structure that did not look like a place that would be a hub of library activity, but since it was the right address Steve walked up to one of the windows and peered inside. There were Venetian blinds that covered the windows almost completely, yet there was a tiny crack in the blinds in which he could just barely see in through. Inside he could make out a large table, some chairs and a few bookshelves. He was about to manoeuvre himself to see if he could get a better look when he sensed a presence behind him.

In general, Newfoundlanders are an inquisitive lot and Steve looked back to find that there were five people behind him wondering why he was looking into the closed building. Slowly he jumped back down from his perch and sheepishly walked through the milling small crowd. No one asked him why he did what he did, that was another trait of his people but they would speculate amongst themselves.

Steve continued on to Water Street where he slowly walked the long street from one side to the other. He passed by Mavericks Sports Cards and Collectibles where he paused for a moment and thought that perhaps he should mention to the owner, Andrew Corbett, that the reason for the fires that burned down his business twice was the result of a long lost buried alien artefact that was located directly under his store and periodically it would erupt into flames for practically no reason at all. The Archive wing of the Inter Galactic Library Board was on the case but typically it would take another fifty years before anyone could be sent out to retrieve the relic. Steve thought better of it and continued to march on.

No matter how many years go by or how much things may have changed Water Street to him would always be the place of his youth where the street was alive with people and commerce. The times in the eighties when the fishery was vibrant and fishermen from around the world set ashore looking for a good time. The Russians were interested in acquiring merchandise such as blue jeans and electronics, the Japanese looked for food, the Greeks and Portuguese looked for booze. All of them looked for women.

Stores such as Sears, Woolworths, the Arcade and the London and Paris were busy selling all manner of items to all manner of people. The street had its own unique personality, a policeman stood in the middle of the road waving traffic, the tower clock would chime, the trains would whistle and the noon day gun would fire and everyone would check their watches to see if they were on the right time. It was a magical time for Steve when he could still have been anything he wished to be. This was the downtown he saw whenever he looked at Water Street and it was while in this nostalgic mood that left him unprepared for what came next.

A gravely toned voice slapped him out of his dreams. “Spare some change?” It was a bizarrely-clad old woman in a strange hat and boots with her short, tattered coat hanging about her miniature frame. Begging was something Steve had never in his life seen before in St. John’s, that was reserved for big cities like Toronto. Even in New York it was on the decline but here in his city he was being asked to “spare some change” and he was taken aback.

Acting on a reflex finely honed in New York, he ignored the woman and continued on his trek. Within half a minute a large, bearded man jumped out of McMurdo’s Lane asking a similar question, “Spare some cash for lunch.” It wasn’t a question as more of a statement but again the answer Steve gave was nothing more than to move on and out of the man’s way. He was stunned by this recent development. Never before had beggars roamed freely on the downtown streets and now here in Water Street, the place where many of his childhood dreams were made, vagrants felt comfortable enough to harass passers-by for income they were undeserving.

"How dare they sully my city with their vile presence?" the angry man thought to himself. St. John's appeared to have gone downhill in his time away from the capital city. There was a time when people would be too ashamed to beg for nickels and dimes; now he was inundated by tramps asking for currency. His period of reflection abruptly stolen, he walked to the war memorial to have a look at what he thought was the best memorial in Canada.

The war memorial in downtown St. John's is a beautiful monument to the people who served in the various wars Newfoundlanders participated in. These days numerous young people hang about the memorial using the site for skateboarding and general loitering as passers-by shake their heads in disbelief. For some reason inexplicable to Steve the city tolerates the skateboarders because they, so far, do not bother the tourists too much, but to Steve it was a disgrace to see people desecrate a spot dedicated to the brave people who died for their country, Newfoundland. Steve walked up and looked at the memorial, someone had stolen the leather strap to one of the statues' rifles and a bayonet was broken off, but beyond that the memorial was still in good condition.

Steve strolled a little further but finally plunked himself down on a convenient bench and began to watch the world go by. On this day a cruise ship had docked in St. John's harbour and hundreds of tourists wandered the streets exploring the oldest incorporated city in North America. Many passed by Steve on their way to one shop or another, some said hello, others simply walked by. The librarian on a bench looked at them all with no meaningful thought in his head other than he wished more attractive redheads would pass by. He became lost in thought, soon he mused, he would have to go to work and it was then and only then would he learn if he had made the right decision in returning home.

Chapter Eight

The Library of Thought

Monday morning means many things to many different people. For the shopkeepers it means opening their stores early to sell to the frantic customers who've forgotten birthday, anniversary and I-love-you-sorry-I-screwed-up presents. For others Monday is the start of a new school week where some go to learn their sums and others go to forget the knowledge they never really had. For still others Monday is a day the world appears to refocus after a hazy weekend, it renews its vigour in hope of a fresh start. Sunday may be the official beginning of a new week, but Monday is the day that gets it all going.

For Steve this Monday morning was different than most Monday mornings. To begin with he was starting his new job and even though he realized he knew very little about the specifics of the position, he was confident that once he entered the library he would be able to conquer his new world. This Monday was also unique as it was the first time in years he would be working in St. John's as opposed to being away or in school. He had made the journey back home where he had actually found a well-paying full time permanent position. This was the dream of thousands of Newfoundlanders who had left their homeland with the hope that one day they would return but for most the dream would never come true.

They had left Newfoundland to seek an education or experience or a stake for a venture back home. Most of these people for some reason hardly ever return, except for the occasional funeral, wedding or Christmas. Steve knew he was one of the fortunate ones, one of the ones who made it, who realized the dream of coming home for good. Hell, no one had gone further away than he had and he had now returned. It was this understanding that made this Monday very, very special for Steve and as he left for work he wore not only a clean suit of clothes but also a very large smile.

The journey to work was a short and happy one. The sun was shining even though there was a hint of fall in the air as if summer was reminding the people that it would soon depart and that the gleeful weather should be enjoyed while it can. This reminder was lost on the man that briskly walked down Long's Hill whose thoughts were firmly fixed on his new job and the wonder of what was to come.

When he reached Duckworth Street he found that the door to his new employ was locked shut. Steve mused for a moment; he was early but not abnormally so, surely someone could have been there to greet him on his first day. The slightly piqued librarian stood outside the door of his new library and waited for someone to show up to let him in. Strangers walked past on their way to work, many said hello or good morning. Even one of the fellows who push rusty grocery carts half filled with bottles in search of refuse nodded a greeting to the man in the suit tapping his foot waiting to be let in to work.

Another ten minutes crept by and Steve became increasingly anxious. "What if this was all a ruse? An elaborate scheme brought about to see me in ruin?" Steve's theories became increasingly elaborate. Ideas raced through his mind and sweat began to trickle down his neck. As the clock struck eight Steve's mind began to flash with scenarios more fantastic than the next. Shaking his head to try and put his paranoia out of him he saw a dark shadow on the ground.

An old man suddenly appeared on the step below him. He said a friendly "Good morning," then walked up past Steve to the locked door. Pausing for a moment, he methodically searched his pockets and fished out a large ring of keys where after a moment of thought he chose one and inserted it into the lock. He walked through the now open door and ushered the waiting librarian inside.

"Welcome to my library!" the man whimsically said. He waved his arms to show to the world that all around him was his. He shook Steve's hands warmly and smiled. "I can tell if people are good or not just by looking at them and I can tell that you are a good man. It's a gift. My name is Joe Simon." Without further introduction, the man led the slightly amused librarian through the cosy hallway and into a very large, antiquated room.

The room smelled of knowledge. There were books everywhere, on tables, on shelves and all along the walls. There was a small office with a computer that looked slightly out of place inside where Steve assumed the librarian would work. There was a reference and circulation area where patrons could come to have a question answered or to take out some materials. It was in some aspects a typical small library, but in others it was one of a kind. For example, there was a large painting of a bearded man dressed in a robe and sandals looking as if he was born two thousands years ago. Its eyes appeared to move as Steve was being given the tour of his new workplace, following him as he walked.

The library he was told by the friendly man held ten thousand books, five thousand journals, a small map collection, four sets of different encyclopaedias, and a reference collection that made up another three hundred monographs. A number of globes were situated around the library that depicted the political makeup of the world in various time periods from ancient to present day. There was a photocopier that was free for the use of the patrons as well as three computers complete with printers and Internet access.

There were also carvings in the ceiling, some grey, gothic gargoyles that hung onto the edge of the walls as if they were holding on for life. Their tongues stuck out of their mouths as if to warn people that their search for knowledge was useless and not to waste their time. The library had a number of interesting paintings and photos, some were of ancient philosophers, some of literary giants and some were of people who were wholly unrecognisable to Steve. The walls were coloured grey and they were of such a grey that if you had a little imagination you could pretend you were in a dimly lit cave. The décor was interesting to say the least. The old man showed him where the catalogue system was, told him the general do's and don'ts of the job and then with a smile he was gone.

The old man made for the door, then as if in an afterthought, turned back and handed him the keys to the library with its machines and walked away leaving a bewildered librarian to his library. Steve explored his new workplace. He was somewhat bemused by the old man's attitude but it also meant that he would not be closely watched over which was a big plus in Steve's book. He didn't like to be over-lorded by some demanding boss who didn't want anything done except on their terms. He had more than his taste of that with the Master of Evil in New York and he did not want a repeat if at all possible. No, it looked like this job was going to be a smooth ride on that front which suited him just fine.

Steve fretted about the library until at 8:33 am he heard the front door open. Immediately, he rushed behind the reference desk waiting to serve. He still did not know exactly what type of library he was running at the moment but he was positive he would get the hang of it very quickly. In through the doors walked a woman of unquestionable splendour. She was in Steve's eyes the quintessential woman. She had long black hair, was reasonably small at 5 foot 6 inches, large but not gigantic bosoms, a thin waist, legs that a man would live for and a face that could have launched two thousand ships, at least. Steve was convinced more than ever that he was going to enjoy his new job.

"Hello, may I help you?" he innocently asked. Steve could not help but surrender to his bestial nature and stare at the beauty in front of him and he prayed that this would be an extremely intricate reference question that might take hours if not days to properly answer.

"Yes, you can start by letting me pass, you're in my way." The woman who was about twenty-four years old walked up to Steve and past him. She took off her coat, sat on a swivel wooden chair that was situated in the corner of the reference area and then relieved herself of her tall, shiny leather boots. Steve was a bit taken aback by this situation but hoped that he was in one of those experiences that *Penthouse* always writes about, the ones where a beautiful stranger appears out of nowhere and has kinky sex with an unsuspecting man then runs away never to be seen again. "What a way to begin the workday," he lustily dreamed.

This lady was the ideal fantasy figure if he ever saw one, especially as she sat there with no boots and her coat draped seductively over the back of the chair. The woman bent down and looked under the reference desk for something. Frustrated, she dropped to her knees and crept closer to where Steve was rigidly standing. "Oh here they are," the woman said.

"This is it!" Steve excitedly thought. The woman at that moment got up with a pair of sensible, black shoes in her right hand. She smiled as she went back to the chair she had been sitting on and put on her shoes. "What the heck is going on?" the librarian wondered. "Just who the heck is this and why isn't she having sex with me right now?"

The beautiful woman stood up, faced the bewildered librarian and held out her hand. "You must be the new guy. Welcome to the team." She smiled such a smile and such a beautifully perfect smile, as there seemed to be no need for anyone to smile again, the smile had already been perfected so no other need give it a try. Steve paused for a moment then shook the delicate hand that was offered.

"You work here?" Steve hesitated before asking the question just in case that this was all a dream and that in fact he had not even woken up yet, got dressed, had his eggs and walked to work. If this goddess was going to be working with him and in fact as librarian she was going to be working under him, figuratively speaking, of course, then this was far too good to be true. He needed to be slapped. Hard.

"Yes. My name is Cecilia Carpenter and I am the library assistant. Didn't the old man tell you about me?" Steve at that precise moment could barely remember his own name let alone what the strange old man said. He gulped before he could drool and, deciding that this was in fact reality, he went with the flow of conversation.

"He told me that there were two assistants, but I didn't know their names or really anything other than that. My name is Steve by the way and, yes, I am the new librarian."

"The other guy doesn't come in until nine. He'll be here shortly. I better get going myself before the patrons arrive." With that Cecilia then got to work by walking to the shelves behind the reference desk and putting books on a library cart presumably for shelving.

Steve watched as she began her chores. "The other guy. Rats!" Steve was disappointed that the other assistant was going to be male, but the odds of two divine women under one roof was too much to dream for anyway. After another glance at the beautiful assistant he went into his office and began to get to work himself. He closed the door to his office sat down in his large, comfortable chair. Fortunately the person who had vacated the position left a large folder filled with copious notes and the work was, if judged by the absence of clutter on the desk, apparently up-to-date so he wouldn't have to play too much catch-up.

The beginning of the stack of notes was straightforward stuff, how much the budget was and how much of it was left to spend for the fiscal year. Steve learned that this was a library that primarily dealt with philosophical matters. The owner was an old man who had made millions of dollars during the course of his work and now wished to help his friends pursue a life of thought and knowledge during their reclining years. The journals and books were focused upon the spiritual and philosophical, the patrons were friends of the owner and those that came in to study carried a library card which was free of charge but could only be given by the owner himself.

The notes began to take a more eerie tone as Steve got deeper in the pile. Some talked of the odd patrons who would spend hours at a time reading the same page, other cryptic notes talked on the librarian's own philosophy and how much she had learned from reading some of the books in her library. The last note was the most notable of all. In it Steve read that the reason the former librarian left was because she was inspired to move to Tibet and devote her life to prayer and mediation. That sounded odd to say the least but he knew more than most that there was more things in heaven and Earth than are dreamt of in philosophy.

Steve let out a gust of air after he had finished reading all the notes. He had gotten a good introduction to the library and what to expect, but he had never before heard of a librarian running off to pursue a dream, which was unexpected and very unusual in the predictable world of librarianship. This library and its wealth of thoughts must have had a profound impact on her. True librarians never dreamed of leaving their posts.

Steve looked at his watch where he was surprised to learn that it was now eleven in the morning. He looked up and noticed an elderly gentleman sitting behind the reference desk calculating statistics. The librarian jumped out of his chair and walked out of his office to greet him. "Hello, you must be the other assistant," Steve deduced. He held out his hand and smiled, "No competition for Miss Delicious's affections here," he mused.

"Good morning sir," the old man said. "My name is Allan and yes, I am one of the workers here. I retired some time ago and this job keeps me from gathering dust."

"Well, I look forward to getting to know you, Allan," the librarian beamed. Steve talked to the man for another few minutes, learning what exactly were his duties, what time he came and left, when he took his breaks and other such necessary information. For now he didn't wish to interrupt the flow of the library. It looked like everything was running fine and everyone beside himself knew exactly what was expected of them. He didn't want to upset the apple cart so early into his tenure.

The rest of the day was spent learning his new duties, checking the time sheets of the two assistants, looking up suppliers to introduce himself, and a number of other simple tasks that were mundane but necessary to ensure a smooth transition from one librarian's regime to the next. When four-o'clock came about he was glad that the day was over, the assistants had already gone home and he prepared to leave. There was only one patron left and he was about to shoo him off.

"Excuse me, but I am afraid it is time to leave. We are closing." The librarian spoke with kindness in his voice. After all he didn't know the man sitting silently in the reading room, he might be a friend of the boss and he didn't want to upset anyone on his first day. The man didn't move a muscle. He merely kept his face down with his eyes staring directly on the book on his lap. The librarian was sympathetic but a little piqued that there was no response. "Excuse me, sir, but its time to go." Once again there was no response.

The librarian decided to make a show of going. Rather than insist, he would begin to shutoff the lights and put on his jacket giving the man another few minutes to finish whatever was so engrossing him. After all was done and Steve was snug in his jacket the man still had not moved. Impatiently Steve walked over to the patron. "I'm sorry but we are now closed and you will have to leave." The man did not move and a chilling thought came over the librarian. He hesitantly placed his hand on the patron's shoulder and the man slumped down, his head smacking the table. "Holy cow! He's dead!" the librarian shouted. "What the hell am I gonna do? It's my first day!" He hauled the man up from his chair to check for signs of life but it was too late. The book that he was reading fell to the floor and by instinct the librarian picked it up and looked at its cover. "Robert Frost? Robert Frost! No wonder you're dead!" the irrational man screamed.

Getting a hold of himself the man rushed to the nearest phone and called 911. Soon an ambulance arrived and took away the first ever patron that he ever served in his new library. One for one, dead. It was a first day he'd never forget for many reasons, but this particular reason was on the top of his list.

Steve was justifiably late on the way home from work and after the day he had wanted to go directly to sleep. No other thought of the man whom he had sent on his way to his otherworldly journey did he bother with. He was tired and needed a rest after his long day. He opened the door to his home and at once the noise struck him like a sonic wave. Shouting and cursing, two of his brothers were arguing over some insignificant thing. There would be no rest for him today.

Rather than struggle against the wind he busied himself with other tasks. He now found the time to actually unpack his clothes from his suitcases that until this time were thrown about in his room opened only when needed. Now, with time on his hands he could unpack properly and begin to truly settle back into his life.

It took a couple of hours to get everything out of his bag and into neat piles, but finally he finished. Now he was truly home, no longer living out of a bag even theoretically, he was now here to stay. There was little thought left for the space library he had left behind. Chubba, Zoe and Cal were things of the past and he could no longer afford to live in the past. The art of living was about to begin.

Chapter Nine

The Big Dark

October is a special month in Newfoundland. It signals the beginning of the end of sunlight and the commencement of a term many refer to as the big dark. The big dark emerges slowly but steadily while the precious sunlight gradually leaves the province not to return for some time. So in October the people of Newfoundland are slightly more energetic knowing instinctively that their time in the sun is fast approaching the end.

Steve had spent the month of September getting to know his library and his assistants. Both of his co-workers were amiable souls and Steve got along well with both of them. The goddess Celica Carpenter proved that she was much more than a pretty face. She was a very able assistant who was willing to get her hands dirty if the need arose. Once he became accustomed with having to work with such a beautiful woman, Steve looked past her physical charms and related to her as a capable colleague who could have easily taken over the library if she had the training and masters degree in library and information science.

Allan was another valuable asset to the team but in a much different capacity that Cecilia. The patrons were drawn automatically to him because of their similar age and they approached him more readily than either of the younger people. He couldn't manage to lift very much due to his bad back and he spent a fine portion of his time studying the books rather than checking them in and out but all-in-all he was a good worker when he was called upon to do his duty.

There was only one characteristic of Allan's that Steve had to call into question. At times when he thought no one was looking Allan would sniff the old monographs. He would open a particularly old book, look to his right and left to see if anyone was around, then his face would plunge into the open pages and he would take a big sniff. He would only chance one inhalation, then he would with a satisfied grin close the book and continue on with his duties. Steve had seen this happen on more than one occasion and thought it almost too strange to bring up, but since it was not against library policy, it didn't damage the books and no one had seen or was offended by it the librarian decided to let the old man have his little odd indulgence. Beyond this little quirk he was an absolute addition to the library and he didn't want to embarrass the old man over a trifle.

Wandering the stacks he noticed a few pieces of paper peeking out of a book. He grabbed the sheets of paper and in a clear, precise hand he found written words. Steve found a chair, sat down and began to read.

A Stranger Calls

The Knights of Columbus Hall offered the same scene every Tuesday evening. It was bingo night and the smoky room held a variety of new comers and regular visitors. The haze of the smoke gave the room a slightly seedy atmosphere, a tinge of impropriety.

I arrived just barely on time, as was my wont to do, and purchased three cards for myself and three for my friend who had left my side to search for a pair of seats. As I looked through the mist I found my companion near the edge of a long table waving to me to approach. I walked forward, handed my friend his cards and sat down.

The evening did not seem unusual. The elderly women chatted amongst themselves, the neglected housewives looked down upon their numerous cards in what seemed to be contempt for what they felt assured would be losers and the middle-aged men with their large bellies shifted impatiently waiting for the balls to drop.

I sat across from my companion with a look of resignation on my face. I thought of bingo as one of those games that old ladies played with cash secreted from their pension cheques and not for someone of relative youth and vigor. Yet I arrived in the same hall every week and all for the same two reasons; first, it was the only time I could see my friend whose busy schedule would make meeting otherwise impossible and second, I had no where else to go.

Suddenly, a loud screech burst out of the hall microphone, everyone's body let out a silent sigh. The squeal of the microphone meant only one thing, an announcement. Announcements were universally despised in our bingo circle, for one they bored people but more importantly they delayed the game. Pat, a short rotund man cautiously approached the phone, wary after he shocked himself with the noise of the feedback from his first attempt.

"Excuse me everyone. I have an important announcement to make. We have a new caller here tonight, a man from away who asked if he could have a crack at calling a bingo. So if you have a bit of bad luck tonight for once you can't blame me." With a smile Pat, satisfied with his performance, proudly walked away from the mike and sat down relieved for the night off.

I had never seen the man who was to call the bingo yet he radiated a sense of good will. The whole room seemed to feel uplifted in his presence; it was as if we had been reintroduced to an old friend that we were delighted to see. All round the hall I heard whispers that people felt that this was their lucky night. Even I felt my mood change somewhat, as if I might be in for some small stroke of fortune myself.

The game began and the instant the first number was spoken there was a sound like that of sweet music that filled the room. I never knew that B7 could sound so lovely to my ear, even if I didn't happen to have it on my cards. As the symphony of letters and numbers continued the players began to concentrate on the melodic call of the bingo. Every few minutes someone would shout "Bingo!" and strangely enough it seemed to me that the most deserving players had won. Miss O'Riely who loved her cats above almost all else won fifty dollars, Mr. Kelly who was all alone in the world won twenty five and old widowed Mrs. Kent won a hundred.

For the first time in my memory no one complained about being on the hitch; instead all the players were happy with the outcome of the games. All the players that is except Mr. Gladstone. Mr. Gladstone is, to be brutally honest, a miser who complained constantly about anything and everything. Tonight he complained from the back of the room that the new caller should speak up as he couldn't hear one number that was spoken from the stranger.

This came as a surprise to those around him who told the man that the new caller had the clearest calls they had ever heard and that he should stop complaining especially when someone new was calling the game.

After this small interruption the games continued and it was at this time that I realized that our new caller was not even using the sound system to amplify his voice, yet this was the strongest bingo call I had ever heard. I thought it odd that Mr. Gladstone could not hear the game.

The night waned and the luck continued to be held by the nicest of the crowd. I myself shared a prize of twenty five dollars with my companion though I found it strange that the sign of the cross would be used instead of the usual T. Another odd moment was when Mrs. Doyle was about to call bingo when the caller stopped her, called her by name and told her that N41 was not out yet.

At last there came the jackpot game. Everyone now became very silent. The caller announced that the jackpot was worth $3330 and with a small smile said "Plus a free pass to heaven." Everyone laughed at this and the game began.

I was close, so close to the jackpot I even now cringe a little when I think on it but in the end it was Mrs. Casey who won the prize. Everyone clapped knowing how this frail individual deserved the cash and were we all genuinely happy that she had won.

It was now time to leave. I looked at the stranger who had called bingo that night. As people filed pass him they paused and asked if he needed a lift home. He refused them all ensuring them he had his own way back.

Finally I left the hall and began to walk to my friend's car. In the background I heard two men talking to each other. "Who was that fella who called the game tonight?" The other replied, "I don't know him from Adam, but he sure could call a good bingo."

Steve put the papers in his pocket. Someone had written a good story and someday that person might want to come back to reclaim it. The day ended like all other days. Steve was the one who locked up the library and went towards home. There was a definite chill in the air now and he buttoned up his coat as he walked up Long's Hill and home.

The month of October quickly fell off the calendar and Steve became more comfortable in his role as librarian in his new environment. He infrequently talked with his boss who never really had anything good or bad to say about the operation. He merely discussed business matters such as the acquisition of new books and materials and the cost of such items. It seemed that as long as there were no complaints and the budget was run appropriately then all would be right on the supervisor front.

Soon October thirtieth arrived and Steve became comfortable enough to suggest a little change from the normal routine. Halloween had become big business in St.

John's. The stores stock their shelves with masks, costumes and a host of pseudo-scary items. It is a time for adult parties, children's trick or treating and the George Street Marti Gras. While Christmas had been commercialised for some time in the province, Halloween had been true to its spirit even if that spirit had been to suck candy out of people and give young children sick stomachs and cavities. Now even this occasion had become the provenance of big business with greetings cards, novelty gifts, sexy costumes for the adventurous and a whole lot more all available to be purchased by those that deemed them essential for their personal Halloween experience.

Steve liked Halloween even though his memories of trick or treating were not entirely fond. On one particular nasty Halloween night a dog chased him through the streets and he fell, badly cutting his hand. Still, the trappings of fun frolic and fear all rolled up into one giant ball of scary fun excited man and his excitement carried over to his work. He entered his library filled with the Halloween spirit.

"Well, hello everyone. I just had an excellent idea. We are going to spend tomorrow dressing up this place in a Halloween fashion."

"Do you think that is such a good idea?" Allan asked.

"Oh pooh. Anyone who can't understand a bit of Halloween fun in a library with gargoyles in it shouldn't own a library dedicated to scary thoughts in the first place. We are going to celebrate Halloween and that is that."

There was a small cash jar that was usually used for small items such as batteries, pencils and miscellaneous things that were needed on the spot. Steve took a portion of the fund and dedicated it to Halloween fun. He asked Cecilia if she wasn't too busy for a trip to the mall during their lunch hour and when she answered she wasn't he was very pleased indeed. The spirit of Halloween would soon live in the library of thought.

It was certainly a thrill for Steve to have such an exceptional beauty hanging next to him during an excursion to the mall. For him the trip could last forever, but for a mere one hour, it was like the Cinderella story without the expensive shoes. Still, being practical beings, Steve and Cecilia headed straight to the stores that sold cheap but nice-looking Halloween supplies. In no time the pair picked out some interesting but appropriate items for what Steve now referred to as the library of thought. Long, black candles gripped by skull holders, a compact disk with scary noise recordings, some candy and other knickknacks that would give a certain air of Halloweenness to the library.

All too soon it was time to go back to the library as the two co-workers exited the mall Steve sighed and thought, "It's always the case that when you want to bump into someone you know there is no one to be seen." The two got in Cecilia's car and drove back to the library.

Allan was sniffing a book on the linear nature of thought when the pair returned with their bags of goodies. He pushed up his glasses to witness their entrance. Both seemed happy as they pulled out their purchases and showed them off to the semi-interested third party. Soon Steve and Cecelia concocted plans to decorate the library and even the nay-sayer helped in the decoration. Tomorrow was

Halloween and for once the library of thought was going to participate.

By the end of the day the library looked wonderfully wicked. He noticed that, as usual, both Allan and Cecilia left together but that Allan seemed very intent on some point as he talked to her. Content, Steve sat down upon a chair that looked out to the front window of the library, a few scattered pages sat down on his lap. The librarian picked up the paper, looked at his words scattered on the pages and began to read. He was inspired by the Newfoundland story that he had found and decided to leave the world of fantasy for a while and write a historical fiction based on the 1948 Newfoundland referendum.

When Sun Rays Crown

She`s cold this morning. The winds off the water are cold, even in July, but in October you can feel it starting to work up something extra special to chill you to the bone. Mornings like this always remind me of my distant youth. My father would drag me out of bed at 5:00 in the morning to begin my work day. He`d come up in the room and haul the blankets right out from under me. "Christ, father! Give it up, I`m going!"

"Watch your tongue," he`d say sharply. "Your mudder might hear ya." Father was never one to spare an admonishment, though he was proud of the way I was turning out. A hard working boy set in the same mould as himself, a chip off the old block.

I`d stagger blurry-eyed down the stairs to the cold kitchen, nearly tripping over the dog in the process. Mother would have been up before either of us getting breakfast on the table, bread, eggs, bacon and tea. We ate an ample breakfast because we would need all the energy we could get for the work ahead. It's funny the things you can remember with such clarity.

After breakfast we would go to the dory and work like slaves until the day was over. By then I was so tired I could have slept right out on the boat. Still, I couldn't wait to get back home for a good supper and a night`s entertainment. Father on the banjo, mother on the accordion and me on the spoons. Then it was up the stairs and on my knees to say my prayers, God bless mommy and daddy, Rufus the black Labrador, and please let the catch be big tomorrow. After prayers it was under the covers and a rest well-earned. I never forgot that child and have fought ever since for his right to exist.

I`m a long, long way from all that now. It`s been many years since the Great Depression, World War II, and, of course, the Battle for the Republic. Yes, it`s been a lifetime since those days when things were so simple, when the existence that I was bred for led me to another life to keep it.

As I sit down in my favourite pub, the Ship Inn, I can remember all the intrigue and plotting that occurred right here near the fireplace of this very establishment. This is partly where it happened, where many of the famous men and women on both sides of the struggle came to discuss strategy over a pint of their favourite. They would come here at all times of the day and over the course of these discussions decide the fate of a nation.

This is where the real history begins, not in the sterile school books that only teach the bare facts but the honest-to-God story. It's a fascinating old tale, full of intrigue, back room politics, all kinds of scandal and a mixture of truth and lies for good measure. It's around this time of the year, right before Halloween, that the story really comes to mind. Maybe it's because the ghosts that haunt me are given more leeway on All Hallows Eve to torment me for all my sins. Now that it's sixty years after the fact I guess it plays a little more on my mind that usual.

Most of the time when I feel like this I head to the pub by myself feeling very lonely and a little bit depressed. It's like that old joke, I called all my friends but he didn't show up. Well, today as I sit here staring into my empty glass, I wait for my old adversary Tommy who is typically late, just like he was all those years ago.

Tommy is and always has been my intellectual superior, at least in terms of formal schooling. I was educated by my father who taught me how to fish, how to fix a net and gut a fish. Practical learning you might say. The only time I was in the school system was when I was too young to be useful to my family so I was sent off to school to read and write, which if I have to say so myself I achieved.

Tommy on the other hand was educated in St. John's and received all the benefits of a full high school diploma so I have to give him the edge over me in the amount of things he knows. Yet, I think that all that knowledge must have rotted-out his brain for he was never the brightest person I have ever met. In fact, I sometimes think that he wasn't all that smart at all. Still, he survived the inner circle of the Republic's various governments for the past sixty years and not many people can boast that. In fact, there is only me and Tommy left.

Finally, Tommy entered the pub and after glancing over in my direction he walked over to the bar and ordered two pints of Newfie Bullet. Moving through the crowded bar, he placed the pint glass in front of me before taking his seat. He knew what my reaction would be but waited silently for it anyway.

"Now, Tommy, you know full well that I drink Guinness," I said taking up the glass.

"Well, you fought for the Republic. You should be drinking a domestic beer," he smiled.

"Yes, that may very well be, but just last month I was on the Newfie Bullet and they now serve fantastic pints of the stuff. In keeping my love for Guinness I'm helping the Newfoundland Railroad to profitability and everyone knows that Newfoundland can't be Newfoundland without the Newfie Bullet. Even former Confederates know that much." I smiled at this and raised my glass. "To the Newfie Bullet, an institution that everyone can agree on." We both brought our glasses together then quietly drained the contents.

Without missing a beat, I was up to the bar ordering two pints of Guinness for my companion and me. In one of life's ironies I was the one drinking imported beer while my friend who had fought for the confederate side was drinking the domestic brands. Life is always full of those little ironies.

After bringing back the pints to the table, we looked at each other and got ready to share our thoughts on the old days. "Old Dick Martin just died. Did you hear about that?" Tommy asked.

"No, I didn't hear. My, that's too bad. He was a sharp fellow in his time wasn't he?" Another one of Tommy's old friends, God rest his soul. "He was always down by the harbour talking to the men working down there for the merchants. Always looking to hear a bit of news." I looked at Tommy slyly as I said this hoping for a reaction.

"You know darn well that he was down there spying for us, looking for any old gossip that could be used against your crowd," Tommy asserted after he took a long swig of his beer. There was still a spark of that old fight-till-we-drop fervour that had worked so well for him those many years ago but which now seemed out of place. While most people accepted the decision after the ballots were all counted, there were still a few like Tommy that still resented the fact that they lost. Well, too bloody bad about it. All's fair in love and war, and the battle for Newfoundland was certainly a war.

To tell the truth there's a lot of things I don't like about Tommy. He is a "Townie" Protestant while I am a Roman Catholic "Bayman." He is pro-confederation while I am anti-Confederation. Yet the two of our lives have been so intertwined over the years that the initial dislike I had for the man eroded into a respect for the way in which he conducted himself. He is honest, loyal to the core and brave, things which in politics make him the man most least likely to succeed. Thank God he was on their side.

The Newfoundland referendum on the future of the island was going to be a close one, no question about it. The British government was sick to death of having to run this backwater place and thought it best to hand the whole parcel over to Canada. When Joey Smallwood arrived in England to ask for support in his bid to become the first Premiere of Newfoundland the ruling Labour party was all smiles. "Of course, Joey, have anything you like, our fields are ripe for the picking, come on in, enjoy." They wanted Newfoundland out of their hands so badly they would have wiped his arse if he had asked them.

The anti-Confederate people, on the other hand, were ignored. The notion of an independent Newfoundland was just a silly thing the ignorant colonials dreamed up. They had had their chance and they blew it. Of course, having blown it on account of saving British hides during the wars was a little aspect they chose to forget. So with no support, it was up to Newfoundlanders and Newfoundlanders alone to save us from the jaws of the Canadian wolf.

Back home on the front, the pro and con forces drew the battle lines and the final fight for the hearts and minds of the people of Newfoundland was joined. Joey was relentless in his quest for power. He seemed to be everywhere talking to everyone on the benefits of a union with Canada. There would be money for old age pensions, money for unemployment and jobs galore. We'd all be rich within a month of confederation. All our troubles would be over. Yes, the pieces of silver were offered and it was a tempting trap for a great many poor souls who for so long suffered on eight cents a day.

I can honestly say that I empathized with the feelings of those people who chose Canada. Who wants to be poor? Yet I also believe in the right for a country to choose its own way to live without begging its master for permission. I firmly believed that and so too did the man who ended up becoming the integral character that determined the course of Newfoundland's history. That man's name was Stephen O'Finn.

No one really knew much about him or where he came from. He kept to himself and was practically friendless. Stephen O'Finn had one thought in his mind and one thought only and that was to save Newfoundland. He knew that without someone with the determination to fight Joey everywhere he went and every time he spoke then the people would ultimately be swayed by the rhetoric. Independence would not have a chance without an equally dramatic speaker in its corner and so without anyone's approval he chose himself to deliver us from temptation.

One day as Joey was finishing beguiling a group of locals, Stephen O'Finn made his move. He strode up to the speaker's podium and without any prelude began to speak. At first slow and halting, he gradually found the voice that swept the people away from Joey and into his corner. The speech he made was passionate and inspiring, appealing to the fundamental things that all Newfoundlanders hold as sacred. The locals who perhaps would have been swayed by Joey's wares were clearly for a free Newfoundland after his speech was made. Stephen O'Finn was the conquering hero and Joey fumed with rage. The battle between these two men of passion became a clash between the titans.

After that first day, Stephen O'Finn's strategy was clear and simple. Every time Joey made a speech he would be right behind telling the people not to be taken in by the words of a Judas. Remember Beaumont Hamel, remember the suffering that our forefathers went through in making Newfoundland the place that it is. Remember that England, the very place that we gave our lives to defend was turning her back on the people that fought for it and was selling us out to the Canadian wolf.

He reminded them that it would be their honour, their heritage and their spirit that would lead them proudly to prosperity. Anyone who was not for independence was a traitor who spit on the graves of their ancestors. It was dramatic words like these combined with the message of a glorious future that Newfoundlanders would forge for their own was too powerful for Joey to match. His fool's gold began to lose its lustre.

I was at that first speech and I instinctively knew that this was the man the Newfoundland people needed to set them on the right path. I immediately zigzagged through the crowds and asked if I could help him in his quest of defeating Confederation. He happily agreed and soon we were on the road together dogging Joey's tracks. We began to get noticed. The *Evening Telegram* published a caricature of O'Finn as a Newfoundland dog with his jaws firmly clamped around Joey's heals. Word soon spread and everyone wanted to see the mysterious underdog who was going to bring Joey down.

It was on the road with Stephen O'Finn that I was to meet a young man who was a part of Joey's Confederation campaign, his name was Thomas Barron. Thomas's job was to try to keep the Confederate campaign on a steady schedule and that all the places that needed to hear the word of Confederation got the chance to hear the gospel straight from the pulpit of Father Joey. He was good at his job and firmly believed in his position, established in his conviction that Confederation offered the best choice for Newfoundland. He and I because of our stances in the cause began to dislike each other but that feeling was nothing to what Joey had felt for Stephen.

Joey hated O'Finn with a burning intensity and it began to show in the personal attacks that popped out of his mouth with increasing frequency. Joey was losing and he knew it. Something had to be done about his opponent.

One incident in particular seemed to be the turning point in the campaign, though before it happened it felt like all the other times the two combatants faced each other. Instead of each man taking turns, making their pitches for or against confederation, a strange incident occurred. As O'Finn got up to speak he bumped into Joey and as they stood face to face with barely an inch of air between them they began to stare in each other's eyes. As the crowd grew silent, a contest of wills between two opposing philosophies grew out of a simple glance and the battle would become legendary. I can't recall how much time was spent engaged in this silent struggle but everyone felt that this clash was a magical moment not only between these two men but also for our country. I was frozen in terror, praying that Stephen would not be the first to look away. I honestly thought that if he was to falter at that moment our cause was lost. Joey would gloat about his triumph all the way to victory at the polls.

As the seconds ticked into what appeared to be hours my prayers were answered. Joey turned away. He didn't want to but he gave up. O'Finn had beaten him. It was an incident that everyone talked about, except Stephen himself. He never once mentioned it.

On April 3, 1948, just two months before the vote to decide the nation's future Stephen O'Finn was found murdered in his temporary home in St. John's, hacked to death with an axe. News of this event shocked the nation. To this day anyone in Newfoundland who was alive during those chaotic times remembers where they were when the news broke. The battle for the Republic had claimed its most important victim and anyone who refused to believe the lengths that the two sides would go to achieve victory had their eyes opened to the truth that day.

The Confederate forces tried to steer clear of all mention of Stephen O'Finn's murder but the ghost of that fine man hounded Joey Smallwood every step of the way. Everywhere he went Joey was faced with the bloody spectre of a dismembered body in downtown St. John's. Signs that read "killer," "blood money" and "remember" were seen at every confederate rally. Colourful rumours, which are always faster and more powerful than cold fact, flew across the island that Canadians had something to do with Stephen O'Finn's murder.

I was not idle in this battle. I began to speak at the Republican rallies reminding people that the ideals that O'Finn had been slaughtered for did not die with him but that a vote for freedom would also be a vote for the dead man who was killed for his desire to see us free. It was a powerful message and many of the people took it to heart.

Even those who could not bring themselves to vote for the Republic came to me to share their sympathy for the death of my dear friend and leader. I knew that it would be this sympathy that would help us at the polls. The murder did not put to rest his ideals. To Joey Smallwood's horror the anti-Confederates now had a martyr that swayed the vote in favour of the Republic.

The vote, while still close, resulted in a Republican victory. There were rumours of vote fixing and ballot stuffing which were more fact than fiction but we had won and that was what mattered. I would have killed a million times to win that election and when the news came that we were free I broke down and cried. I felt that at last I had saved my people from a fate worse than it could have dreamed of.

On June 3, 1948, the Republic of Newfoundland was born. I have never seen the jubilation in the people's faces quite like the joy that I saw that night when the result was finally told. We were our own country once more and the relief that the people felt was palpable. Even those that voted for confederation had a glimmer of that alleviation in them. It was felt we had all dodged a bullet.

There was a great deal to be done before the nation would be able to prosper again. Open wounds that were caused over the battle for the republic had to be healed. Stephen O'Finn, was given a statue in Bowering Park and was hailed as a hero first by the Republicans, but soon after by the entire country. The people, once the initial shock of freedom wore off, soon took to the idea that they lived an independent nation once again and looked forward to settling their own problems.

Joey, who was defeated in his bid to become the first premiere of a new province of Canada, faded into the background for a few years then got his taste of power as the second President of the Republic of Newfoundland. That man was almost the ruin of the country and with one defeat and an air of vulnerability already under his belt he was soon handed a second. After the dreadful way he ran government, people shrugged their shoulders at the thought that he almost led us into a deal with Canada.

All that was sixty years ago but the consequences of those days still define the present. Without that hero who stepped into the breach when his country needed him the most I shudder to think of what would have happened to our nation.

Back in the present, the beer was going down well, but Tommy, who never had a strong stomach, was beginning to have his fill of both the alcohol and the recollections of the days of the past. Tommy's head was slowly nodding into his chest and I realised that the time for the past was over for the night. I gulped down the last of my Guinness and rose to my feet simultaneously stretching my arms out wide.

The young Newfoundland people don't fully understand the fierce struggle that divided the nation. They take it for granted that Newfoundland made the right choice. That it would have been downright stupid, just for a few dollars, to have given up our native land to a country that looked down on us. As I helped Tommy into a taxi and send him on his way I still have a tinge of doubt over the part I played in the whole affair. There was no way that referendum could have been fair and square, there was too much at stake to let democracy take its course, especially with the odds stacked squarely against us.

Yet, as I look back on all the hardships that we had to endure on account of my stand against the Canadian wolf I wonder for the briefest of instants if I had been right all along. Then I see the Pink, White and Green flags that fly so proudly over head from all sides of the country and I'm comforted. I'm certain that if I had to do it all over again my choice for freedom would have been the same. Long live the Republic and come near at your peril Canadian Wolf.

The End

The next day, October 31, was not just another day for the excited librarian. Today his assistant Cecilia promised she was going to dress up in a special costume for the occasion. Steve was going as Indiana Jones. His shirt looked good and rough, he placed his hat tilted on his head and he strapped a fake gun to his waist. All in all he imagined as he looked in his mirror that adventure had a new name, and that name was Steve.

For many parts of the world the last day of October is a special day on which anyone can dress up as outrageous as they like and no one will say two hoots about it. A girl can go out dressed as a cat in a hat and a man can go into his office dressed up like a leaf on a tree and everyone will smile. Try doing that in the middle of April.

So with his eggs lapped up and a smile in his heart Steve bid adieu to his fellow residents and briskly walked out the front door. Covered up in his coat there was hardly any costume to notice, Indiana Jones is hardly as conspicuous as

Dracula anyway. He glided down Long's Hill to Duckworth Street, reached a door, pulled out his key and swept himself inside. At the moment he was alone but soon the others would come and the fun would begin.

Anticipation swept over Steve and he could barely handle opening up the window blinds and the turning on the power to the photocopier before Cecilia arrived. While he was resolved to the fact that she was a co-worker and as such out-of-bounds, none-the-less a dressed up Cecilia was something to get excited about. At nine o'clock the door opened and Cecilia arrived. She took off her coat as usual and revealed her ordinary dress. Steve was utterly disappointed. How dare she tease him so cruelly? His fantasy of Cecilia in a cat suit or toga or red devil dress was about to die before ever truly having been born. Tears almost welled up in his eyes which he knew was totally disrespectful to the image of Indiana Jones, but his disappointment knew no bounds. He was about to say, "Where the heck is the goodness?" when the girl took out a bag, smiled and said she would be right back.

"What was she doing? Where was she going with that bag? It had to be something naughty if she wouldn't wear it in the street, perhaps she would be too cold." These thoughts and a hundred others filled the librarian's head as he waited for the beautiful girl to return. The wait was interminable and Steve almost gave up on never seeing the girl again when he heard a shuffle coming from the door to the library. He turned in readiness to drink in a health dose of cleavage when he gasped in disbelief; it was Allan arriving for the day. Allan showed up dressed in a flowing robe and sandals. "Who are you supposed to be?" the librarian asked.

"Who am I sir? I am one of the greatest philosophers of all time. I am Socrates!" With a hammy raise of his arm, he twisted his hand in the air as if he were about to make a piece of oratory history. He stiffened a bit, thrust his head up, turned his head a bit and yelled, "Great gods!" His eyes and that of the librarian's seemed to pop out of their sockets when they saw the sight that suddenly appeared in front of them. What they saw was Cecilia clad in black leather boots, leather corset, throat chain and a whip. It was a dominatrix outfit if there ever was one.

"What's the matter, I thought you boys liked Emma Peel?" Seeing that the two men were frozen to the spot she added, "It's from *The Avengers* episode "The Hellfire Club." Does that help any?" she asked.

"Best show ever," Steve weakly said. Allan felt a tingle in his left arm and his heart throbbed momentarily. The sight of Cecilia was enough to take anyone's breath away. The pair found it hard to take their eyes of their enchantress; it was only after a long pause that she cracked her whip to restore their tongues to their proper place in their heads. The pair would have preferred to stare indefinitely at the gorgeous woman but work still had to be done and soon there would be patrons to help.

The pleasantly surprised patrons of the library got more than an eyeful. Cecilia played the role of tantalizing temptress to the hilt smacking her whip on the floor of the library and ordering Allan and Steve around as if she was used to being in the role all her life. Her inner dominatrix came to the surface and both her menservants were tickled pink to be her thralls.

In the afternoon Steve spotted a group of children trick or treating with their guardians and decided to invite them into the library for treats and a story. For the first time in its history children had been welcomed into the library of thought and everyone seemed pleased with the result.

Allan told stories of the adventures of long ago where dragons were real and men rode on white unicorns. Cecilia passed out some of the candy that the elderly patrons refused to touch on the grounds that their dentures would explode. Steve helped organise the children and moved tables and chairs so that they would be comfortable. For an hour twenty children from ages eight to twelve were entertained by three enthusiastic people who were very, very glad to be delivered from their everyday routine. Seeing the happiness all around Steve thought that lives can grow stale when the rust of routine sets in.

The children, candy-filled and thoroughly enchanted by the wizardry of Allan's storytelling, left the library delighted. Their guardians, who continually were amazed by the very existence of a library in downtown St. John's of all places, were happy as well to let others take over their duty of keeping the children entertained for an all too brief hour. As the children left the library they all promised to come again next year. The day ended, everyone had enjoyed a great time and Allan, the man who was against Halloween in the library at the beginning, was the one who anticipated the children's next visit most of all.

The big dark arrives in late October but it is truly entrenched in November. It is a period of time in Newfoundland when anyone can wake up in the morning and see blackness outside, go to work in a haze then get walk out of the office after work and still be in darkness. People can and do go without seeing the sun for months and it is a deeply depressing time for some.

Steve truly hated the big dark. It sapped his energy and set him upon the bleak path of depression, even more so now that the sheer amount of time that he spent living in the dark reminded him of his time in space. Superman would never have been able to live in Newfoundland, even more than humans; the alien from Krypton needed sunlight to live. Those that can, schedule business trips during the big dark. It is a time where the weeks lose meaning and people hibernate and gain a lot of weight. Steve felt the expanse in his pants and knew that his new diet was not working.

His eating habits had been in decline ever since he left New York and went back home. Although he did indulge in a pizza nearly every Friday night the rest of the week he ate sensibly or not at all. Here in St. John's living so close to a multitude of fish n' chips emporiums, he succumbed to the lure much too often. After not having fish and chips for so long, he engaged in eating it sometimes four times a week and now the results were showing.

This tightening of the waistline only led to more depression that led to more fish and chips that inevitably led to the continuation of the circle. The big dark now contributed to this morbid sequence as there would be more time to stay indoors and less out in the non-existent sunlight. Sleep became a big time hobby for the man as his psyche began to tire more easily than before. There dreams came of castles and creatures both strange and mysterious. It was sleep that was on his thoughts when the phone rang one day in late November and slapped him out of the arms of Morpheus. "Hello? Who is it?" he sleepily asked.

"It's Duane. Are you free for a pint or twelve?"

Still tired but realizing that it was only eight o'clock, he replied, "Sure, what the hey." Soon it was arranged that Duane would arrive and they would go out to one of their favourite pubs. Steve hoped he might get a few winks in before he arrived.

The Duke of Duckworth is one of the more popular pubs in downtown St. John's. Located at 325 Duckworth Street McMurdo's Lane, it is a place where everyone and anyone can relax and enjoy a well-poured pint of Guinness. Terry, the owner, is a friendly individual who doesn't mind signing, dancing and general happiness in his pub.

Steve enjoyed going to the Duke. It was his home away from home, a place where he could sit back and relax without the deafening noise that many other pubs seemed to enjoy cranking out. This night Steve entered the pub with his friend and fellow librarian Duane. Duane was part of the new breed of librarian, the breed that actually didn't need a library to be employed. He worked with databases, computer systems and a whole host of other electronic stuff that Steve either couldn't or wouldn't understand.

The Duke was crowded as they entered from the cold, dark night and they had to settle for a table in the middle of the pub. Steve went up to the bar and ordered a pint of Guinness and a pint of Smithwicks. Soon the $15.50 plus tip was exchanged for two pints of the foamy stuff and Steve tiptoed his way back to his table. "Ah, here you go guy, something to help salve your problems." Steve enjoyed his little pun and passed a Smithy to his hardly-amused friend.

It was rare when both men found the time to visit with each other, but when they did they made the most of it. Drinks flowed freely and the conversation went more freely. They talked about their respective careers. The Library of Thought, why did it exist and to whom did it benefit, fascinated Duane, "It has to be some kind of tax dodge," he concluded.

" I dunno, I think that there has to be more to it than that. I hope so," Steve said.

The world of librarianship was a multi-faceted one. There were children's librarians, reference librarians, collection librarians, school librarians, preservation librarians, medical librarians, special librarians, space librarians and a host of other types of librarians. Each separate branch had its own unique tongue and when a group of librarians got together it was a wonder they understood each other at all.

The two librarians seated for a relaxing pint understood each other perfectly though. As the pints flowed their conversation went from the complexities of the Dewey Decimal System to collection development to how the Miami Dolphins never make the playoffs to why Formula One needs to change their fuel from gasoline to something more environmentally friendly.

It was after the sixth pint that the conversation turned towards the familiar topic of sex and the library. Duane was recounting the story of how one day he found a couple of library assistants having sex in a university stacks. "It was in the religion B section for goodness sakes!" he laughed as he said this, as anyone who knows the Library of Congress classification system B is for religion and certainly the pair in question were getting to know each other in the biblical sense of the term.

"Oh, I tell you, you should see the assistant I have in my library. There's one woman who you would love to get in the B section. She wore this unbelievable outfit for Halloween that was too sexy to describe. I almost had to be alone for a couple of minutes if you know what I mean."

Steve would have gone on about his assistant's wonderful Halloween attire but he heard a shuffle behind him. He turned to see Cecilia get up from her chair that had been situated directly behind his. She gave him a look that if she had been a Gorgon he would have immediately been turned to stone. As it was he had turned red and before he had the chance to apologise the girl got up from her chair and left her friends, her Guinness and the pub altogether.

"Oops," Steve said to his companion.

"That was her? Holy God, I can just imagine the trouble you are going to be in tomorrow. She looked like she wanted to eviscerate you. She was hot though."

"So you think she might have heard then?" Steve optimistically asked.

Duane shook his head and gulped back another healthy dose of Smithwicks. Steve, with an aching in his head, decided that after just one more round he would go home and wish the incident away. By closing time he had just about had enough pints for the night and with an adieu to the friendly bartender he got in a taxi with Duane and made it home.

Steve crashed down on his bed and immediately went to sleep. It was not nightmares or dreams that filled his unconscious thoughts. It was the same, chilling haunting theme that plagued his soul every night for no reason. It was the image of a storm battering his soul, it was the picture of nuclear holocausts disintegrating everything around him; it was horror and destruction and death and blood. The most chilling part of all was the knowledge in the depths of Steve's soul that it was the entire experience was extremely and utterly real.

The next morning, hung over and repentant, Steve got out of bed and moved slowly towards the shower. He couldn't eat his usual eggs and settled for just a diet pop and a pair of aspirin before leaving for work. The world seemed just a little bit darker and he knew that he was going to have a few awkward moments when the time came for Cecilia to arrive.

The clock ticked slowly until finally the door opened and the girl who was offended showed. She refused to talk to Steve, preferring to stave off any attempt at communication by turning her back on the man. Soon she was off in the stacks of books and Steve, not wishing his head to "accidentally" fall off, decided the best approach was to let her come to him. What did he really say that was so offensive anyway? That he thought she was attractive? That he wouldn't mind enjoying her company at some time? It was just his luck that of all nights he went out that she would be sitting behind him just when the conversation turned to the attractiveness of his assistants. Just his luck.

Allan soon arrived and as if picking up some strange psyche energy he shivered. Something was in the air and it was not good. The entire day was one of avoidance, Steve avoided Cecilia, Cecilia avoided Steve and Allan avoided the pair of them preferring to let sleeping dogs lie. If someone wished to discuss something with him then they would have to come to him and at three thirty, after Cecilia had left for the day, someone in the form of Steve did.

"Well, I guess you are wondering what is going on," Steve matter-of-factly said. He needed to talk and since Allan was there why not make use of him. "She's a bit upset because she overheard me in the pub talking to a friend of mine saying she was hot in that Halloween dress. I can't understand why she is taking this to heart. Man, if she doesn't cool down I might get into trouble with the owner Joe over this."

"Oh, I wouldn't worry about Joe if I were you. Just let me fix it. Everything will be all right." Allan smiled and walked out the door leaving Steve to ponder just what did Allan know that he did not.

Chapter Ten

Merry Christmas

The next week ran mostly smoothly in the library. Steve managed to apologise to Cecilia and all in all she took it well and things, while not entirely back to normal, began to work again. Allan continued on the way he always did, sniffing books and staying out of trouble. Once Friday came Steve was more than happy to see the end of this particular week. The day went about as well as the rest of the week, Cecilia was off quietly doing her own work, Allan was busy sniffing Boethius' *The Consolation of Philosophy* and Steve was filling out forms to buy some books. Only a handful of patrons entered the library. More and more there were fewer and fewer filing in through the front door. The only thing that had remained the same was that Allan still felt the need to hide away and sniff his old books.

Twelve o'clock came. Cecilia left for her lunch break and then as one-thirty approached Allan put on his long, heavy coat and prepared to leave. "Goodbye Steve, I am not feeling very well so I think I'll go on home. Have a good weekend." Allan turned then as he neared the door he suddenly let out a gasp. His arm shot out and he knocked down a row of books upon himself as he fell to the floor.

"Holy cow!" the startled Steve said. He immediately called 911 then rushed over to his assistant's side. "Are you all right, Allan?"

The old man gasped as the blood ran freely from his mouth; help it seemed would come too late. His trusted librarian held him in his arms and tried to comfort the dying man. "No, no, don't worry about me, if it's time it's time and I can't think of any other place I would want to go but in the presence of the books which gave me so much pleasure. Some people think that they can own a book but that's impossible, it's just borrowed knowledge. The book goes on longer than the writer or those that read them."

Steve didn't know what to do or say so he merely kept silent and listened to the final words of his friend. "I guess I'll soon find out which one of these guys, if any, was telling the truth." The weak gentleman slowly raised his arm and waved it at his beloved philosophers who sat silently on the shelves.

Soon the ambulance arrived and the emergency team rushed in the door with equipment and a stretcher. Steve moved aside so that he would not be in the way. In less than a minute he was rushed away. The visibly upset librarian could hardly move from where he stood. One minute his assistant was there, the next he was gone. Who knows if he would return? What could he do?

The librarian waited quietly inside his office until Cecilia returned from her lunch. He told her the terrible news that the old man had been taken to the hospital and it did not look good. The woman took the information poorly. She broke down immediately and cried. She was a strong woman but Allan had been her friend from the first day she arrived and if he was to die it would be a terrible blow to her.

It was decided that she would go directly to the hospital to see if there was any hope. Steve would stay in the library in case a call came there. The two parted with a hug and once again Steve found he was alone. He strolled through his book aisles with emptiness in his heart. Alone again, it seemed that was his lot in life, Dave the security guard, Melinda, Cecilia and now even Allan all left him alone. What was life really all about? He looked at all the dusty books around him and wondered. "Do any of you have the answers for me? Is even one of you worthy of the paper you are printed on?"

Books for such a long time had been a part of his life that they were always considered necessary but he now wondered if now they were actually worth anything. Was he or the people who came to this private little library kidding themselves into thinking that they were doing anything but wasting their time? Were the mocking gargoyles on the walls right? Was the meaning of life actually sleeping in these parchments or were they just distractions or excuses from actually experiencing the real thing? Did this Library of Thought have a real purpose?

All these questions and a thousand more came to Steve as he fretted over the fate of his friend. Despite himself he thought of the practical implications of Allan's death. Despite the spinning of wheels in his head Steve tried to put all his questions out of his mind. What was important now is the condition of his assistant. For two hours he waited. He hung on to hope that all might be well when finally the phone rang. "Hello, hello?" the librarian anxiously asked.

"No, I'm sorry but that book is out right now. Please call back some other time. Thank you, goodbye."

The phone remained silent for the next hour. Steve spent the time shelving the books that had been knocked over during Allan's fall. His mind was blank now. He worked on things that came automatically to him, such as shelving and adjusting and dusting, work that required no thought but still something that justified his pay. He didn't want to close the library until it was four o'clock, which was something that Allan would have wanted.

It was at four o'clock that the phone rang again. By this time Steve had been in a trancelike state for hours and he had not heard the phone at first. The ringing went on and on and on until Steve finally regained his senses and answered the phone. Lifting up the receiver he pulled it to his ear and prepared for the worst. "Hello."

"Where the hell were you? I've been waiting for five minutes!" Cecilia shouted.

"Sorry, I was a bit lost. How are things?"

"Surprisingly well. Allan will pull though. He's had a mild stroke, but the doctors say he will recover given enough time and rest. Isn't that excellent news?" Cecilia sounded happy on the phone but Steve was quiet on the other end. It was all too much for him. In the past three months he had two people drop in front of him in the library. One man made it, the other didn't. Was this to be a normal occurrence for him while working in this library? He bade goodbye to the girl on the phone and hung up. He was relieved but still disturbed by this incident.

Now that the waiting was over he decided to close up shop for the day. He had enough excitement for one evening so quickly he put on his jacket and shut the door. The night had already established itself and as he trudged up the hill in relative darkness he thought dark thoughts which held no dreams of the future.

The rest of the day he sat on his bed thinking. The old man had taught him something, not by his philosophy but by his near-death experience. That thought kept Steve awake through much of the long, cold night. Many of the experiences that he had with the space library, New York City and finally at home were bizarre and were beginning to take a toll on him physically and mentally. He shut his eyes and tried to get some rest.

All of November Steve and Cecilia worked away in the small library. They answered questions, shelved and tidied and time marched on. December arrives, the cold set in and little changed. It was only when the nineteenth of December appeared on the calendar that the library pair were greeted to a happy sight. Allan opened the door to the library and greeted everyone with a big hello. Steve and Cecilia leapt up from their chairs and rushed to his side.

Allan began to regale his two friends with the stories of his hospital stay when he stopped suddenly and asked, "Where are the Christmas decorations?" beyond the usual trappings of gargoyles and pictures of biblical proportions there was no sign of holly leaves and nary a hair of Christmas trees. "Don't tell me that you went all out for Halloween and haven't done a fig about Christmas yet?"

"Well, I like Halloween. Christmas can be depressing." Steve folded his arms and slid back in his chair, a pout on his lips. The thought of Christmas in the library didn't fill him with cheer. Did he have to buy presents?

"Well, we can't have that now can we?" Allan laughed and it seemed that for the first time in weeks a spark of life had been brought back into the library of thought. Over the next few days things got progressively better. Christmas rapidly approached and the three got ready for the big day in the library. They decided to have a celebration on December 23rd, the last day that the library would be open before the holidays. All Allan's friends and patrons would be invited. People would come for the party and the Library of Thought would be alive for the first time since Halloween.

Allan and Cecilia bought the decorations as Steve stayed in his office and brooded. "Humbug!" he said to himself as the pair left for the outing. He knew what was wrong with him, but he still was not sure if he had the courage to say something. In the silence of his office he decided to take a chance. He was going to ask Cecilia out.

Soon in came the two with bags loaded with decorations and food for the coming tide of people. Allan had told all his friends to show up for some drinks and cake and that they were not to disappoint. In a matter of an hour the library was filled with people both young and old having a wonderful time. Drinks were poured out and everyone congratulated Allan on his speedy recovery.

Steve, emboldened by three glasses of moderately expensive red wine, decided to make his move. Summoning up all his courage he walked over to the laughing Cecilia and asked, "Listen, would you like to go to the Duke after this is over?" the librarian inquired.

"Thanks, but I'm meeting my new boyfriend," she answered.

"Hey, let's all sing a song!" Allan shouted to the group. Within an instant "Auld Lang Sygne" was kicking into high gear. People were laughing, singing and raising their glasses to the holiday season that muffled out the lone, sad cry of "Rats!" that managed to escape the poor, sad librarian's lips. One more love was not in the cards that he had been dealt.

At last the party was over and after clearing up the mess it was time to go home. Steve dejectedly put on his hat and coat and began to walk out the door. As he was about to leave something seemed to tug on him so he turned as he came to the entrance and looked at his library. Upon reflection he began to put the mad year in perspective. He thought about his year without context. No matter what would happen in the coming days, months and years he knew he had contributed to this library. He changed the lives of not only the two people who worked there but also all the patrons who daily came looking for some meaning to their lives.

Perhaps the old men and women who came there were simply looking for company and not the meaning of existence but at least they had somewhere to go when the world had left them alone. This was the thing that he would hold in his heart after the year was over. His space library had been destroyed by persons or creatures unknown, he was stranded in New York City with hardly a dime and made it there and after a choice bit of luck ended up where he wanted to go all along, home to new and old friends.

He looked back upon all the changes that he had made during the last six months. It began with being dropped off from a space ship, to living in one of the most famous cities in the world where he was desolate and lonely. It ended with him coming home to work in a place that for all intents and purposes didn't exist to the outside world but where he was for the most part content. Perhaps the New Year would change the way he felt about the Library of Thought but for now, right now, as he looked at his library he felt something he had not felt in a long time. He felt that he belonged. Steve turned out the lights, opened the door to the street and turned his back to the wind.

Tomorrow would be Christmas Eve and for many people one of the most magical days of the year. The night was just beginning for Steve. He had invited some of his friends to join him at the Duke of Duckworth for a few beverages to toast in the season. For years this was a traditional event that all his pals looked forward to with great anticipation and tonight would be no exception.

The gathering at the Duke was full of life. The place was packed with men and women dressed up as Santa Claus or one of his many helpers. There were many beautiful young women running about in their red, green and white costumes trading kisses for beers. Steve and his companions were enjoying another night of freely flowing conversation and even more freely flowing beer. This was a chance for those who rarely had the opportunity to get together to compare notes of the year gone by and plan the one to come.

Steve sat back and listened to the stories of his friends around him. The two old men in the corner who usually never talked drank to his health and he returned the gesture. They all had a similar mix of hope and disappointment. After the drinks had been put away and all the Santas had evacuated Steve and some of his friends decided to go to another bar to tap off the night. Most of the bars by this late hour had closed so they took a long walk to a bar called the Piccadilly Pub, a strip joint on Duckworth Street whose claim to fame was that they featured local talent.

Alcohol and the desire for the night not to end led them to the pub's door and beyond. It was dark inside and surprisingly for the time of night there were many people. The group of five men walked up to the bar and ordered their drinks. Steve received his Black Horse beer and then looked at the show on the small, dimly lit stage. The girl gyrating to "You Sexy Thing" by Hot Chocolate was attractive but hardly what would be considered energetic. Steve thought that at least she would know that Newfoundland was not part of Vancouver.

Everyone seemed happy in this little bar, sure some of them hooted at the pretty girl on stage but they were happy hoots. There was a festive mood in the air and at two o'clock in the morning on a Christmas Eve that seemed more than appropriate. Steve finished his beer and as his friends bid him goodnight he paused, looked back at the odd scene in the bar and to stay behind for one more beer.

"Give us one for the road luv," he called out to the bartender waving a twenty-dollar bill. The beer quickly followed and the change added up to $15.95. It was as Steve pressed his lips to the bottle while simultaneously looking at the patrons of the establishment that he came to a realization. It was more of a feeling than something he could articulate but something significant was there inside him. He looked about him, at the men who were staring at the naked girls, at the woman bartender who was busily tending bar and to the girls who roamed about with smiles on their faces seemingly glad to make a buck. There was a connection there and somehow in this bar on a fresh Christmas Eve something began to fit for Steve.

All these people that he met over the past few months had some something in common. There was a singular thread of humanity that tied them together, which bound these diverse people tight in a shared world. It was this realization that came over Steve like a wave of spiritual relief, as if something that had been bothering him had finally been fixed. His experiences helped him to understand something about humanity that sometimes things are because we are. His love for planet Earth had come back to him and his heart beat with a pride that being all alone in the stars he could not manage to find.

All creatures great and small, Steve felt he had met them all. The past few months had made a great impact upon him. He looked back and remembered the time he lived in New York City and while it was for the most part a boring experience it was something that he would never forget. In his brief trip to Toronto he was glad for his chance to reunite with special friends who kept their culture alive with frequent visits to the homeland to bring back precious supplies of Dominion Ale. His new position with the Library of Thought had opened his mind to ways of thinking that previously he hardly knew existed. Even the men and women he met in the bar on the beginning of Christmas Eve, these people were decent folk in a place where decency some may think would be an unknown quantity.

With a final look back at the happy people Steve left the strip bar and began to wander his way home. He past a few people in the cold streets, wished them a merry Christmas, and continued on towards home. Finally he made it to his front door, fiddled with his pockets until he produced a key, inserted the object after a few unsteady tries and then finally opened the door.

Steve entered his house, took off his outerwear and headed up to his room. With a clear mind he got into his cosy bed, pulled the sheets over his body and went readily to sleep. That night he dreamed of the sun on a clear and calm day. The wind was cool and everything seemed right with the world. For Steve, his dreams for the first time in a long time were something beautiful to remember.

Chapter Eleven

Revenge of the Vampire Zombie Bunnies

Her body was more than willing as he put his strong arms around the beautiful woman and gently pulled her towards his eager lips. There was no protest or hesitation, and when their lips touched there was a wave of love between them that could not be shaken by the whims of time. After an all but too brief moment Steve looked into the beautiful woman's eyes and said "Oh Cecilia, you are so beautiful and this night is so perfect. It all feels like a dream."

Cecilia looked at the man, gently put her finger to his lips and said "But of course it is a dream, my dear." Then she slowly shimmered and faded away to be replaced by a small monkey with a bunch of bananas. "Bugger," came the reply from the still sleeping man.

Steve woke up from his warm, comfortable bed at slightly before high noon on January the first and began slowly to open his eyes one lid at a time. It sounded to him that they creaked as they haltingly rose from the rest that they so obviously enjoyed. First the right eye then the left opened and slowly focused on the ceiling of his room. His right arm raised itself and patted the body insuring that all limbs and essentials were unharmed and intact.

Plunking the arm back down it smacked on something hard. Feeling around the object told the hand that it had in fact struck a bottle of some sort. Without further information from the other senses the hand guessed that it had been a wine bottle that it had been holding only hours before.

Five minutes elapsed, then another ten. Finally, as the rest of the body decided that there was no reason to disturb itself from its happy repose, the hand, knowing that the eyes had already thrown in the white towel and closed, gradually fell to the side of the bed and relaxed. The New Year had begun.

January first, the beginning of a new year and a fresh start to life for everyone, like a clean slate the year begins free of clutter. For the librarian in charge of the library of thought the day was especially significant. Other years were pestered with self-defeating thoughts and worries about how the year would unfold, but this year was different. This year would be good. Gone was the thought of space travel and all that madness. This year promised stability, it promised a real job in the city that he loved. The year of promise began.

At two in the afternoon Steve had finally managed to get himself out of bed and into the shower. The first shower of the New Year and a well-needed one at that for the haze of smoke that his body had maneuvered through the previous night had penetrated into his skin and Steve hated the smell of smoke. The cascade of water and a healthy lather of soap soon put paid to the emanations that arose from his body, now if only he could do something about the drummer boy in his head.

Popping out of the shower Steve dried himself, put on his new pants and sweater that his mother had bought him, and proceeded to plan out the rest of his day. Food at the moment was out, there was no room for it and the disturbance it would create in his stomach would not be long tolerated. No, he decided that it was best merely to take a brisk walk around the neighborhood to clear his head off all the cobwebs. So grabbing his winter coat and putting on his boots he was off to inhale some fresh, cold air.

The crisp snow crackled under the man's boots as he walked through the fresh coating of snow. He could see from the haphazard trails along his path that party goers had staggered their way to and fro coming and going from one home to the next in search of the elusive New Year's Eve magic. Some of course found it but they were in the vast minority. Most woke up the next morning feeling like hell and disappointed in the night before but already making plans for the next one. That is what it is like to chase the New Year's Eve dream.

This was all moot to Steve. He could not recall quite what he had done on New Year's Eve but he was sure that he must have had an entertaining evening. He did recall that he was talking to an enchantress by the name of Penny and that she was tall and plentiful. What the conversation was about he did not remember but he was sure that it was delightful. Afterwards it all got a tad hazy and his recollection ended. In time he was sure that it would be brought back to life but as Steve walked the silent street of downtown St. John's his mind was a blank slate just like the New Year.

As Steve was strolling down non-memory lane Ms. Cecilia Carpenter was strolling along the opposite side of the same street, like ships passing in the night. Steve, lost in his own thoughts never looked up to notice his co-worker. Cecilia, on the other hand, looked intently at her co-worker, muttered something to herself and walked on.

After a week of holidays Steve was looking forward to once again returning to the Library of Thought. While the break was excellent he knew that too much time away from the library would mean that he would get ever fatter on Christmas cakes, beer and oh those lovely rice crispy cookies that his brother made. The best cure for the rapid expanse in his pants was to return to work where the routine of the day would put a halt to snacking during all hours.

It was a cold, dry morning that greeted Steve as he walked down Long's Hill and towards his Duckworth Street library. He was looking forward to seeing Cecilia and Allan again and exchanging stories of how their respective holidays went. He wondered how after the break the feelings he held for Cecilia would have changed in any way. Would they still be a strong or would they have faded in any way? It would not take long to find out as he marched himself through the morning air.

The morning had started out so well that Steve instinctively knew that it was bound to fall to the dark side sooner or later; it was just that he didn't know just how hard the fall would be. For the first time since he had returned to Earth he had managed to put the space library behind him, his memories of that part of his life had become something of a mad dream than actually reality. The plain fact of the matter was that if he ever told anyone about his wild experiences as a space librarian he would probably have been put away as a crazy person also helped to keep the memories at bay. Not being able to share his time in space with anyone on the entire planet helped to make the memories seem less real and more of a dream.

The loss of that life didn't much matter to him on that happy, crisp morning as he cheerily crunched his feet under the freshly fallen snow on his way to the library of thought. He smiled at people with a genuine smile and he nodded to every passerby, life was getting good again and while he knew that there were slings and arrows to come he was prepared to meet them head on and fight for his right for happiness in a cruel and unjust universe. Little did he realize just how cruel and unjust the universe really was but he was about to get his first clue.

As he opened the front door and walked into the cool library he found himself confronted by a sight that he had hoped he would never see again. Standing menacingly in the darkness was the large form of his onetime Manhattan branch library boss the Master of Evil with her huge arms folded and a look of utter pleasure on her enormous, evil face.

Steve shook his head in disbelief sure that this sight before him was the result of the congealed gravy he had splashed on the micro waved chips that he had eaten for the morning's breakfast on the account that his bread had all run out and he wanted something to eat before going to work. There was no way in hell that his former boss from the New York Public Library was standing in his downtown St. John's library looking like she had eaten the canary and the cat too.

"Not possible." Steve could not believe his eyes yet here was absolute proof that the universe was simply against him. What in God's name could she possible be here for? Steve slowly circled the large woman before asking the obvious question. "What the hell are you doing here?"

The smile that came from the woman wasn't one born of happiness, it was pure malevolence. The Master of Evil did not say a word but clicked her fingers and Allan walked out from behind the librarian's desk. He stood to the right of the woman and both began to smile menacingly.

"Ok, I am officially asleep having one bizarre nightmare," Steve said. He looked at the pair that just stared back at him and he realized that the other shoe was about to drop right on his head. He took a step back as the two advanced on him until his back was to the front entrance that only moments ago he so cheerily entered.

Allan looked into the eyes of his former co-worker and stared into the face of the librarian. After a moment he spoke not in the friendly tone that Steve was familiar with but a voice tainted with menace, "Oh, for so long we have waited for this moment, so long have we watched and waited. No more."

"Ok, what the hell is going on here and why is that woman here?" Steve demanded but with a slight tinge of fear in his voice as if Allan had disturbed him with his unusual delivery. He put his hand in his pocket probing for anything that might be used as a weapon but there was nothing save his keys that he didn't think he could use against Allan.

"It's simple, we want the book," the large public librarian said.

"Could you be a little more specific? We have a lot of books here," Steve replied.

"We want the book of the dead, the book that gives life to the unliving; we want the Tome of the Lost Ones!" Allan shouted out. Steve was mystified. No one on Earth could even know of the book's existence let alone come to the one person on the entire planet that knew where the book was being held. No one from Earth that was.

"Oh..., that book." Steve smiled and turned to face not the front door as he had hoped but a smiling Cecilia who looked for all intents and purposes like life was unfolding as it should and that nothing was wrong. Steve told her to run but she just stood there smiling as if she was oblivious to the world around her. Steve tried to move her physically out of the way but there was no way he could move the rigid form in front of him, he was trapped with enemies on all sides.

"I thought that might surprise you. Cecilia is a robot placed here to keep an eye on you during your non-working hours. Or did you think it a coincidence that she was behind you in that pub all those months ago?"

"Alright, alright. Just what the hell is going on here and how do you know about the book?" Steve was in the first stage of being in a state of rage. Just when he though life was going good something out of the blue comes along and rips his contentment from him and if what he was now thinking was true then his whole life upon his return to Earth had been one big fat lie.

Cecilia led him to a chair and the three surrounded him. There in the cold January early morning he was told the truth of how his library space ship was trailed to Earth by the followers of Gregos whom Steve had unintentionally overthrown as supreme ruler of the cosmos. They were upset that their place in the universe had been disrupted and the people of the planet Maladred wanted to go back to being kings of the hill.

Allan looked into the eyes of the now-angry librarian and said "We want the book. It is the ultimate weapon and any planet that stands against us will feel the fear of their dead return to life to consume! We, the people of Maladred have thrown off our lethargy and will once again take our rightful place as ultimate rulers of the universe!" A stray spate of spit hit Steve's chin as he listened to the last part of the raving library co-worker but as he tried to stand up to punch Allan in the face Cecilia violently pushed him back into his chair. Steve looked up to meet her eyes but all that met his was a cold and indifferent stare. No change there then he thought.

"I really do not wish to make this an unpleasant affair," Allan continued.

"Well, then this is really not going well for either of us is it?" Steve replied.

"But I want that book and since your actions have not led us to it we are forced to show our hand. Give us the Tome of the Lost Ones! Give it to us now or we shall destroy the Earth! Our people may no longer have the military capacity to rule the galaxy but we certainly have the strength to wipe out one miserable back water planet!" Allan's eyes had changed from the kindness that he had usually showed to a level of madness that Steve had never before encountered.

"Well, it is not like you are giving me much choice in the matter. Give you a book that will help you and your mad people regain power over the galaxy or the destruction of my home planet. What kind of assurance will I get that you won't simply take the book and destroy me and my people?" Steve asked the increasingly drooling Allan.

"You have my word as the heir of Gregos that I will spare you and your people from destruction. We have no need to destroy this backward planet. All we want is the book and we'll leave you alone. But any tricks and we'll at least have our revenge on the great 'Liberator'." Allan laughed at that word. If only the people of the free universe could see their fabled hero now. A small, pathetic creature living in a wretched planet that didn't even have a decent beer let alone interstellar transportation.

Steve looked at the trio of menace around him and knew that for the sake of the Earth he had to comply with their demands. Yet the code of conduct of the Inter Galactic Library Board stirred deep into his veins and he simply had a terrible time letting anyone take a book without checking it out first let alone the most dangerous book in the entire universe. Unfortunately, the fate of the Earth was in his hands and there seemed to be little choice. The creeps in his library may not be able to do what they say they could but any space faring race had to have technology far more advanced than that of Earth. They certainly had the capacity to do a lot of damage.

Having experienced their planet firsthand there was every chance that the warlike crazies of the planet Maladred had decided to take another crack at ruling the universe. What better weapon than the silent killer that everyone feared? There was indeed magic in the universe and unfortunately in this particular case it was pure evil. Giving it to the power mad people of Maladred would destroy a hundred worlds but how could he let Earth suffer for the actions of just one of its inhabitants?

"Ok, I'll get you the book. It isn't here. We'll have to take a little walk." Steve looked at the perfect form of Cecilia and after a nod from her master the beautiful robot let Steve up from his chair. The librarian got up and began to move to the front door, this time rather than being stopped he was followed out the door and onto the cold street.

The deep silence during their small walk would have unsettled even a veteran academic librarian, Steve walked along Duckworth Street with the strange trio of a large woman, an elderly man and a beautiful woman/robot all following close by. It didn't take long before the group arrived at their destination, 141 Duckworth Street, home of Downtown Comics. "Of course, the comic book store! Who would have thought of ever having an important book in a place like this?" the Master of Evil spat out.

"I bet you have never even read a comic book or graphic novel," Steve said to the Master of Evil.

"No, never and I am glad I never did!" she squealed with righteousness.

Steve stopped in front of the large window of the comic book store and turned to Allan. "You know, technically the book is the property of the Inter Galactic Library. You wouldn't happen to have your library card handy just so I can cover my behind with the board do you?" Allan looked at the sincere librarian with slight shock. He replied that he never had a library card in his life and the pretense of loving books for months made him physically ill. Steve shook his head at the willful ignorance and turned to the door of the panel-loving bookstore.

All four entered the building. Steve quietly strode up to Jason the owner and asked for that special book that he had been holding for him. At first Jason handed Steve the *Illustrated Companion to Bettie Page* but quickly Steve pushed that away and said, "No, not that special book, the other one." Jason looked at the three people accompanying Steve, and looked thrice at the lovely Cecilia before getting up from his chair.

Jason got out from behind his counter and went to the backroom. A moment later he reappeared with a small white box. Steve took the box gingerly from Jason's hands and handed it over to the grinning Allan. "Here you go, the Tome of the Lost Ones now get the hell out of my life."

Allan took the top of the box and looked inside. Nodding to his companions he replaced the top on the box and the three left without another word to Steve. Steve watched the three leave, walked to the front door and made sure that they were gone. He returned inside and walked up to Jason. "You know, some days can be good, some days can be bad but today just blew most of them days out the water."

"I can't believe it, I can't believe you gave them the book," Jason said incredulously. "I can't believe anyone would simply give away a mint, hardcover copy of *Seduction of the Innocent*. It was a first edition for goodness sake! At least you kept the dust jacket. Here it is protected in Mylar." Jason held out the cover of the controversial book that helped destroy EC Comics and hindered the natural progression of comic books as an art form for decades.

Steve smiled to himself. He played a hunch that neither Allan nor the Master of Evil actually knew how to read. It was obvious that the people of Maladred had a lot of catching up to do when it came to doing things for themselves and reading was one of them. He remembered that the Master of Evil was rumored never to have read and Allan always sniffed books so perhaps he didn't have a clue about them either. Anyone with a brain would not have fell for the ruse of switching books but they fell for it hook, line and sinker.

It was a ruse that if you had written it in a fiction novel no one would have believed it but truth is often stranger than fiction. The book he gave them was old, smelt like it had been around for some time and hidden in a comic book store where few people actually buy text books. It was the perfect hideout for a tome of great power.

The switch wouldn't last forever though, as soon as the three got back to their home world someone with more on the ball would figure out that they had been had and would come back looking for revenge. Steve had to act quickly in order to really save the Earth. Fortunately his pal Jason was there to help him out. Within the walls of Downtown

Comics was the actual Tome of the Lost Ones which Steve sent to Jason very soon after landing in New York City.

Steve had kept the book on him after the crash. Despite being asked for its whereabouts by the Inter Galactic Library Board he maintained that it had been destroyed in the crash. No one knew that he had it, though obviously people had suspected, but since it was the most dangerous book in the universe, and what's more he really wanted a souvenir of his time in space, what better person to have the book than a dedicated librarian?

Sending the evil book to Jason at the comic book store was the only thing he could think of to avoid anyone such as the Inter Galactic Library Board trying to discover if he really did have the book. Once the heat was off then he could collect it from his friend and put it in his own book collection.

Unfortunately he didn't count on the persistence of the Maladred people who obviously weren't the forgive-and-forget types. Now he had to do the one thing that he really didn't want to do; he had to ask for help from the very person he wished to avoid for a long time to come. He had to call Bogatta.

Sitting down in the Downtown Comics' small office Steve opened the box containing the true Tome of the Lost Ones and within the box there was a small, square device that looked like a little television. Steve turned on the device and silently waited for a response. It didn't take long.

"Liberator!" shouted a very happy man who appeared on the screen. It wasn't that Steve didn't like Bogatta, it was just that both times he met him the fellow just got too excited for words. If the man could manage to calm down a little perhaps he would be a fine alien but until that day Steve would have preferred not to give the fellow a call, but considering the unique circumstances he didn't really have a choice in the matter.

Steve explained the situation as quickly as he could. "So now I gotta find the fastest ship in the galaxy to pick me up and then head to Maladred to stop them from getting their revenge on the Earth. Can you help me Bogatta?"

Bogatta had become the representative for Quan on the newly formed Galactic Council after the fall of Gregos, which was a position of some power. Bogatta immediately made arrangements for Steve to be picked up in a fast ship and then taken to Maladred where he was on his own when it came to ending his troubles with the people of the planet. The small force of ships that the Galactic Council had was about as efficient as a bunch of monkeys hired to write Shakespeare and even less accurate.

Maybe the universe was simply filled with slackers, or perhaps eons of total rule under one dedicated slacker had made the whole universe sluggish when it came to initiative but after the initial revolution against Maladred and the subsequent kegger had ended few planets had followed up on the actual getting down and getting their hands dirty in running the galaxy. According to the Inter Galactic Library Board's own news website most planets ran almost exactly the same way as they had during the time of the supposed tyranny. In consequence there was little to no effect on the Inter-Planetary Library Loan policy or IPLL.

That also meant that Janet Eke of Champaign, Illinois had only three more weeks to return a book on gardening that she accidentally received in the mail via her local public library. The book was, in actuality, on loan from a library in the Davros Twelve system whose librarian S. Magfly just so happened to be particularly brutal when it came to delinquent borrowers. Such unfortunate things happen when loaning library books becomes a universe-wide operation.

Steve turned off the small device that Bogatta had insisted on giving to him during the fast revolution and for which Steve was now thankful he did. Having no other way of communication with the outside galaxy that little device might have been the instrument that saved planet Earth. After checking out the latest comic book releases, which for once actually arrived on a Friday, Steve prepared himself to leave the Earth and do battle with murderous aliens.

Only a madman or a librarian could handle such a job as save the Earth from destruction and fortunately Steve was a bit of both. He had precisely two weeks to prepare as he learned from his space acquaintance that even the fastest ship still had to travel a large portion of the galaxy in order to arrive on Earth. Steve's hope was that Allan's ship was just that much slower.

The librarian decided that it was best to return to the scene of the crime and look for clues back at the library of thought. Bidding Jason a fond farewell he began to walk back to his library in order to rummage for anything that would lead to the deadly trio's comeuppance. As he neared the library of thought his chest sighed with the instant realization that he wasn't going to find anything of use.

Fire trucks sat near what was once the Library of Thought. Brave firemen fought the terrible blaze that Steve was sure was the act of two mad aliens and a sexy robot. With crazy thoughts tumbling out of his cranium there was only one thing to do. It being now noon it was time to go to lunch. What else was there to do? He had to wait for the spaceship to arrive in order to go to Maladred and in the meantime there was nothing to do but wait. Besides he wanted a roast beef sandwich.

Steve walked home and immediately fixed himself a snack. With the possibility that he was going to go into space again with a probable result of him never returning he was extra careful to ensure that this particular sandwich was especially tasty. The bread was toasted, the meat was warmed and it was indeed delicious. Who knew a good sandwich would be so hard to acquire in outer space? The reason for this was that the Phelan Corporation of the Barron Cluster fame had bought out the entire sandwich making competition in the universe. Once a monopoly had been established there was very little in the way of choice and the quality of sandwich declined in the known universe.

Steve relaxed, walked to the television and hit the on switch knowing that the work week was over. This was the exact extent of his planning for saving planet Earth from certain doom. He had no plan, he had no secret weapon, he had no real idea on how he was to save Earth but he did have one thing on his side. Time. He had a whole two weeks to figure out just how to get the hell out of the predicament that he found himself in. Two weeks in which to save the Earth. Two weeks to rid the universe of a planet full of killers and two weeks to enjoy a full life on Earth in case he failed miserably.

When you know that you may have only two weeks left to live before getting murdered by a bunch of revenge crazy aliens you tend to spend a little more time on reflection. Sure you think that you'd rush off to Las Vegas and spend all your cash on booze, wild parties and doing all those things you know you shouldn't but that hardly ever turns out to be reality. Plus Steve couldn't actually afford to do any of those things so settled for sitting home thinking and watching DVDs.

He also spent his remaining two weeks being reflective. He talked and actually listened to his family and friends, he made sure his affairs were in order and that anyone and everyone that meant something to him had gotten a piece of him before he left on his insane journey. While he had been on some insane journeys before being returned to Earth, after coming to terms with his life both in space and on his home planet meant that life seemed a bit more real to him. This was this first time he felt that he actually had something to lose.

With this in mind he decided to make an extraordinary call to the spaceship that was coming to pick him up. He requested that the ship make a slight flight detour that would hardly make a difference in the ship's arrival time to Earth but would make his journey towards possible death a lot smoother for him. Plus, as he said to the pilot before signing off, misery loves company. The pilot, having never heard that particular expression before, filed it away in the back of his head for future use.

The day finally arrived when Steve had to leave his home and head towards the planet Maladred once more. The arrival had been arranged and three am the spaceship would land on top of Signal Hill, one of the more historic sites in a city filled with history.

Steve said goodbye to his three brothers Derm, Martin and Michael and his mother Betty and opened the door to adventure once more. Steve walked up the hill towards the spot where Marconi received the first trans-Atlantic wireless communication. He carried a bag with him that he regretted was so heavy as he neared the top but he would need the things he had if he was to save Earth.

Upon arrival he sat down on a concrete wall near Cabot Tower and looked at his watch. Looking up at the night sky he saw a star falling straight at his head, the people in the cars that lined the picturesque view of the city didn't even bother to look up, their minds occupied with matters of the flesh at the popular make-out spot. So when the small but fast ship from outer space landed in the middle of a parking lot on top of historical Signal Hill no one bothered to look or even take a photo. The entry ladder emerged, Steve climbed on board and the ship, with hardly a noise, lifted off the ground and headed once more into the black of space.

Steve felt a million times better once the ship had cleared the atmosphere and headed off into deep space. The waiting was not very good for his stomach but once the adventure had begun the anxiety that he felt simply vanished. He made his way to the flight deck where a group of people waited to greet their passenger.

"Well, well, well. The human who just can't help but stir up a whole load of trouble has finally graced us with his presence." The woman who spoke with a raised voice wanted to appear to be angry but in truth she was not. She was actually pleased to see her old boss again but she did not wish that information to swell his head. As for the other creature that stood there it said not a word, as he physically could not, but he radiated a sincere warmth that was felt all through the pilot's cabin.

"Good to see you guys again, too," Steve said. He looked at the pair before him, Zoe his former library cataloguer and Chubba his technician. Both of them he had relieved of their new burdens for the Inter Galactic Library Board and put on this special mission to save Earth. To at last get their hands on the Tome of the Lost Ones the Board would bend a bit and could forgive much. Steve had promised the book to the Library Board as compensation for help, nothing was said about his withholding the book from them in the first place.

Steve held a quick meeting in the pilot's cabin as he wanted not only his two fellow library workers to be fully aware of the situation but also the pilot Colonel Sanders, who didn't really appreciate Steve's laughter when he was introduced. Still, there was no laughter once they had all gotten down to business and the deadly consequences should they fail their mission.

Steve's plan, which he had formulated while standing in unusually long lines at the Merrymeeting Road supermarket, consisted of picking up his pair of library workers partially because he knew they would be useful in a crisis but mainly because he knew it would get under Zoe's skin to be recalled during acquisition season at her new job. Then they would travel to Maladred where he would inform the authorities there of the criminal activities of Allan and his band of thugs. Surely, Steve believed, not everyone on the planet of

Maladred were vicious killers intent on ruling the galaxy. Once he had gotten this mess straightened out he would go to the Inter Galactic Library board to hand over the Tome of the Lost Ones, and hope that he could latch on to another job as his former one had went up literally in flames.

With that all spelled out for his companions Steve clasped his hands together and waited for the congratulations. Obviously his plan was simple but simple was what worked most of the time as far as Steve knew. The less complicated the better. The blank look on Zoe's face said it all. It read, "You sir, are one crazy bastard," a million times over.

Even with a history of mad ideas this one was a doozie for his companions to take, even Colonel Sanders had to shake his head in disbelief. This was the guy who was the famous liberator? How in hell did he manage to dismantle the evil empire of Maladred the first time round he thought to himself as he flew straight on to Maladred where he now knew all that awaited him was certain death.

For his part Steve was oblivious to any distain for his plan. He knew that his plan wasn't perfect but what the hell it was a start and who knows it just might work. If not he wasn't prepared to tell anyone about his second option, the one that was more dangerous and totally unethical but just might be able to save the planet Earth and all its inhabitants.

The journey to Maladred was the most enjoyable space ride any of the passengers had ever experienced. The ship came equipped with many of the amusements that real space cruisers had such as: virtual reality bubbles where one could hop from one alternate reality to another, Ultimate

Massage where every muscle in your body gets soothed and relaxed and of course everyone's favorite checkers. Oddly checkers had become a very popular game in the galaxy due to its uncomplicated nature. There were no buttons, no view screens to look at, just plain disks on a board and the simplicity appealed to many in a technological universe.

The ship arrived in virtually the same spot where they had previously landed with the space mobile so long ago now it seemed to the library staff. The scene had dramatically changed from the previous journey though. This time all the populace seemed to be in furious activity. This was a far cry from the lackadaisical people that they had encountered before. These people meant business.

No sooner than the last occupant of the ship exited than a hundred armed soldiers surrounded them and led them away through streets lined with cursing, hissing people to a hill where a large, scorched building rose into view. It all happened so fast that none of the library staff had time to protest as they were pushed and prodded along a steep hill.

"This all looks vaguely familiar," Steve said.

"It should, you Earth bastard. This was once the grand palace before you blew it up. Now look at it! The grandeur is gone and we are left with a mostly hollow shell all thanks to you!" one of the angry soldiers with a large gun shouted at him. The tension mounted as the group kept walking towards the palace. The hatred towards Steve and his band was clearly evident.

"Oh right. It all comes back to me now," Steve said in a low voice to no one in particular. He was viciously kicked in the small of his back for his remark and he fell face first into the dirt. No one was allowed to help the man get to his feet but he quietly managed on his own. The march continued towards the Tower of Gregos which was a dilapidated shell of its former self.

The trip to the dilapidated tower was not an overly long one but was made unpleasant due to the rude and somewhat unwarranted remarks of their hosts. Through the halls of beautiful artwork of the violence and crimes against all creation did the group march forward towards their final destination. By the time they had reached the inner hallways of the palace Steve remarked that their hosts were far nicer their first journey to their planet for which he was given another swift kick in the back.

At last the four arrived in front of a stern militaristic group of thirteen men and women sitting upright behind a very stern looking table. The vibe was definitely hostile and no one bothered with formal introductions. Steve was surprised to see Allan and the Master of Evil sitting almost in the middle of the table. They were no random terrorist but members of the government. The middle itself was reserved for a small man who snarled at the approach of the four visitors. None of the counselors looked friendly.

Perhaps they were not friendly but they were recognizable. They were all patrons of the library of thought! These were the folks who attended the Christmas party! No wonder not one of them knew who Santa Claus was! Why all of them sniffed books rather than read them! Steve thought it was just what old people did but now it all made sense.

Not only that but they also didn't even leave one beer left for the cleaner the next day. That itself was an indication of their evil.

"These are the creatures who initiated war against the people of Maladred?" the man asked somewhat rhetorically. There was a murmur of agreement from the twelve uniformed people at the table. The man looked to either side of the table then focused his attention to the four in front of him. "We are a fair and noble race and thus even scum like these before us who are obviously guilty will have the privilege of addressing this court before execution."

"Well, as long as everything is fair," Steve said in an obviously sarcastic voice despite the translation. Zoe didn't even wait for the guard to kick him this time but did the job herself. There was little said after the initial harangue from the thirteen uniformed people, the council talked and threatened while the library party listened. Every time one of the party tried to speak they were silenced immediately so after a while they no longer bothered.

The trick of the book had been discovered very quickly upon Allan's arrival on Maladred. While Steve's ruse had indeed worked thanks to none of Allan's party knowing how to read there was one section of the populace they did retain the knowledge, the civil service. The civil service had always been a part of the empire, running it and maintaining it throughout the hundreds of years of its existence. Unlike the majority of the true citizens of Maladred they actually had to work in order to keep the empire going. It was here that the true evil lurked.

The workers of this particular group still had the knowledge to read, write and do all the things that were necessary to keep control over the galaxy. The revolution had upset their little house of cards and now they wished nothing less than to regain the power that the corrupt and lazy citizens of Maladred had lost for them. This time they would ensure that the reign of Maladred would last for another thousand years.

Throughout the brief courtroom drama there was no chance for the library team to defend themselves and there was little evidence presented except for a recording of Bogatta's recognition of Steve as the liberator at the time of the great revolution. Once the video had finished the kangaroo court simply screamed at the four and promised revenge.

The council's mock trial did reveal one disturbing fact to the library four. They did not destroy the space library. The council insisted that they had nothing to do with the destruction of branch number 6941 and as they were a bunch of braggarts they surely were telling the truth. This led to a whole host of questions in the library party's heads but the bang of the gavel shook those questions out of their minds.

"It is in this council's judgment that you all have acted against the people of Maladred and will be punished. You will be held in the dark palace prison until sentence is decided. Take them away!" the council members all shouted and hissed as the library group was corralled and taken to the dungeons below.

Soon the four prisoners were marched down to holding cells in the basement of the former palace. "Well, that did not go as well as I had hoped," Steve remarked as he sat down on a bunk in the cell that he was confined in. Zoe, Chubba and Colonel Sanders all were silent. The energy had drained out of them as thoughts of a quick execution filled their minds. Steve was the only person who realized that torture would be their lot until the location of the book, the true Tome of the Lost Ones would be revealed. They would not be killed until the ultimate weapon was in the council's evil hands.

Once locked safely in their cells it did not take long for the threats to multiple against the library party. Earth would be destroyed; all the family and friends of the library workers he endangered would be forfeit, etc., etc., etc. Steve had heard it all before and he judged the amount of dedication and voracity of the threats by the amount of spit than came from the mouths of the creatures who were shouting the threats. The prison floor needed a good cleaning after the interrogators had left.

Chubba was taken away first and all could feel his agony through the waves of pure pain that emanated from his soul. Chubba was the strongest and if he could hardly take the pain then what chance did any of the others have? All the library crew was afraid. Colonel Sanders thought of the girl he left at home, Zoe thought of her family on her home planet and Steve thought of his family, his friends and the chicken sandwich he left on his kitchen table back home. "What a waste," he thought, all the while Chubba silently screamed.

Zoe, then Colonel Sanders and finally Steve were taken one by one from their cells and tortured for information to the location of the Tome of the Lost Ones. The torturers were relentless. For days the parade of pain and questions were trotted out and for days the library workers said nothing.

After a week of intense agony Allan walked into the holding cells and spit at the library party. They were informed that one of them would be killed unless the secret was given up. Allan looked directly at Steve as he talked then smiled and walked away. In response Steve silently shed a tear but it was not for himself or indeed even any of his friends.

By now the full realization came to him. From words spoken from guard to guard the story of Maladred's evil slowly dawned upon the human who previously had truly believed that there had to be some divine spark of decency in any sentient life form. He realized now that he was utterly wrong. There was only cruelty and a desperate evil living on this planet and it had to be stopped. Steve spoke just three words to himself in a low tone of voice and then went to bed.

That night the door to the holding cells swung open by itself and then mysteriously closed once again. There was a definite presence in the room but no one could see or hear anything. Zoe wondered if the ghosts of the space book mobile had returned to haunt them one last time and even whispered "R-Man, is that you?"

Steve cautiously got up from his cot and walked over to the middle of the room. "Weed." Steve quietly spoke and the space between him and the door began to shiver. What was once an empty space filled with the figure of Cal, the space library computer that had once taken the routine reference questions at the now destroyed space library branch # 6941. Amazingly Cal had not been damaged by the blast that demolished the space library. Everyone chalked it up to the superior research and design skills of the American and Canadian Library Associations' research and development teams who had been contracted out by the Intergalactic Library Board to develop futuristic reference tools.

The R and D teams had a number of silly ideas about database systems and survey results but the one idea about the robotic reference aid really caught the attention of the Board and they had run with it. Taking the ideas of the ALA/CLA research teams they had built a select few robot prototypes and had sent them off to various libraries as a first steps project. Cal had been one of those models and he more than lived up to his function.

Cal had been fitted with an invisibility shield and a noise dampener so that patrons studying in the quite areas of libraries would not see or hear necessary book retrieval from the reference areas of the library. This technology was practical and functional but its uses were widespread. One of these uses would now save the lives of the library computer's co-workers.

Steve smiled as he asked Cal for the book that was contained within the small book bin in its innards. Cal reached into its middle and handed the book to Steve who took it and patted the head of the computer while ordering it to once again turn invisible. Steve then got up and produced the Tome of the Lost Ones for all his friends to see. He figured he had about ten minutes to actually use the book before his captors returned so he regretfully opened the book and began to recite.

Zoe, Chubba and Colonel Sanders all remained silent as Steve cried out the words that would raise the dead of the Maladred race. Anyone who had recently died on the entire planet would be brought back to unlife and attack the living for their flesh. A great gust of air immediately swept into the cell as the strange words rang out. Steve's voice became louder and louder as if the words had taken hold of his body and made his voice their own.

The whole palace began to shake and crack. The weakened foundations slowly started to crack and crumble as the librarian reached a crescendo. At the climax of the spell Steve's eyes had turned completely black and his head was thrust back in an unnatural state. Chubba reeled in pain as he tried to get the furthest away from the wave of evil that emanated from his former head librarian's soul.

Finally, Zoe managed to stagger to Steve and look in his eyes. The manic, black pools could not recognize the terrified woman holding his head on either side right in front of him. There was no trace of the librarian that she knew, only a foul creature tainted by otherworldly magic. As in a trance the man continued the enchantment until the last word was spoken.

At last, the abominable words were silent and the strong grip that held the librarian released. Steve fell to the ground like a puppet whose strings had been severed. The palace stopped shaking. The world fell silent, at least for a moment time paused as if to catch its breath. Steve's eyes returned to normal and for some reason a look of calm came over his face. Then a hint of recognition arrived in his eyes as he realized what he had just conjured.

"What have you done?" Colonel Sanders asked from his sitting position in his cell his voice filled with fear and confusion.

"I gave them the hell that they wanted to inflict on the entire galaxy. It was either all our worlds or them and I made the choice. Now let's get the hell out of here. We still have to get to our ship before these bastards come down to finish us off."

The anger in the librarian's voice was not contained. He truly hated to inflict a plague on the population of the planet. He still felt deep in his heart that despite all the torture he and his friends had suffered that there had to be people who were innocent of the crimes of the rulers of Maladred. Yet despite this he could not see another way out. Maladred had to be stopped once and for all if Earth and the universe were to be spared from the wrath of Allan and his cohorts.

Steve shouted an order and Cal ripped open the cell doors with ease. Steve patted the machine on its head as he walked past it and up the stairs leading his library team towards freedom. Up the group ran, past gruesome torture chambers and special death rooms. The stench was sickening and it made Steve feel just a tiny bit better about his decision.

Zombies were already seen on the outskirts of the palace, a grisly reminder of the new regime's policy of silencing all resistance. Now the evil dead had come back to haunt their executioners. The guards were busy lining up their defense against the undead and it was an easy task to slip past and into the large chamber where only a week previously the thirteen leaders of the now falling command centre held court. It was in this room that the library group found themselves surrounded by ten of the thirteen council members with Allan in the middle looking directly at Steve with a burning hatred.

They slowly advanced on them with murder in their eyes. Steve halted them with one wave of his hand. "No, no, no, no, no. I think that is far enough. One more step and I'll be forced to do something that I really, really might regret."

Allan and his group halted as they pondered what to do. Despite all their theatrics the group still had little in the way of leadership ability and that is why their instinct to follow orders kicked in when they heard a commanding voice. It gave Steve all the time he needed to reach into Cal once more and produce a small box with a button.

"I really think that you should now concentrate on your problems rather than attack myself and my friends. I am giving you one more chance to save yourselves from certain destruction. Let us go in peace and never, ever try to get revenge on Earth or any other planet." Steve waved his hand over his head and waited for the response.

Allan spat on the floor and laughed at the librarian. "You fool! What the hell do you take us for! Idiots? We were not fooled by your simple ruse on Earth. We knew that the book you gave us wasn't the right one but we also knew that you would follow us so you could play the hero one last time.

We have studied you for months and knew exactly what you would do. Those stupid romantic ideals in your head have ruined you at last. We even wanted you to use the book so we could thin the herd of the weak and battle ready our troops. By the time they are finished clearing up this zombie chattel we will be ready for the invasion of the galaxy!"

"That may as well be," Steve replied. "But I don't think you are ready for what I have got in my hand. One warning then I will push this button." His hand was still raised in the air as if a terrible fate was clasped in the palm of his hand. The council members all stood back fearing what was in Steve's hand, all council members that is, except Allan.

Full of hatred and arrogance Allan rushed towards the librarian and pushed him down on his back. He grabbed for the box in Steve's hand and inadvertently pressed the button. A loud buzzing sound came out of the air. Steve kicked off the furious Allan and returned to his feet. While everyone else wondered what would happen next, where that deafening sound was coming from Steve stood upright in nervous anticipation. Only he knew what was about to happen because he made it happen.

Within moments smoke appeared out of thin air followed by an intense swirling light. The brightness got wider and wider until a small living thing hopped out of the vortex. The light and whirlwind then faded into nothing leaving a creature with dark fur, sharp teeth and red, hollow eyes crumpled on the floor of the former palace. The library workers recognized the thing immediately. It was the vampire bunny king and it was quickly regaining its senses.

Steve walked in front the vampire bunny king and bowed. "Your gracious lord, I have fulfilled my end of the arrangement. I present to you a new planet in exchange for New Bunny World." Steve, still bowed low, slowly retreated to a safe distance while the vampire bunny king sat up and stared for a moment into Steve's eyes.

The bunny king sniffed the air and its eyes grew wide in recognition. A slight grin appeared over its dark ruby lips as it began to speak. "We shall take this world in exchange for leaving our home planet. The colonists shall be spared and the gateways will now open. We bunnies shall finally have revenge on the makers. Those uncaring beings that so long ago abandoned us on a world so far, far away and hunted us for sport will now learn of our vengeance!"

"What is this? What is that creature?" demanded Allan his arrogance unfazed. Steve was more than able to fill Allan in on the picture.

"You see, a long time ago your ancestors tried to colonize a world that is now known to the universe as New Bunny World. For centuries the planet had been lost as a wave of vampire zombie bunnies infested the world and as a result almost wiped out the people living in the cities. It was only through the courage and might of a leader named Major Allan Strong, who held back the horde of the undead that led the colonists to victory or at least to what they believed to be victory.

A hundred years later the last communiqué with the colony mentioned that they had an infestation of vampire zombie bunnies crawling out of the ground, rising up to attack. With that the colonists were heard from no more and your Maladred Empire, rather than head up a rescue squad, decided to quarantine the planet and leave the colonists to their terrible fate.

Hundreds of years later my library team found the ancestors of the colonists. We retrieved the Tome of the Lost Ones that had partially caused such awful damage to the once docile bunny rabbit and saved the ancestors of the original colony from further attacks by the undead bunnies. Thus only a horde of vampire bunnies remained and with only the remaining few colonists left to feed on I had to make a deal to ensure their safety."

"What kind of deal?" the angry Allan demanded.

The vampire bunny king answered. "In exchange for the lives of the colonists we were offered a new world to populate, one where we could live on not a mere few colonists but a host of new victims."

Steve continued. "I had intended to find a planet uninhabited by sentient creatures but the irony of the situation and the horribleness of your people led me to this final solution to the vampire bunny problem."

"What do you mean irony?" Allan asked suspiciously.

"Don't you get it yet? The original colonists who brought the bunnies to New Bunny World in the first place came from Maladred. I knew it once I had a chance to study the artwork within these walls one more time. They are your ancestors and these bunnies that were exported from here have come home. All the bunnies are now on Maladred while your kin, those who used their vigor for peace and for hard work rather than violence, are now safe to live in a world free from the terror of the vampire bunny and your horrible influence. The evils that you have done to the universe have come home and that coupled with your new zombie plague will stop you and your people from ever again becoming a renewed threat to the universe."

"But we have never had these creatures on this planet! We never had such creatures, we never had bunny rabbits!" One of the council screamed as fear began to take hold of his body.

"No, that's true up to a point but then that really isn't their true name either. These creatures were not originally called bunnies. They were called Jummies! Oh yes, the cloud lifts. The creatures that you hunted, killed and ate almost to extinction are now back in numbers to hunt, kill and eat you. It is only fair after all. Jummies, bunnies or whatever you want to call them are now back on their original home to get their revenge!"

Steve was very proud of his speech, especially the last bit where his voice had reached a crescendo. With zombies attacking and vampire bunnies flooding the planet from ruptures in space he was quite aware that attention spans might be very limited but the council had heard every word and now the realization struck that the dark evils of the past had at last returned to haunt them.

An explosion woke everyone up from their amazement and Steve and his library team prepared to move out. Grabbing up the Tome of the Lost Ones Steve motioned for his companions to leave the Maladred people to their fate. They needed to get off the planet before it was entirely consumed in vampire evil and zombie madness.

Allan, who watched the librarian in utter rage, had other thoughts and rushed towards Steve with the sword of the Divine Gregos clutched firmly in his hands. The vampire bunny king saw the man running towards the librarian and leapt up on the collar of the leader of the Maladred people. Allan grasped at his neck as the vampire bit down and sucked the blood from the man who would be king.

The library team halted only for a moment as they saw the man disappear in a cloud of his own blood. Steve's eyes met those of the man whom he once trusted and there was no pity. Allan had just the strength to raise his head and utter one last warning to the head librarian. "He is coming!" with that he fell to the floor dead.

The group turned from the body and began to run. Racing down the corridors of the former palace Chubba, Zoe, Colonel Sanders and Cal all followed the lead of their head librarian. Dodging laser fire and the odd lumbering zombie they had made it out of the palace and into the open wilderness. It didn't take long before they reached the spaceport where their space ship rested. "Let's get the hell out of here!" Steve yelled as the group all entered the ship and closed the horrors behind them.

The ship lifted off the ground, rose into the air and within moments had climbed out off the atmosphere and into space. From their vantage point you could see lights going out on the planet, in one portion a huge mushroom cloud appeared. It seemed that the world was rapidly dying and even though they all held some portion of the blame for this none could say they that they were entirely at fault. The Maladred race had to be finally stopped otherwise their villainy would ruin the entire galaxy.

With the threat to Earth and the galaxy over each member of the library team retired to the living rooms station to try and get some needed rest. After spending over a week together locked in a dungeon and previously another week or so confined on a space ship they needed some me time. There was no one who was unaffected by their experience and all needed to take some time to sort out their feelings.

A few hours later Zoe stepped into Steve's room on the living quarters space of the ship. "You used the book didn't you? I can't see how there was any other way of opening up those portals from New Bunny World to Maladred. You had to have used the book. But how the heck did you use it with a communicator device?"

"Well," Steve began as he got up from his bed, "I left one device with the vampire bunny king telling him that I would one day send the spell that would send his people to an inhabited world where he could feed all he wanted. I used the technology of a library book reader that recorded the spell in the communicator. Once the button got hit it transmitted the spell along with the destination to the bunnies. And viola! "

"But you didn't physically open the book. How did it work?" Zoe was confused. She hopped on Steve's bed, lying across with her legs swinging back and forth up in the air and her face buried between her clenched fists. Steve sat down next to her and continued with his explanation.

"Well, when I used it the first time I realized that the book itself isn't all that magical. It is the spells that have the power." Steve was getting fairly used to magic books by now and he had learned a few things in using the Tome of the Lost Ones. "All the wonderful grandeur, all the impressive toys in the universe and it is the simple power of words that come out on top. There is a lesson to be learned there"

"You could have sent them to an uninhabited world to starve. It is not as if anyone would have blamed you for ridding the universe of vampire bunnies." Zoe walked over and sat on the bed next to her friend. She looked into Steve's eyes wondering what to make of this strange man. Here was a human who could leave an inhabited planet to be destroyed by undead creatures but would not destroy a host of ghoulish bunnies when he had the opportunity. Humans were very particular in their morals.

"That wasn't the deal I made. Besides, even the vampire bunny king wasn't truly evil. He was the victim of some other creature, a vampire. He didn't have a choice in what he became but the populace of Maladred did. I couldn't do it to him. I had to give the vampire bunny king the chance to survive. It was the right thing to do. At least I think it was. Who knows? Maybe the whole thing will bite me in the ass one day."

A week into their journey back to the space library Steve called a quick meeting of the crew. He told them that they were all brave for enduring the tortures that they had gone through. While he could have used the Tome of the Lost Ones at any time he wanted he had to make sure that it was the only thing that could be done to save the universe from evil. Steve was only sorry that anyone else had to suffer. The head librarian then called on the computer Cal to come forward to receive a special commendation for bravery and devotion to its library team.

There was a certain irony in celebrating Cal's role in the adventure. Library technology had saved them but it had also doomed an entire planet to a slow but inevitable death. None of the library team felt any pleasure in this but the truth of the matter was that it was either them or the universe as no one would have been safe from the menace of Maladred. There was simply no reasoning with the utter hatred and contempt the creatures of the planet had for the rest of the universe and now that hatred would only consume each other.

The threat posed by Maladred was going to be over. Those few who survived the zombie plague and vampire bunny onslaught would not have the military might to threaten anyone, not even a defenseless planet like Earth. Still, Steve communicated with the Inter Galactic Library Board asking for them to contact the correct authorities to set up a quarantine zone around Maladred to ensure no one infected got off the planet.

After the celebration all left the room except Zoe. "So, we still have no idea who actually blew up the library?"

Asked Zoe to the librarian. Steve paused a moment before answering, his mind seemingly far away.

"Nope. I guess we'll have to wait and see what the inquiry at the Library Board turns up after all. Strange, I thought for sure that those crazies on Maladred had done that. I would have put good money on it but I guess not. They had no reason to lie about it," Steve replied. "Still, we better be on our guard. Who knows why someone would destroy an entire library? It might have nothing to do with us personally at all, just someone trying to make some sort of point. There is always some loser who wantonly destroys public property to get their jollies."

"And just who is the 'He is coming' that that lunatic was telling us about with his dying breath? And where was the master of evil and her sexy robot? We never saw them in the chamber. Could they have escaped ?" Zoe asked the uninformed librarian.

"Look, all I know is that we saved my planet from certain destruction and our library is well underway to completion. It was a miracle that the rare book collection survived. Who knew that shielded, condensed shelving was the perfect defense for a neutron blast?" Steve shrugged his shoulders at all the other questions that Zoe asked him. He had no answers for her inquiries, all he did know was that there was some menace out there that might have it in for his particular branch of the space library and one day he was certain he would find out why. Until then it would be business as usual, his team would go to work fixing up the new space library and going about their lives as best as they could.

During the voyage Brenda, library technician # 7439, contacted the space library staff with some good news. The Inter Galactic Library Board had declared that the space library branch # 6941 was now officially in service and all staff could return to their old positions. Steve's world was beginning to take shape and his life as a space librarian had at last been returned to him. As he clicked off the communicator he relaxed in his seat and stared out into the vastness of space. His life had come full circle and for once he acknowledged the special circumstance that he was in. He was a human in outer space working with aliens and being the best darn librarian any space library could ask for. He smiled, closed his eyes and went to deep sleep.

A few days later the space ship landed on the asteroid that they called home. The new library, gleaming in the sunlight as the large rock turned into the direction of the sun, was larger and more beautiful than the previous library that had once existed on the same spot. The upgrade was simply amazing and every staff member's face beamed as they had their first look at the new and vastly improved complex.

The trio of library workers along with their new friend Colonel Sanders walked into the fresh library from the space book mobile landing pad and set straight into their new lives. They had all faced terrible danger and incredible obstacles to get to this magnificent point, none of them had ever considered the possibility that library work was so full of adventure and danger. None of that mattered now though. The space library branch #6941 was back in business and no matter who or what was gunning for them the team of the space library would be ready. Optimism reigned in the new library and its inhabitants beamed with pride and joy.

Steve stole himself away from the festivities to contact home. His real home in St. John's and he told his mom and brothers everything. They were happy that he got a job but remarked that it was a heck of a commute. Steve smiled, bid his family goodbye for now and entered his new circulation area where his friends were busy looking at all their new library toys. With the new, much faster, space book mobile in the hanger Steve could go to Earth within any reasonable length of time. Despite being in outer space he was closer to home than ever.

The sun set on the rocky asteroid and Steve, Zoe, Colonel Sanders and Chubba all retired to the living quarters of the space library. Cal the reference computer turned on his night vision and silently answered reference questions from other computers out there in the universe. The dark silence of the library reflected the shadowy stillness on the asteroid itself. Cal roamed through the library stacks and shone its light through the collection. Everything was as it should.

Not too far out from the new library near the wreckage of the old branch library a small, bruised hand worked its way through to the surface of the crushed and tattered rubble. An arm crept up and then finally a body, the body of a living female who managed to get to her bleeding feet after climbing out of the mountain of library remains.

Her eyes were hallowed and her breath non existent, yet her voice could still speak even in airless space. Her decayed, cracked lips spoke exactly three words. In a hushed, almost reverend tone she whispered over and over again "Alberon must live."

She moved her shrunken, torn legs slowly towards the gleaming space library. As the tired library workers slept in their comfortable new beds they sensed nothing of the danger that lumbered menacingly towards them. Unknown to them the fate of the universe was once more at risk but that adventure would have to wait until morning. For now the library was closed.

The End

Appendix

Illustrations

This book was originally conceived to be a little lighter than it actually became. Writers do not write the characters the characters write us and thus the illustrations that were originally conceived to connect the chapters were too light hearted for the text. I include them as a reference to what might have been.

Here is an example of how the space library might have been seen from patrons first entering the library.

Here is an example of the original art for the fight scene between the wise old man, the White Knight and the dragon of Alberon.

Here is a lonely librarian walking the streets of Toronto looking for hope and finding none.

This is a scene of the Times Up! Funeral parlor where a deranged Steve thinks he sees things that isn't there. I cut this scene out of the book in order to highlight the emotional play between the characters and give the scene a more grounded feel.

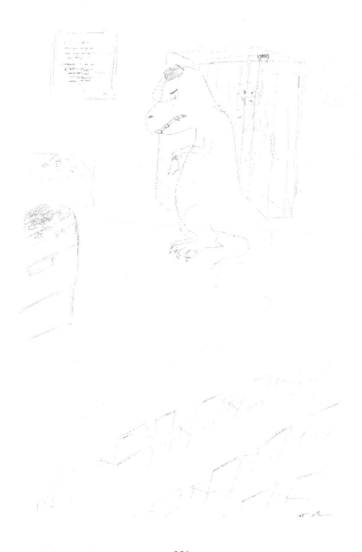

Here is a happy JC calling bingo. The idea came to me that in this life anything and everything can happen if you open your eyes and heart to it. There is probably no more odd moment in your life than having the Big Guy call a bingo.

Concept art for the cover. The idea of power coming from the vampire zombie bursting upward from the grave gives excitement to whole book.

Here is a wonderful image of the vampire zombie bunnies who are wandering around, they don't really look exactly like bunnies but since they are truly jummies it works perfectly!

Here is another image of the book cover concept art. Again the idea of power for bursting into the scene is what I hope to accomplish on the final cover design.